Praise for Ernesto

The Second Death of Única Aveyano

"This gorgeous tale of the last days of the aptly named Única Aveyano is a tropical garden of a book, lush with histories, miracles, and ghosts. With the deftness and humanity of the great magical realists, Mestre-Reed makes an ordinary life into legend in language so lyrical it takes your breath away."

—Patricia Chao, author of *Monkey King*

"Ernesto Mestre-Reed is a masterful observer, the creator of dazzling word portraits: here the manifold details of family and romantic life, the subtlest shift of facial expression, the minor disappointments of any day, the most elusive yet crushing emotion, are all captured in poetic and daring prose. This novel, the story-fable of one family caught up in the tragedy of contemporary Cuba, draws its authority and unforgettable emotional power from that luminous intimacy."

—Francisco Goldman, author of *The Ordinary Seaman*

"Ernesto Mestre-Reed is among the most gifted and accomplished storytellers to emerge from the Cuban diaspora. Mestre-Reed's Cubans—whether in exile or on the island—are as deftly drawn as Philip Roth's Jews of Newark. *The Second Death of Única Aveyano* makes clear to all this author's soaring artistry and power."

—Ann Louise Bardach, author of *Cuba Confidential*

"Ernesto Mestre-Reed's beautiful and often elegiac novel reminds us that the story of Elián Gonzalez is everyone's story: the journeys of Única and her family are driven by the burdens of remembering and of forgetting. This book is important, even daring, in its weaving of the magical, spiritual lives of its characters with historical and political realities surrounding them. The yearnings and resolutions of these characters—Única especially—remain with us. By the end, we know for certain that going forward can be a difficult move, but returning—to the homeland, to those people who stayed behind, to the old stories that raised us—is probably the hardest thing one can ever possibly do. The novel is gorgeously sculpted and breathtaking in its scope."

—Carolyn Ferrell, author of *Don't Erase Me*

"Mestre-Reed is a lyric novelist of uncommon power, creating a memorable portrait of a woman wracked by longing and memory yet fearlessly embracing impending death." —*Booklist*

ERNESTO MESTRE-REED

The Second Death of Única Aveyano

Ernesto Mestre-Reed was born in Guantánamo, Cuba, in 1964. His family emigrated to Madrid, Spain, in 1972 and later that year to Miami, Florida. He is the author of the novel *The Lazarus Rumba,* teaches creative writing at Sarah Lawrence College, and lives in Brooklyn, New York.

THE SECOND DEATH OF ÚNICA AVEYANO

A Novel

Ernesto Mestre-Reed

VINTAGE CONTEMPORARIES

Vintage Books
A Division of Random House, Inc.
New York

A VINTAGE CONTEMPORARIES ORIGINAL, MARCH 2004

A brief portion of this work was originally published under the title "After Elián" in the anthology *A Whistler in the Nightworld: Short Fiction from the Latin Americas* (Plume, 2002).

Grateful acknowledgment is made to the following for permission to reprint previously published material:

Alfred A. Knopf: Excerpt from Fragment 95 of Sappho's poetry, translated by Anne Carson, from *If Not, Winter* by Anne Carson, copyright © 2002 by Anne Carson. Reprinted by permission of Alfred A. Knopf, a division of Random House, Inc.

Viking Penguin: "Book 7: Phaeacia's Halls and Gardens" from *The Odyssey* by Homer, translated by Robert Fagles, copyright © 1996 by Robert Fagles. Reprinted by permission of Viking Penguin, a division of Penguin Group (USA) Inc.

Library of Congress Cataloging-in-Publication Data
Mestre-Reed, Ernesto.
The second death of Única Aveyano : a novel / by Ernesto Mestre-Reed.—1st Vintage Contemporaries ed.
p. cm.
ISBN 1-4000-3316-0
1. Cuban American families—Fiction. 2. Cuban American women—Fiction. 3. Cuban Americans—Fiction. 4. New York (N.Y.)—Fiction. 5. Miami (Fla.)—Fiction. I. Title.
PS3563.E8135S43 2004
813'.54—dc21
2003052544

Book design by Debbie Glasserman

www.vintagebooks.com

Printed in the United States of America
10 9 8 7 6 5 4 3 2 1

To Andrew, por todo

"Stranger,
I'll be the first to question you—myself.
Who are you? Where are you from?
Who gave you the clothes you're wearing now?
Didn't you say you reached us roving on the sea?"

Homer
The Odyssey, book 7

but a kind of yearning has hold of me—to die
and to look upon the dewy Lotus banks
of Acheron

Sappho
Fragments

PART ONE

SONG OF THE STREETS

SHE RECITES THE NAMES OF STREETS.

There is Cranberry and Orange and Pineapple, she says.

And she climbs their steep slopes to the wrought-iron benches on the promenade.

Maybe someday she can hold her grandson's head in her lap again, brush his lambswool hair as he falls asleep in the afternoon, like she did in the courtyard of their house in Cuba, and years later, in the little concrete patio outside their cramped apartment on Meridian Street.

There is Poplar and Willow and Vine, she says.

And in the park under the overpass some whispery aspens and leafy cottonwoods that she will not see bloom.

He used to let his hair grow long just for that—so that she could untangle it with her brush and with the ends of her fingers. He hid under her long skirts when his mother chased him, snipping her giant metallic shears in the air like a mad sheepwoman.

There is Love and Grace, she says.

And she follows each to its end, crumbling brick walls meshed in ivy. El culo del saco, se lo comió Paco.

She picked living things out of her grandson's hair as if she were digging memories out of his skull. A brown beetle to forget his father. A wingless moth to forget his homeland.

There is Pearl and Water, she says.

And a desolate beach that hides under the Brooklyn Bridge, which will not fall down, will not fall down.

He fell from the boat, from the overcrowded boat. His long hair floated on the olive sea like a clump of sargasso weed. He fell from the boat and her husband fell over after him.

There is Montague, she says.

But no Capulet.

DANCE OF THE WILD BOYS

ÚNICA AVEYANO HAD LEARNED to go almost without sleep. Sometimes she slipped the painkillers that she had hidden under her tongue into her husband Modesto's daily dosage of pills so that he would not worry about her wandering the halls at night, pressed to the walls like a mouse. The other pills she took. Especially the little egg-shaped Marinols, which were supposed to combat nausea and make her hungry, but which made her jittery too, and daring. Later, they were to blame it on them, on the little egg-shaped pills, as if it had been the first time.

The nursing home was a six-story building, two blocks away from the fashionable beach. Storm shutters hung halfway down over the windows at all times like droopy eyelids, so very little light ever managed to get in. When the windows were left open, Única could hear the music from the oceanfront cafés late into the night. Sometimes she asked a night nurse to bring her a chair, and she sat in the hallway, crouched by an open window, and listened to the sounds of life outside. She hadn't been to the beach in ages.

One night, a week before Elián had been taken away, in the middle of April of the year 2000, she made up her mind to see the ocean as it is when the moon flirts with its restless surface. When Modesto fell asleep, she took her cane (which she rarely used) and made her way to the end of the hallway. She stood by a window, pretending to listen, and waited for the night nurse to forget her presence, and then she lumbered into the stairwell. The two flights did not prove as painful as she'd imagined. She planted both feet firmly on each step before proceeding to the next one, one hand on the railing, the other firmly on her cane, each step as precise and deliberate as a musical note. If this were all, she thought, her arthritic knee, her brittle bones. Before the chemo, her cane had always stood in one corner of the bedroom she had used in their daughter-in-law Miriam's house, what had once been her grandson Patricio's room. When she made it up to the top floor, she was surprised to see the door to the roof ajar, a breeze passing through it. She had not been outside in weeks, since the last time she was in Jackson Hospital and the treatments had been temporarily stopped. The night air sneaking into the stairwell felt as precious and as dangerous as something stolen. She wished she had woken Modesto and brought him up. He missed his long afternoon walks to the bodega, strolling patiently on the edge of the roads near Miriam's house. Única had accompanied him once and was surprised to see that most of the way to the bodega had no sidewalks. Nobody walks in this part of town, Modesto explained proudly, as if he were the last practitioner of an art long forgotten. Sometimes Miriam came on weekends and took him out for a stroll on Ocean Drive, but the nurses forbade Única to go unless she used a wheelchair. They said she was still too weak from the treatments. A wheelchair! As if she were an invalid. ¿Y qué? He always came back from his walks more depressed than when he left. He told her in two words that he didn't like to be apart from her. Miriam had wanted him to stay in her house, and that's how he had responded, with the same two words, "No puedo." As a parting gift, she had given him a Walkman to listen to his classical music tapes. It's true what they said about old age. He was turning into a boy again and he needed Única as simply as a child needs its mother. Just to be there. Única gave a good push to the roof door and then climbed the last step and stood in the doorway, loving the way the gentle breeze teased the new nap-like growth on her skull. She had not looked at herself in weeks, had hung a hand towel on the mirror over the bathroom sink (which her nurse Lucas kindly rehung every morning after Modesto was finished shaving), and now she wondered how much grayer her hair was. The doctors had said that it would probably grow in that way, thicker but grayer, maybe even a little curlier. It was more difficult once she was out on the roof, having only the use of her cane. She wished she had worn something other than her slippers and her ratty night robe (but she wasn't sure if she still owned any shoes, and whatever old dresses hung in her closet always went unused). She had refused also, after the first phase of the chemo, when they were still living with their daughter-in-law, the use of those monstrous contraptions that they called walkers. She'd rather stay in bed all day, she told Miriam, rather have her bones in a sack.

"You don't listen to anyone," her daughter-in-law had told her the night after Thanksgiving, the day after Elián had been found, floating on an inner tube. They had just eaten turkey sandwiches for dinner. "You never have. That's why it's better that you have daylong professional care. Them you'll have to listen to, coño. It is for your own good, mamá."

What use living in a country where family can say such things? How dare she call her mamá?

There were a couple of lawn chairs on the roof, a beach towel draped over one of them. Maybe the nurses came up here to sunbathe on their breaks. For a moment, looking at the chairs, Única lost her direction. Which way was the ocean? She hobbled on the sticky tar, leaning on the cane with both arms, to one edge of the roof and grabbed tight to the low concrete parapet. Below, there was only an alleyway, and across, an abandoned building, its windows shuttered with flimsy plywood. She found it odd that there were any buildings so near the ocean left to sit useless. In one of his few talkative moments since they'd arrived here, Modesto had told her what a great job they had done with all the hotels on Ocean Drive, how they had restored them to their original splendor. Twenty years before, when they had first moved to their little apartment on Meridian Street and Miami Beach wasn't as fashionable, clusters of the old lounged on the hotel porches, waiting for a guagua to oblivion, the buildings' ratty structures crumbling, the wood perforated with termite damage. Única was very eager to see how much the buildings had changed, but she did not let Modesto know. The breeze picked up and she heard the irascible rumbling of the ocean. She stayed close to the parapet and moved towards the sound. When she saw the tall palms that lined Ocean Drive, their fronds swaying lazily as if they heard nothing of the troubled ocean but only the music from the open-air cafés, she dropped her cane and grasped the edge of the parapet with both hands. She moved along faster, her back foot skittering up to the front one and then the front one sliding forward. The sea continued its rumbling and its constant perturbation inspired Única—this will to never let anything stay as it is. She dismissed the blood pulsing like an alarum on her swollen knee, the hundred needles of fire pricking at her bones, the suspicious feeling that her tongue could easily reach up and lick the seat of her brain. She made it to the corner and felt the sea's presence before she could cast her eyes on it, its brackish breath assaulting her. She raised her chin.

"Sí, sí," she said, as if she were welcoming Modesto (as she never could anymore) in his still too-frequent attempted incursions into her ruined body, where he would end up doing everything himself, spilling his tepid seed on her thighs, on her belly, on the fleshy hollow between her collarbones. (No child then.) She could not remember when she had stopped loving him. She felt she no longer had access to all that had been joyful and worthwhile in their life together, and though the moments themselves had not vanished, though she could summon the images in her mind, one by one—all the way to that evening in Varadero, the second night of their honeymoon, and the manner with which Modesto had held her naked body at first, his arms wrapped around her waist, just held her, whispering his praises, till her skittishness fluttered away and a wave of fluid heat passed from her chest to the caverns of her lower parts and she felt she could not stand it anymore with just him holding her, as if she were a lifeless muñeca, so her hips shifted, thrust obscenely, she thought, and an ocean breeze made the hair on her inner thighs stand on end, so that she wanted all of him, part by part, hour by hour—they existed now only as shadows beyond the impenetrable haze of her present days.

But again, surprisingly, she wished Modesto had come with her, though he would have certainly refused had she offered, called her una loca, as he often did these days. At seventy-eight, and though on plenty of medication (twelve pills a day), he had never spent a night in a hospital, and now he was confined to a nursing home because of her. Yet, he had never had the strength to stand up to their daughter-in-law (she bought him off with a Walkman!). He had lost all vigor on the morning Única was given her diagnosis, had suffered all the doldrums and depression that the doctors had told her were her due. Única was glad, very glad that God hadn't made her a man. If it had been her, her the healthy one: Ay, the fight she would have put up!

She moved along the front parapet, keeping an eye on the sea. No moon tonight, but from the glow of the streetlamps she could make out the white of the foam crashing on the sands like spilt sugar. A pair of men wearing only sandals and shorts strolled by holding hands. They too were listening to the embroiled sea. The bounty of that day's sun still stuck like sap to their burnt shoulders. Then a pack of pale wild boys ran by them, screaming obscenities, and for a moment the friends lost hold of each other, and for such virile young men seemed too easily parted, cowering till the wild boys had passed quickly and clamorously as an afternoon thunderstorm—and the friends found each other again and made their way towards the darkness of the shore. Única thought about her grandson. She wondered if he ever held hands with his friends. Maybe that's why he had moved to Key West. It was safer there; they were less outnumbered.

If she leaned forward enough she would just stumble off the roof to the pavement below. Maybe the two friends would find her on the way back. Maybe the pack of wild boys. She let go of the parapet and found her body surprisingly light, as if she were floating in the warm sea. With her bent fingers she undid her robe, pulling it up to reach the lower buttons. She let it fall off her shoulders, and the sea air draped in around her, it whistled on the catheter above her breast. In the moonlight, the wan cast of her skin took on a ghostly appearance. She had forgotten what a great joy it was to go without clothes. She could not unclasp her bra (the nurses always did that), so she pulled the straps over her arms and slid it down to her waist, twisting it around her till she found the clasp, but still she was not able to undo it, so she left it there and slid her hand under the band of her bloomers and let them drop, and she stepped out of her slippers and slid over, leaving the bundle of clothes aside like a shed skin. She felt feverish. As dangerous and as daring as the young friends holding hands. She laughed as if she were being tickled. She raised her hands in the air and called out to the friends, "Aquí, aquí, mis vidas!" But no one heard her, so she moved farther away from her pile of clothes. She wished she could get rid of her bra but it would not go down below her belly button, even though she was, as Miriam said, thin as a lizard. It hung above her waist like garters, like a dancing girl, so she lifted her feet off the ground, one at a time, trying to keep rhythm to the song rising like a prayer from the street below. How she wished Modesto had come with her! She would relent. She would pretend to love him again. She would reach back and grab their old joy by its tail. They would do it right here, coño, on the roof of the maldita nursing home. Why not? She would give in. He would hold her on the ledge of the parapet and fuck her and fuck her until both their bodies crumbled at last. He would fuck her till they tumbled over together and they were no more.

Fuck.

She loved that word. It was one of the first English words she had learned to say, though she rarely got to use it—a few times on her daughter-in-law—but she was going to use it tonight if anyone tried to stop her.

"Fuck you," she mouthed it, pounding her fist into her palm in mock fury. "Fuck me."

Sometimes English to her was like one of those thin-headed shiny hammers used for precision nailing.

Única kept dancing, her bare twisted feet hardly lifting off the ground, the sea air like another's breath on the new soft hairs running up the inside of her legs, under her armpits. She would never shave them again. In Key West, she had once met a friend of her grandson Patricio, a short stout woman who let hair grow all over her body, except on her skull, which was buzzed like a soldier's. Única wondered how much she looked like this woman now, this woman she had then found loathsome, unnatural. Now, comadre. She kept on dancing and giggled provokingly, like someone who is holding back a great secret. And when she laughed, she covered her dry rotted mouth, so as not to infect the guiltless night with all the ills that had befallen her.

Many songs rose from below, ballads whose words she could not quite hear but whose gist she understood by the baleful abandoned voice of the crooner, by the desperate plucking of chords—así es la vida, señores y señoritas, only our wounds, our wounds, awaken us, make us compelling—and then the songs stopped and all she could hear were the sighs and the broken laughter of those who had still not gone home, so she danced to the uneven beat of their noise. She had never in her long life been drunk, but this was what it must be like, the poisons transfigured into this windy riotous joy (she raised her empty hand in a toast)—and then the laughter stopped and all she could hear were the waking groans of the ocean, calling to her.

A light, soft and hushed as the steps of a lone ballerina, appeared at the frayed edges of the mantling sky; it should have comforted her, she knew, but she suddenly felt the excoriated folds of her innards and became frightened of the gentle glow. She grabbed the parapet again and shuffled over to her cane. She took it and left the pile of clothes and made her way to the stairs. Pieces of stone dug at her soles, and just before she reached the doorway, she fell to her knees. The light grew, more suggestive now, as if others, more vigorous, more grounded dancers, had joined the lone airy ballerina. Única was on all fours, the pain at her bad knee and the hidden wounds within her and the young morning all denouncing her mad excursion, so she crawled into the shadows of the stairwell, dragging along her cane. By the time she got up, both hands on the railing, dangerously close to the precipice of the stairway, the light fell on the roof like the waves of a thunderous symphony that had no use for dainty ballerinas. There was blood on her knees, which she touched with her fingers and spread on her breasts and on her cheeks. She slid along the wall with her hands, smearing it, and picked up her cane. She was as patient going down the stairs as she had been coming up, first the cane and then one foot and the other on each step and then the next step and the next one. She imagined the notes of Bach's *Goldberg Variations,* played in an impossibly slow tempo, each key struck one by one, as if the notes existed alone, independent of each other. (Modesto had listened to the Glenn Gould recording again and again on the night they had found out about their son's fate.) But the farther she got away from the garish morning light, the more she felt lost, forgetting which floor she was on (had she passed one doorway, two, three?) and the colder the concrete steps became, sending a chill up her legs, up her spine, till she was unsure of whether she was descending or climbing. She lost hold of her cane and heard it tumble eagerly away from her. And for a moment, she leaned forward and thought she would follow it. But this passed. She turned and faced the wall, grabbed the railing with both hands and continued, sideways, both feet on each step, passing her cane, which she spitefully kicked aside twice (till it tumbled farther down the stairway). She passed doorways that looked out onto empty hallways and kicked her cane along when she felt it graze against her feet, till she reached the bottom door and, ignoring the warning in bold red letters that this was a fire exit and that an alarm would sound, she pushed it open and heard nothing of what had been warned and felt the morning's warmth again, and she thought she had just traveled in a loop back up to another roof. She picked up her cane and made her way out.

It was an alleyway, which she followed to its opening, not questioning how there could be streets on a roof, as if a whole deserted city and its nearby beaches could naturally sit atop some great renovated art deco building. She stayed close to the walls of the buildings, hiding in their shadows, her whole body turned away from the waking world, from the prying sun, as she plodded up the street towards the sound of the ocean. Someone called to her from a balcony, and then that someone called to her God, "¿Dios mío, Dios mío, qué es esto? Una viejita sin nada." She had to hurry; they would surely send someone after her, so she quickened her pace, pressed closer to the walls, as if she were blind now, ignoring the honks from cars and the bleary looks of those who, like her, had spent the night sleepless and were in various euphoric stages of undress. But when she made it to the corner of Collins Avenue, the wide street seemed as impassable as a rushing river. At the corner of the last building, she pressed her cheek to the wall and let her feet rest in the strip of its shadow and looked out across the expanse of Collins Avenue, knowing how close the sea lay beyond it.

"No puedo." Then, "Sí, coño, ¿cómo que no? Todo se puede." So she went on—admonishing herself for what a fool she was and with the same breath calling on all the saints to whom she had not prayed in ages not to abandon her in this quest—this way and that, till she whispered a quick plea to Saint Lazarus of the Wounds and she found the courage to venture away from the wall, at first holding on to the frame of the rusty fence that surrounded the building's front garden, at whose center sat a lone majestic almond tree, and then with only her cane as aid, both hands wrapped around it and the insufferable weight of her years bearing down upon it. She did not make it far. Before she had reached the curb, she fell again, this time unable to break the fall with her arms so that her chin bounced on the pavement and she bit hard on her tongue and on her lips. The roof of her mouth rattled in its place and felt as if it had come loose and settled back in askew. She pushed her head up and then her torso till she was again on all fours like an animal. Bright drops trickled from her mouth and splattered on the sun-bleached sidewalk with a shocking splendor. If she let go now, she could just let it happen here, on this corner, at this sparkling hour before the morning truly came, before anyone but those who had not yet gone to bed were awake to bear witness. Her cane had bounced away from her and she could not see it anywhere. She could not recall where she had been heading, but something, the raw briny primeval odor, perhaps of nakedness, of a thing just killed and laid open, told her she could not be far. Here. Here. What better place? She crawled into the garden, under the shade of the almond tree, and pushed off her arms and sat back on her bottom, her useless legs folded in front of her. (She was going to a place where she would not need them.) Again, she smeared blood on her cheeks and on her breasts. More cars passed by now, but they ignored her unless they were stopped at the light. She heard vulgarities about her drooping breasts, about her age, about her tortillera's haircut, about her shriveled sex, and they called her what Modesto would have called her, loca, loca de remate. No one stopped to inquire what she was doing at dawn, wearing her bra as a garter belt, seated and bare-assed, a trespasser in the garden. So why not here? Why not on this spot where no one would ask any questions? Here, here there would be no two-faced daughters-in-law, no conscientious nurses, no stone-hearted doctors to get in her way, to tell her of the need for patience, for fortitude, for faith, who talked as if these things were something one put on as easily as one smeared blood on one's cheeks, on one's breasts.

It was funny, the way they talked to the condemned.

So on her little spot of private grass, she laughed vehemently, but this time did not bother to cover her mouth. Her shoulders shook, her bloodstained breasts jiggled, her breath fouled the salty air, her peals filled the hushed morning, and now, when cars stopped at the light, the passengers would cast their eyes from her, and the driver would let the car inch up dangerously towards the intersection, away from her, and she was sure that no one would ever be brave enough to come near.

The boys were still dancing when they approached—the same wild dance that they had begun when they ambushed the friends who held hands the night before—dancing still, in a whirlpool, arms flailing, chanting their own song, as if casting a spell on the soberness of the new day, summoning back the outlandish night. There were five, six, seven of them, or more, she could not tell because by the time she noticed them, they had already surrounded her, some on their knees like supplicants, some rolling on the ground like fallen creatures, some hanging off the almond tree like monkeys, and some, she thought, hovering above her on their tiny wings, whispering in her ear, blowing kisses on her neck and passing their soft hands on her bare scalp; and, except for their threadbare loose shorts, they were as naked as she was.

"¿Qué pasa, abuelita?" they whispered. "¿Qué pasa?"

One of them undid her bra and passed it to another, who wore it tied under his chin like a bonnet, and it was as if they had put on him a crown, for he forthwith became their leader. He tucked his long dark hair behind his ears and straightened his milky lanky hairless frame. He barked orders simultaneously at those on the ground, those on their knees, those in the tree, those in the air, his reptile eyes boring intently into them, as if their existence depended on his seeing them, waving one hand around like a conductor, keeping one finger of the other hand pointed directly at her, as if to signal, for those dumb enough or stoned enough not to get it, who his orders were about, and then, in a sugary voice that was half-pitying, half-mocking, he spoke to her:

"We're taking you, abuelita. We're taking you where you were heading." He reached down and touched the catheter above her breast, was confused by it, and then with his thumb he wiped some blood from her lips and traced a circle on his scrawny chest and smeared his tiny brown nipples. "Vamos, vamos," he yelled, turning from them and raising his blood-stained hand in the air, "take her!"

She felt their hands under her armpits, grabbing at her waist, pushing up on her rump. Others reached into her mouth and took her blood and smeared it on their chests like the leader had done. Her arms flailed as she rose. "My cane, coño," she protested. "Why can't you find my cane?"

The leader, who was already halfway across Collins Avenue, turned and stared at her. Cars passed him, swerving wildly to one side or the other, as if he were made of some substance that repelled all physical objects. He nodded and moved back towards them, ignoring the screams and the horns blaring at him, and returned to the garden. He surveyed its grounds and hopped up on the almond tree, leaning one way and then the other, passing his hands over the branches, till he found the right one and with one quick turn of his wrist broke off a young branch, as easily as if he were cracking a chicken's neck. He peeled off the leaves and branchlets and handed it to her. "Your cane, abuelita," he announced, and then bowed, before he was off again. And with her new cane, the others surrounding her nakedness, pressed so close they kept her from stumbling, she followed him, across Collins Avenue, across Ocean Drive, towards the sea, and none dared stop them.

On the beach there was an early-morning jogger who would later tell those in charge at the nursing home and the police investigators that he thought it strange that a naked bald old woman was steadfastly making her way across the wide stretch of sand towards the water, leaning on a long crooked staff, determined as a prophet crossing the desert towards Jerusalem, but that this was a crazy town and that he had seen crazier things before, so he didn't stop her. She seemed deranged, caked in dirt, maybe even blood. Perhaps she was homeless, going for her morning bath. Maybe she had just murdered someone. At any rate, he had been either not interested enough or (more likely) frightened too much to do anything but keep on jogging.

And there was no one else on the beach?

No, no one else, just the crazy old woman, and a pair of half-naked gay boys sleeping on the sand, wrapped around each other.

"There was no one," her nurse Lucas said to Única. "You appeared on the beach by yourself. There were two men sleeping there. They saw you go in the water and, like the jogger, they thought you were una loca, desnudita como el día así como estabas, going in for a morning swim."

"Ay, Lucas, some people need to be blind. Those little wild angels came to get me, not anyone else; that's why the jogger couldn't see them. You can tell yourself that you saved me when others wouldn't. If it makes you feel better."

So she told Lucas all that had happened just before he came and rescued her, all that had happened that the jogger and the two friends sleeping on the sand couldn't possibly tell him about.

Their numbers grew as they approached the water. Some she thought had surfaced from the foamy shore and were coming towards her. These were also naked, but thinner and darker than the others, and their skin glistened with droplets of broken light, like shimmering scales, and their hair was strung with seaweed, and their eyes spread wide on their heads, and their sex livid and heavy as ripe plums—these were all the other little ones, Única thought, who had had no band of dolphins to protect them, no mothers prescient enough to give them a bottle of fresh water, who had never made it across the treacherous straits and had grown older with the creatures of the sea—and they seemed ill at ease on the sandy earth, wobbling, their arms thrust out for balance, ungainly as newborn calves. They approached her, carrying handfuls of seashells that they tried to shove into the folds of her body to give it a drowning weight. The other boys joined them—joined her—in their nakedness. They slipped off their threadbare shorts and cast them in the air with a whoop. The boy who was their leader threw off his bra-bonnet and also cast it in the air, and when their shorts and her bra rained down, he was like them and they were all like her. And they whooped in unison.

Maybe that's when the friends who had been holding hands the night before noticed the wild boys, because the friends had been sleeping (on that detail the jogger had been right), wrapped around each other, the sand covering their lower halves up to their belly buttons, so that it seemed that they had been struggling up out of the earth and had perished just when they were almost there, had perished without letting go of each other. But at some point the two friends must have awakened (perhaps because of the whooping of the boys), because one of them raised his head and called out to Única and that's when the wild boys left her. They seemed astonished that there was anyone else on the beach besides them and her. They crouched. They dropped their handfuls of seashells. They fell to the sand, grabbing at it as if it were a sheet. They looked up at the sky, at the sea, back out to the hotels on the street, their bright eyes wide and darting end to end. The ones that had come from the sea fell from their stagger and crawled on the ground back to the shore and disappeared into the foam. The others, once they had figured out where the voice came from, moved towards the half-buried friends and surrounded them in the same manner that they had surrounded Única under the almond tree. Some dug under the sand and crawled beneath the two friends, others lay beside them and tangled their long limbs with theirs and others yet tarried above them like days to come.

Única moved on without them. When she had made it deep enough into the water, with the aid of a rope that floated out to a faraway buoy, she let go of the almond branch. It was dragged back to the shore. The warm sea slapped off the blood from her breasts, from her cheeks, it gurgled in her catheter, it stung in her mouth, and it lifted her and dropped her as casually as if she were a windblown scrap. She held on to the rope until her feet could no longer graze the bottom, and when she let go, she felt little hands grabbing at her feet, at her thighs, kelp-like arms wrapping furiously around her waist, tugging her outward, and it was as if a world of little fish-like saints had grabbed her and with all their diluvian cunning were whisking her to her glory.

LIKE CARY GRANT

SHE MADE UP HER MIND, a week later, the morning they took Elián away. She said the same thing many Cubans in Miami had said that balmy late April Saturday, after watching countless replays on the special reports of the puta marshal carrying the horrified boy away, "I can't live in this country anymore. Yo me voy." Leaving. All leaving this city they had invented, this guajiro resort town that they had transformed into a sleek international metropolis in less time than it takes to build a cathedral. Pero claro, none of them had really meant it. Leaving? ¿A dónde carajo? Where could they go?

But Única Aveyano knew where to go. That Saturday evening she asked Lucas to let her use the computer in the supervisor's office. She thought Lucas looked like Marlon Brando in *On the Waterfront,* young and oddly handsome, already a little balding, but not quite as pudgy. She often told him this (though she left out that middle part). When he thanked her, his voice was lispy and girlish, like Brando too. He had won her over almost from the day she had arrived with her husband, Modesto, after the first intense phase of the chemo, looking like a mad gypsy with a motley scarf wrapped around her head. Miriam had decided it would be better if they had daylong professional care. That's how she put it—in a methodical, even voice that sounded as if she were reading directly from one of those dreadfully blithe pamphlets from the Leukemia and Lymphoma Society, or the American Cancer Society, or Jackson Hospital, which after her diagnosis appeared almost daily in all their festive bird-like colors, stuffed into the wrought-iron mailbox like a cluster of Christmas cards.

They arrived in the nursing home a few weeks before the celebration of the new millennium. When they were set up in their room, each with a bed (which was fine with Única—during the last weeks in Miriam's house, after she had come home from the hospital and dutifully returned to be by his side, she had had to master the art of dozing in and out of her nights on the very edge of their shared mattress), Lucas told her if there was ever anything she needed, to ask, sin pena ninguna. And she did ask, for the thing she needed most then. There were four or five thin white hairs growing from her chin, and her husband would not pluck them anymore. Somehow they had withstood the chemo. Could he do it? Could he pluck them, por favor? Modesto let out a little noise, as if he had just dropped something small and fragile; but Lucas nodded and quickly returned with a pair of tweezers, and took her face in one hand, carefully, as if handling a newborn, and plucked her unsightly hairs. And from then on, he did it every third week.

On that night, after they had taken Elián away, Única assured Lucas it would only be a minute. She wanted to order something on the Internet. She reminded him that she had her grandson's credit card, his password. It wouldn't show up on his bill for another month. She whispered this in Lucas's ear, using her most practiced vanquished voice. Lucas was clearly Patricio's type—what happens to all these men, she often wondered, that they forget about the joys of a woman?—so every time she mentioned her grandson's name, his face softened, lost all its boyish tension.

"O sí, sí, Patricio," he said, his ears reddening, his serpent-green eyes cast away. And he let her into the supervisor's office, walking her to the wide mahogany desk and sitting her in front of the computer. He stood guard outside. It took Única less than half an hour to find what she wanted. The empty late-night hours that she had spent on her daughter-in-law's computer had paid off. She found it appropriate that the company that made the inflatable raft was called Caribe. Without a motor, it came to $289.95, plus shipping and handling. She charged it to her grandson's credit card. It would arrive at Miriam's house in eight to ten days, which was a little too soon, she thought, but at least it would give her time to plan, to tell Modesto (if she had to, if he ever talked to her again: his silence these days was as menacing and oversized as a butcher's knife). She would tell Miriam that it was Patricio's birthday present. She would ask her grandson to come visit them for his birthday, which was in May. She had already convinced Miriam to let them stay at her house again for a few days, like she had been promising for weeks now. Once there, it would be easy. Patricio rarely talked to his mother (though Patricio's silence was different from his grandfather's; he wore his silence like an athlete does his medals, as something hard fought for, deserved), so he wouldn't call her before he left Key West, and that would give them the time they needed. She thought all this through before she stepped out of the super-visor's office, and the only thing that bothered her about her ingenious plan was that she would have to lie to her grandson. She had never done that. She pulled out one of the forbidden cigarettes from the secret pocket in her robe and smoked half, till her dentures began to hurt. Her palate felt like the soft rot-ted roof of a rain-soaked bohío, at any time ready to collapse from its own weight. Then she put the cigarette out on the sil-ver ashtray and left it there. She leaned on the desk and on the walls on her way to the door. She knocked lightly and heard Lucas jangling his keys before he let her out.

"OK?" he said.

"OK."

"What were you ordering?"

"A birthday present, para mi nieto." She took his forearm.

"What did you get him?"

She dismissed his question with a flick of her hand. "Some-thing." She stumbled.

"Where is your new cane?"

"¿Quién cojones sabe?"

"It's not funny." But he laughed, as he always did when she cursed in Spanish. Like so many young Cuban-Americans born in this country, Lucas didn't speak Spanish too well. So she spoke to him mostly in English, which she had forced herself to learn to speak in her old age, mostly by watching American movies that she had first seen during the early years of their marriage, when Modesto acted as if he were still courting her, surprising her with gifts, which he would hide in their tiny apartment in Guantánamo and she would find only after he had left for work: in the mop bucket under the kitchen sink, potted violets whose tiny flowers were as delicate and unfathomable as their new life; hanging by a meager thread from the lightbulb above her mother's fire-scarred four-legged bathtub, a miniature gilded box of coconut truffles, succulent and lingering as grief; taped under the sewing machine that had been a wedding present (the only one) from Modesto's half sister, Rosana, an envelope with love notes written on pressed and dried magnolia leaves. Those first years, he courted his own wife as if he were not sure that the law of man meant anything as far as they were concerned, as if the tragedies that had immediately preceded and followed the day of their wedding had rendered their union void, annulled, as if she were not yet, and could never be, his.

One day, not long after their honeymoon in Varadero, when Única could hardly do anything else, adrift with sorrow, could scarcely manage to get out of their marriage bed before dusk, Modesto arrived from his law offices and found her wandering the rooms of their apartment, checking in drawers and cabinets and cupboards, as if she had lost something, barefoot, her hair in tangles, her breath rank, a look in her eyes that made him fear she had no idea who he was. He gathered her in his arms, gingerly, afraid he might harm her with his touch, and guided her to the bathroom, stripped her and stood her in her mother's bathtub, which he filled up to her ankles. With a warm soapy washcloth he cleansed her as if she were an invalid, calling out each place in her body out loud—the long slope of the neck, the hollow between the clavicles, the muted space between her breasts and the breath hidden in her belly—summoning her back to her own body. Then stepping into the tub with her, still in his shabby work suit and dropping to his knees, he continued to call out the mystery of her body (now as if to make it his own), the slant of her hips and the fragrant dark hairs of her sex (as he pressed his cheek against it), the secret hollow behind her knees and her long toes with their unpainted nails. Única looked on him distractedly and let her hand rest on the crown of his head.

"You are getting all wet," she said. "What will you wear to work tomorrow?" But then she was back, she was there with him again for the moment.

On Friday nights, he took her to el teatro on Calixto García to watch American movies. The badly dubbed voices always reminded Única, as she watched the oblivious yanqui actors, moving their lips and saying nothing or screaming with their mouths shut, of the possessed man in the Gospel of Luke. And when she watched these movies again, so many years later, to learn to speak English so she could talk to her own grandson, the actors having regained their voices (their very selves, it seemed), it was as if in the intervening years, the Lord had touched them and cast out all their demons.

She had learned to read English a long time ago, as a girl, with the books her stepfather, Dr. Esmeraldo Gloria, took from the library in the yanqui naval base for her to keep, with his patient tutoring, and with only the best, as he said: the noble doomed language of Thomas Hardy and the voluminous excursions of Charles Dickens and her favorite, the drunken prose of William Faulkner. But speaking English was surprisingly more difficult than she had imagined—all those silent letters hidden within syllables, scarring pronunciations like a salty wind. But Única persisted, as she had done with Faulkner, until she was better at it—speaking it, reading it, writing it—than most native speakers. At first she had thought it was a shame that so many young Cubans were losing their native language, but such things mattered less and less as time passed. She adapted, and now she spoke so much English that some of her laziest thoughts—about the weather, about the movie they had watched the previous night in the rec room, about her necessities—appeared to her like clouds of mosquitoes in that menacing tongue.

She stopped and pulled out Patricio's credit card from her robe pocket. She pointed to the little photograph in the corner.

"He's a good boy, coño."

"Yes, and very handsome," Lucas said, which should have bothered her, but it didn't. She nodded and looked into Lucas's startling green eyes and then again at the little picture of Patricio, the swarthy complexion he had inherited from his mother, the spilt-ink eyes set against the toothy bright smile that he used to disarm others, and that he wore always, like a favorite wrinkled linen shirt.

"Bueno, así es . . . maybe . . . ," but she couldn't finish her thought, so she took Lucas's forearm again and let him lead her back to the rec room. "My mouth hurts again."

"You shouldn't have smoked, then."

She wasn't surprised that he smelled it on her. "I wish some-one would get them for me," she said.

He ignored this, as he always did her requests for the things that would kill her, the only kind of request he would ever ignore. He led her to an examining room, put on some gloves and a mask and put his fingers under her chin and examined the week-old wounds in her mouth. "Open." He stuck his fin-ger in one side of her mouth and stretched it out gently. He peered in and she could smell his citrusy breath through the mask. "You're lucky, you could have really hurt yourself."

"I left the butt in there," she said when he let go of her mouth. "Left it right on her ashtray." She nodded once, as if to make a point, but she knew that Lucas hadn't been talking about the cigarette anymore.

"I know. I'll clean it up before morning."

"Poor boy," she said.

Lucas didn't respond. She had heard him speaking to some of the other nurses about Elián, how he thought the boy be-longed with his family in Cuba. She wondered if Lucas had had a good father. Then she thought about her own son, who never had much of a chance to be a father, good or otherwise.

"Poor boy," she said again, though Lucas couldn't know she wasn't talking about Elián this time.

He tapped her hand. "Anyway, they're due to fit you for new dentures next week, aren't they?"

"I won't need them."

"Please, señora Única, no se ponga dramática." He addressed her in the formal mode, the Spanish words spoken almost syllable by syllable, as if he were inventing them. He took off his gloves and put out his hand. "Now, give me the cigarettes."

"No," she whispered, as if there were anyone else there from whom to hide her contraband.

"Give them." He wiggled his fingers. He had long feminine hands for such a well-built boy.

"Ay niño, por favor, what good is it not smoking now?" She wished she could pull away from him, leave this room, but she was afraid she would fall before she reached a wall. "Ya, ya, the price is paid. Anyway, if you take them . . . I can get more."

He lowered his hand. It always worked; whenever Lucas challenged her, she summoned the specter of her illness.

"I want to see my husband," she said. He nodded consolingly.

Modesto was asleep on the couch in the rec room. The headset of the Walkman that Miriam had given him had slipped down his neck. She could hear the tinny notes of his music as she approached. His mouth was set in a pout, a dribble down one corner. His glasses had fallen off his nose and lay on his belly, strands of his neatly greased hair had come loose from the top of his head and hung over his forehead, and his long legs were splayed out in front of him like a pair of loyal sleeping hounds, but his hands were neatly folded over his chest (just like when he took his siestas). Lucas led her to the couch and politely asked one of the younger residents, a russet-skinned woman from Alabama, to make room for Única. She took his glasses, folded the arms, put them back on his belly and shut off his Walkman.

No movie tonight. The television was tuned to the Cuban stations, still blaring with news about Elián. A photograph, whose authenticity the newscaster questioned, had just been released: Elián in his father's arms. His famous smile. Única soon found herself translating the news bits for the woman from Alabama, as competently as she translated the old American movies for her husband. At first she agreed with the newscasters: the picture was certainly a fake. She knew what could be done with computers these days. But then she wondered if Elián wasn't the type of boy who could be happy anywhere, with his beautiful cousin, with his comunista father. There was an art to it—this living in happiness. One had to be born with it, she supposed, like an ear for music. And develop it, lest it wither.

"Too bad," she said to the woman from Alabama, "we won't see how he turns out."

The woman looked at Única over the rims of her glasses, her cloudy eyes puzzled, her lips wet and parted, as if she were waiting for a translation, though Única had spoken in perfect English.

Modesto stirred beside her, his hands unfolded, and he grabbed her wrist frantically. She winced. Ever since the chemo, her bones felt as if they each had been dropped from a great height, shattered, and then hastily pieced together with the incompetence of a child gluing together a broken vase. Her kidneys were ailing, the doctors said, but there was hope; the cancer was taking a beating. They spoke of it like a wounded boxer. She imagined it otherwise. She imagined it leaking like a juicy rumor from the fatty part of her bones to every region of her unsuspecting body.

"Estoy aquí. Aquí estoy." And she turned and translated for

the woman from Alabama. "I am here. I am here for him." She shrugged and the woman smiled. Única pried her husband's fingers off her and made a note to trim his fingernails. If he ever let her near him again.

When he noticed how his hand had instinctually reached for her, Modesto quickly let go and grabbed his glasses. He pulled his heavy legs toward him, took out an old plastic comb from his pocket and passed it through his waxen hair, until it was all set back in place. He turned his music back on and put on the earphones. He didn't ask Única where she had been. It had been over a week since he had said anything to her. He grunted as the TV showed one more replay of the events of that morning and then cut to the smoky streets, erupting in riots. Everyone in the room seemed captivated and disgusted at the same time. Some eagerly looked for a glimpse of their grandkids at the riots, others cheered the rioters on, and one old man got up and poked the screen, pointing out someone he knew. Única wished they could watch a movie as they usually did on Saturday night, but Lucas hadn't even bothered to rent a video, knowing the news about Elián would take precedence. Única had wanted to watch *Bringing Up Baby* again. There were parts of the movie (her favorite because of how they lightened Modesto's mood), such as when Cary Grant is forced to wear the lady's nightgown, when Modesto laughed so freely that Única did not need to translate at all. She had heard that Cary Grant too had been like Lucas and her grandson, but at least he had been married, which is what they all should do, and keep their dirty little things on the side. De todos modos, all men did it. Oh God she knew! Their dirty little things. That's how God made them. Of that she was thankful, that God hadn't made her a man, as gawky and as jittery and as foolish as Cary Grant singing about love to the wrong Baby, who could cleverly assemble his outsize dinosaur monster but not notice love when it was biting him in the cheeks. She looked up again at the endless reel of Elián being carried away, his boxer shorts slipping from his hips, his little hands like a frightened kitten's paws on the shoulders of the marshal, and she wondered what lucky girl would one day take his virginity from him, and how happy the young lovers would be that night and how far away this night of terror would seem.

WHAT YOU CAN TELL A NEW YORKER

THE STRUGGLE FOR FREEDOM, Única Aveyano explains to them, sipping her black tea in the garden of Dr. Abdel Alirkan's Brooklyn town house, is one of eternal vigilance.

They have come here as a last resort. The doctor, her grandson's friend, has pulled a few strings and has generously welcomed them into his own home. Única is now being looked over by the finest cancer specialists in the world. She is reminded of it daily by her grandson and her husband, in a humorless tone, as if they were casting a spell not only on her illness, but on her every misfortune.

She sits cross-legged on one of the wrought-iron benches. The garden is like a room with half a roof. It is late May, and someone has already been busy planting and beautifying. Morning glory vines creep up the lattice fences and a blooming wisteria braids the overhanging trellis. Heavy terra-cotta pots of all shapes and sizes and brimming with flowers crowd

the edges of the garden like ponderous spirits afraid to roam.
She looks for the ghost of her stepfather hidden amongst
them. A gas lamp burns almost unnoticed in the extravagant
late-afternoon shadows. She is not sure that they understand
her. Her grandson looks at her with a bewildered face, as if she
were pronouncing some inscrutable prophecy.

Her nurse, Lucas, her private nurse now, imagínate eso, has
also come with them to New York. He leans with one arm on
the flank of the lean angular bronze horse that is the center-
piece of the garden, his lustrous eyes cast downward. He had
gone out on his skates looking for her and now he is barefoot,
one foot on top of the other. His toes are as long and elegant as
his fingers, the nails neatly trimmed. When he looks up, he
stares at her cup of black tea. She continues: If you take it
from me, now, this freedom to go as I may, pues vaya, then you
might as well have left me in Miami, might as well have kept
me locked up in that maldita nursing home. Her nurse looks at
her, wounded, as if this comment had been meant specifically
for him. Her grandson crouched beside her, his face turned
away now, breaks off a succulent branch of a yellow begonia.
His rage has subsided, but he is not convinced.

She had disappeared that afternoon for the first time since
coming to New York—on one of her walks where she recited
the names of streets—and when she'd returned some hours
later, her grandson had screamed at her, had said his mother
was right, pulling out Única's wicker suitcase and throwing all
her clothes into it as his grandfather watched in silent terror.
No one had ever seen her grandson like this. They were going
back to Miami that very minute, he had said, unless she promised not to disappear again.

Her husband does not want any part of this conversation. He is inside now, in the front room, reading the Spanish newspapers that her grandson buys for him daily, listening to the classical music station on his Walkman in case any of their voices should seep into the basement of the town house.

What are you afraid of? she says. She sets the teacup down on the wrought-iron bench and extends the fingers of her right hand and embeds them in her grandson's tangled dark hair. That I'll go and disappear forever one day? He places his hand over hers and hunches his shoulders. The broken begonia branch hangs limply from his fingers. She imagines that his eyes have begun to water, but she cannot see his face. Do you think you can prevent it if that's what I want?

Her nurse walks over to her, takes the cup from the bench, sits beside her and finishes drinking her tea. You shouldn't have too much caffeine, he says.

Later, at the dinner table, Dr. Abdel Alirkan will have the final word. He makes sure that they have dinner together at least four times a week. She must feed herself well, he says, strengthen herself for the renewed chemo treatments.

Oh, it is bad manners, he says in his melodious voice, little grains of arroz con pollo stuck to his lower lip; you should never tell a New Yorker when she can come and when she can go.

HALF A FRUIT

THEY HAVE TAKEN ELIÁN. On that night, they sit in front of the television and watch the scenes in succession as if it were a bad dream they can't stop from having. Elián is screaming, but you can't hear him, just like in a dream. Modesto stares at the television and grumbles and then falls asleep. When he wakes up, he tells Lucas that he wants to go out to the streets to protest, that he wants to go to the riots. Then he starts talking about his days at the University of Havana, about all the protests that he organized against all the corrupt powers of the capital. He tells him how once the government police fired into their midst, tells him how exaggeratedly warm another man's blood feels when it splatters on your cheeks.

Most of it is true, Única thinks. He doesn't need to invent.

After he graduated from law school, Modesto Duarte spent three years living in a one-room tenement in La Habana Vieja. When not at the office or at court, he would spend his free hours outside, lounging like the bands of wild black cats on the steps of the Catedral de San Cristóbal, whose solid magnificence inspired more faith in him than any creed ever could, or wandering under the balconies of the colonial houses of Calle Obispo, peeking in through parted shutters out of which wafted the smell of sofrito and the chatter of families getting together for the weekend, or paseando in the cracked and salt-weathered walkway of el Malecón, which wrapped in limestone around the shoreline of the city as if to keep it from dissolving into the sea.

At night, when he returned to his shabby room, he took a bath hunched over the kitchen sink, wiping his underarms and his privates with a little towel, eating dinner on the single mattress thrown on the floor, strewn with law books, whose dictums and precedents were entirely ignored by the Havana judges, as if they were the scriptures of an ancient dead religion, and during the day he represented the poor and the outcast who lived in the tin-shack barrios on the outskirts of the city, looking almost as ramshackle as them in his grease-spotted shirts and single pair of pants that had grown so threadbare at the seat that he had had to borrow a brightly colored shawl from an upstairs neighbor and tie it around his waist as a sarong. He thought himself a great idealist.

And then one summer he came back to Guantánamo to visit a dying aunt (who along with his half sister, Rosana, was all that he had left of his family) and he saw Única Aveyano from across the street, sitting on the veranda of her mother's house on Narciso López Street. She was still nothing more than a child pretending to be a woman. But he did not notice this at first. When he saw her, her body turned away from the street, her legs pressed together, the side of one foot resting against the lower calf, lifting the hem of her lacy dress, he thought it was Única's young mother, Marcia, who long ago, it was known, went mad over lost love, and now it was said seduced the most desperate and forlorn of men in town. Modesto reluctantly crossed the street to offer a cordial hello and be on his way, for he did not want to linger too much in the presence of this foolish woman whom he hardly knew. He kept his gaze lowered as he made his way towards her, so it was only when he had reached the opposite sidewalk and looked up that he noticed that it was not Marcia sitting on the veranda, that instead a child was looking back at him. His vision suddenly became blurry and all he could focus on was on the child's round face, bounteous as a split ripened fruit—this was definitely the image that came to his mind, because even though he could not take his eyes away from her face, in the penumbral haze surrounding it, he imagined that the girl was holding something out for him to take, so he raised his hands to grab it, thinking it was a fruit of some kind, half a papaya or mamey. But then he heard the girl giggle and saw her empty hands rise to her mouth to cover her smile.

"Are you a beggar, muchacho?" she said.

It was not an outrageous assumption, Modesto thought. He could not remember when he had last shaved or bathed, and must have reeked of impending death from the days spent at his aunt's bedside, and the raggedy wardrobe that was the cause of so much amusement for the learned Havana judges now pleased the young girl as well. He lowered his hands and thought but did not tell her until many years later (when one day her flesh abruptly refused to receive him) that he might as well be a beggar in her presence.

"De ahí empezó," Modesto says to Lucas.

That morning was the ruin of him. A week later he moved back to Guantánamo, into an upstairs room of his half sister's house, and began planning the arduous courtship of the madwoman's daughter. At first unsure of how to even approach her again, countless times passing the veranda of the house on Narciso López Street, only to encounter there what he thought he had seen the first time he passed by, the madwoman herself, eating her afternoon pastries with her friend, the mousy doctor. Modesto would salute and continue on his way, though more than once he lingered, or paused and turned after having gone a few steps past them, but had no gall to formulate the question that now lay at the core of his being. Where was she? Where was the girl? That vision that had made him return to this flat, insipid, sun-punished pueblecito? And then one day, as he was making plans to return to the capital, Rosana called from downstairs announcing he had a visitor. Modesto had no friends left in this town, so he could not imagine who it was. The doctor, the madwoman's friend, was standing on the front porch; he was still wearing his medical scrubs and would not step into the house, so they talked on the porch.

"This will not take long." He introduced himself. He said he was like the girl's father, and from the way he spoke about her, with the shortened breath with which one would speak of a beloved, Modesto believed him. "I imagine you want to see her." Modesto nodded meekly and lowered his eyes.

"It can be arranged."

Y bueno, after that, the poor of La Habana were left forever without their protector, for things happened, vaya, all those unavoidable misfortunes and unquestionable blessings that glaze over any life—the death of a parent, an unexpected illness that doctors diagnosed as grief, the birth of a child—and they postponed their move to the capital, once and twice, and then canceled it altogether.

He tells Lucas all this while they watch the endless newsreels, the marshals butting down the door as if the little house were a fortress, shoving people out of the way with their rifles to get to the boy. "Qué pena," he says. "For this a mother dies." He watches and rages about it to Lucas. He tells him stories, but he will not talk to Única.

It has been a week now since Lucas found her barely floating in the sea.

THE CRACKED MARACA

HERE IN THIS WORLD, Única Aveyano writes to Patricio, affliction occurs as naturally as the bubbling of thick coffee in the morning. And we must react to it as such. What use pretending that we are living in an unparalleled nightmare, when whatever woe has befallen us has befallen others hundreds, thousands, millions of times?

In her long nights of insomnia and freedom, after the residents have gone off to their purgatorial sleep, she takes one of her little egg-shaped pills and imagines herself as replete with stories as Scheherazade.

The long night before Easter, on the day they had taken Elián away, under the sparse light of a miniature book lamp, she writes again to her grandson. She imagines that the stories she tells have not changed at all over the years, that she repeats them just as she remembers them, just as she heard them from her stepfather, but that is the wonder of the cracked maraca of her imagination: the stories rattle in her mind from beginning to end, from end to beginning, and everything is and is not fully what it had been; things are skewed a little, off-center; characters are haunted by the jarring noise that invented them.

The second time she saw the ocean was during her honeymoon in Varadero. At sunrise, she sat on the balcony of their hotel room in her shabby suit of mourning and watched the waves, and the tiny blur of her husband's figure, his arms doggedly slashing through the infinity of the sea.

After her mother's sudden death, both her stepfather and her future husband had decided that the wedding should go on as planned, even though the hurried funeral and the marriage ceremony had been less than a month apart. She had not fought them, but she had not been surprised when the pall of her mother's death (pobre muchacha, with half a life yet to live and her heart stops just like that) cast its shadow over their wedding day, in the consoling stares of the congregation, in the cheerless manner that Father Gonzalo had asked them to repeat their vows, in the just-nibbled-on pieces of coconut wedding cake, in the countless bottles of wine and champagne that had turned sour, so that each guest had to settle for just a few drops from whatever good bottles were left, and in the half-finished dances, the music dwindling note by note, instrument by instrument going silent, as the pairs shambled from the dance floor. But most of all, Única felt the pang of her mother's death throbbing at her temples, in any audacious claim she might stake on her future happiness, in any foolish hope that all those toasts that they raised their almost empty

glasses to—to long life and longer love, to loyalty and a devotion that finds joy in the crannies of every hour, to fulfillment
in each other, through the flesh and beyond it, and vaya, to
family, chico, to many children and many, many grandchildren—might somehow, somehow be honored.

On their honeymoon, after his swim, her husband would
come to her, still wet, half-naked, and sit cross-legged on the
floor beside her.

"Why is it that you married me?" he asked one day. She was
surprised by the gentleness with which he was able to ask such
a weighty question, but she continued to look at the waves.

She hunched her shoulders. "It was the first thing I ever
really wanted, ever really needed, to be with that lovely gangly
beggar who approached the veranda that afternoon."

"Would you have waited for me if someone else had asked
you first, pues, if someone else had come to take you from that
house?"

She continued to look out at the waters. It was true,
throughout her childhood she had been like a prisoner in that
house. "Imagínate," she said, not even imagining an answer to
her husband's question, "living in a nook of the most beautiful
Island in the world, and at nineteen years old this is only the
second time I have seen the sea!"

She had left their pueblito only once as a little girl to travel
to the southern coast of the province, because somebody had
told her mother, Marcia, that they had seen Christophe Evesque
there. That was her father—she knew—though he was not
often talked about in Guantánamo, especially in their house.
That was the beginning. Years before, he had breezed through

town and in less than two weeks had fallen in love with Marcia, proposed to her, given her a thin silver band of an engagement ring, impregnated her and abandoned her. It was true, sometimes a whole lifetime of tragedies can be lived in less time than it takes to hatch an egg.

Marcia's mother, Única's grandmother, was horrified.

Her name was Pilar. She was an erect, pale-skinned, sable-haired woman, the features on her face a bit off balance, and most perfectly composed when she narrowed her eyes, as when disbelieving something, so that she was most handsome when most ravaged by doubt.

Pilar kept Marcia hidden in the house, the heavy drapes drawn, as if by keeping out daylight she could keep out the long gaze of el chisme. But it was impossible to keep light out of their airy house. It flooded in as it does into all Cuban houses, as if by pressure, pouring in through the open-air courtyards, rushing through the grille of wrought-iron doors, via the stained glass of geometric mediopunto windows (without losing any of its vigor), trickling past the slits of closed shutters, seeping in between clapboards, and even by biding its time stealthily just beyond the deceptive shadows of verandas.

When she saw that she could not win her battle against the light, Pilar put a padlock on the outside of her daughter's bedroom door, which she opened only to slide in her meals and to clear the chamber pot that Marcia was forced to use for her necessities. She would not let her out, Pilar announced to her daughter, till she found a doctor to come to the house to terminate the pregnancy.

Marcia wouldn't eat any of her meals, afraid that her mother was poisoning the food to kill the baby. She receded to the farthest corner of the room, from which the breezes that normally passed through the house had been banished, and a feverish air, tainted by the reek from the chamber pot and heavy as her mother's mahogany furniture, prevailed.

"Good," Pilar said, taking away the heavy plates of food. "I hope you both starve to death! ¡Puta será si nace! Puta como la madre."

But she wasn't always this harsh. Vaya, she loved her daughter, and sometimes, Única thinks, as she recalls the stories piecemeal and labors to write them out for her grandson, love gets pretty ugly. Sooner or later, everyone finds that out. So one night Pilar left open the door to her daughter's bedroom and set down a blanket just beyond the doorway, laid out with a sumptuous dinner of plantains and roasted chicken, and shrimp stuffed with carne de cangrejo, because she knew her daughter loved seafood, and sat there on her haunches and pleaded for her daughter to come join her, begging for forgiveness, explaining that she had just been thinking of her future, that she knew well the anguish of raising a child on one's own, of the evil tongues that would speak against her, of the stenchy solitude of knowing a man only once, because that's exactly what would happen, no man would ever again approach her knowing she had borne the child of another, and who could blame them, to have to be reminded every day, by looking on such child, no matter how lovely, that your wife was once in the arms of another, her mouth shucked open by some other tongue, her breasts suckled by other lips, her . . . Bueno ya sabes, mi pobre hijita, perdóname, pero así es.

And so ended Pilar's contrite soliloquy: "I don't have to tell you. When all you have to do, all you have to let us do, me and the young doctor who is coming soon, is . . ."

But by then, by the time Pilar had decided to be gentle and loving to see if that would work, Marcia had already hardened herself. It was an astonishing transformation that took place in less than a week. Whereas before she had been a flighty love-lorn child, her character unformed, her aspirations minuscule, the twin blows of the abandonment by Christophe Evesque and her mother's heartless insistence on putting the unborn child to death had steeled her, had given her a new sense of what it meant to be alive, even if at first it all seemed like a glorious madness.

"I will not share a meal," she said from the oppressive shadows of her room, "with someone who wants my baby dead." So Pilar stood up and squinted, so that all her features fell naturally into place. She brushed herself with the back of one hand, as if dusting off all responsibility, and backed away from her luxurious picnic dinner without touching a morsel and left the door open. She did not imagine that at one point during the night this feast would tempt her daughter.

"Mira, coño," she said, "ya estoy cansada de esto. No sé. You are free to do as you want. I have called a doctor and he is coming, because I love you and because it is the right thing to do, but I am leaving all the doors open tonight and if you are gone from this house in the morning, it shall not surprise me at all."

But Marcia was still in her room the following morning, though it seemed as if a pack of dogs had gone at the meal laid out in the blanket. There were bits of dried food splattered on the walls, pots were overturned, glasses shattered, the blanket itself shredded into frayed strips. Pilar ran into the room afraid that Christophe Evesque had returned during the night and finished the desecration of her daughter. But Marcia was alone in the room, on her knees, gnawing on a rolled-up photograph. A trail of food and sauce and bread crumbs and bone bits and shrimp tails and a muddy drool led from the blanket to her knees, up her ruined nightgown, to her aghast face.

"Is this what love is like, mamacita?" she asked, chewing on the edges of the photograph, one hand on her belly. "Is this what it is?"

And Pilar, for the first time in their life together, addressed her daughter as an equal:

"No, mi cielo," she said, wrapping her arms around Marcia's clammy body, letting her daughter's unwashed head—the locks of hair snagged with shrimp heads and chicken bones—rest on her shoulder, "this is not what it is, but this is what it feels like sometimes."

She took the photograph from her child, spread it over her breast and let her daughter press her cheeks to the image of her beloved. Única Aveyano still had that picture somewhere. Maybe in Patricio's house in Key West, where Miriam had sent her boxes for storage, among her books and ceramic statuettes of the saints. One day, she writes to her grandson, she would show him the picture, show him how much he looked like a Moorish version of his great-grandfather. She never got her mother to talk much about him. Marcia talked endlessly about the days of her pregnancy, about her struggle to keep her baby, told that story to anyone who would listen, but about Christophe Evesque, about their brief and doomed affair, she never said much. What Única knew about Christophe Evesque she knew from that dreaded doctor who was coming to end her mother's only pregnancy, the cursed angel whose role was to bring Única Aveyano her first and earliest death, but who was instead to play such an immeasurable and tender role in her life.

Christophe Evesque was a navy man. In the hand-colored photograph, he is wearing a crisp uniform and his hair is trimmed very short on the sides and thick and black on top. It is a profile and he is looking far off into the distance, his pale green eyes burnished with youth, his eyelashes thick and long as a lady's, his nose just blunt enough to keep him from being too beautiful. His chin is pressed to one of his hands and his lips kiss his index finger, but it doesn't look as if that is a gesture that Christophe Evesque would do naturally; it is a pose, intended to give him the air of a pensive young man, a pose perhaps intended to cloak his brash nature. I always imagine, Única writes, that he seduced my mother in the opposite fashion with which your grandfather seduced me. Whereas I was drawn in by Modesto's almost pitiful sincerity, his absolute guilelessness, my mother must have been dazzled by Christophe Evesque's inventiveness, by the way he transformed himself and all those around him.

Pero bueno, that was another story.

Two days after Pilar found her daughter on the brink of madness, a young doctor arrived from Santiago de Cuba. Marcia would later tell Única that as soon as she saw him walk into her room (whose drapes had now been parted to let in the afternoon light and whose shutters had been forced open to allow passage to the tropical breezes, the room freed of the haze and nostalgia amongst which had hidden the treacherous memory of Christophe Evesque), she guessed that the doctor, with his narrow rodent eyes, his skin sticky and rosy as the pulp of a persimmon, his scrawny bent-over figure, his cat-scratch of a mouth and his hairless eyebrows, his halo-like bald spot that all the downy hair from around his elfish skull could not begin to hide, was clearly a man sorely in need of love. And, Marcia thought, with the mere promise of it—or perhaps even with the future possibility of the promise of it—she could save the life of her unborn child. So she asked her mother to be left alone with the doctor so that they could discuss the procedure. In less than an hour, she had arranged the ruse with which Única's life would be saved. Dr. Esmeraldo Gloria (that was the hapless savior's name) would leave that evening pretending the procedure that he had been summoned to perform was a complete success. He would return in the rainy season, when his lie would have become apparent, and whisk Marcia away to live with him as his wife in Santiago. Marcia sealed her end of the promise with a kiss.

"And he could not kiss me back," she told Única many years later, sipping from her white teacup, with him sitting right there next to her on the veranda. "The poor man had no lips. So really it was only half a kiss and the deal was never closed."

And so, as if knowing of the forces gathered against her in the outside world, Única Aveyano grew almost imperceptibly in her mother's womb, completely unbeknownst to Pilar, who once again had taken to parading her daughter before a society to which she had never quite belonged due to her own unwed state, and to her own father's rash act before dying, inventing stories of how her daughter had been bitten by a mosquito and come down with a virus from the darkest regions of the Nile, to which everyone snickered, knowing very well that the mosquito that had bitten Marcia had likely been passing on infections from near the banks of the Seine, not the Nile. And yet, to men and their mothers alike, Marcia seemed to have been transformed from that inconsequential little girl with as little cultivation as a mustard seed to an assured young woman who carried herself with an air of authority, as if the few French phrases she had learned from Christophe Evesque and now used freely served as ballast to her bearing, who—it was obvious now—could one day as gracefully and ladylike give orders to servants as please her husband in bed. And she must have been aware of her new advantages, for all who approached her with offers and invitations were kindly turned away.

But Marcia and Dr. Esmeraldo Gloria could not keep their secret for long. On the first day of her second trimester, a month before the start of the rainy season, while her mother was away at the market, Marcia stood naked before the full-length mirror in Pilar's room. She was caressing the roundness of her belly, for the first time since Christophe Evesque had abandoned her, indulging in the fleeting pleasures of her nakedness, of her bare feet on the cool terra-cotta floor, of an itinerant afternoon breeze brushing so tangibly past her, it felt as if she were not alone. She jumped on her mother's wide bed and wrapped herself in the linen bedsheets that smelled of her childhood when she had been allowed to sleep with her mother. It was then that she heard a rustle outside the drawn curtains. She covered her nakedness with a bedsheet and tiptoed to the window, pulling on a corner of the curtain to find, on his knees on the brick floor of the patio, his trousers halfway down his hairy thighs, his snail-like organ shriveled in his hands, the drunken and spent figure of Dr. Esmeraldo Gloria. They were later to celebrate this day (since they had no other) as their anniversary, the only day of the year when Marcia would drink, lifting a glass from the bottle of Montrachet that Dr. Esmeraldo Gloria purchased from a certain colonel at the naval base and laughing together at this memory as if it were someone else's farce. Pero, coño, that day nobody thought anything was funny, and Marcia wasn't the same helpless little girl who had met Christophe Evesque less than four months before; this was now a woman to be feared, as Dr. Esmeraldo Gloria, huddled outside on the brick patio, was about to find out. Marcia searched and searched her mother's closet for a man's belt, which was a hard thing to find in that house rarely frequented by men. No man had lived there since Marcia's own grandfather Agosto, in a fit of revolutionary zeal, had joined the mambises—those great Cuban revolutionaries in the wars of independence against Spain, fighters who were mostly guajiros and ex-slaves, as fierce and stealthy and deadly as scorpions—and been promptly shot down from his horse and killed on his troop's first confrontation with the Spaniards. Though Marcia knew her mother kept one, the very belt that Agosto had been wearing when he was mortally wounded in the soggy land of the Battle of Dos Ríos (just minutes before José Martí himself had been shot down). The leather was stained with mud and with her grandfather's blood. She found it in a box in a corner of the closet, where the rest of her grandfather's shabby mambí outfit was neatly folded, the countless holes where the bullets had struck sewn together so expertly they were barely noticeable. She wrapped the buckle end tightly around her hand, wound the bedsheet around her torso and went out to the patio in search of Dr. Esmeraldo Gloria. The poor man did not lift his pants, did not cover his privates, did not raise a hand to defend himself when Marcia thrashed him with her grandfather's bloodied and muddied belt. When Pilar arrived some hours later, she found them on opposite corners of the brick-floor patio: the wretched Dr. Esmeraldo Gloria curled up like a sunburnt fish, next to the giant outdoor brick oven, facing the southern wall, his hands covering his head, his pants still halfway down his legs, long rosy welts on his thighs, back and buttocks. He was whimpering about his endless devotion to Marcia, of how this and much more he would endure for her. Marcia sat atop an overturned rum barrel on the opposite corner, her hair standing on wiry end, the bedsheet fallen from her shoulders to reveal her enlarged breasts, her burgundy nipples, her elbows on her knees and the belt still wrapped tightly around her hand and dangling in front of her.

"The pervert was watching me," she told her mother, looking vacantly into the distance, "and I am not finished with him."

Pilar approached her daughter, unwrapped Agosto's wide belt from her hands and set it aside. She raised the bedsheet to cover Marcia's nakedness, and while she was adjusting it she let her hand rest momentarily on Marcia's belly. She looked over at Dr. Esmeraldo Gloria and at once understood.

"¿Qué han hecho?" she asked, shaking her head in disbelief and narrowing her eyes so that all her features fell perfectly into place and she became, abruptly, beautiful. "¿Qué carajo han hecho?" She raised a hand to slap her daughter, but when Marcia did not as much as flinch, her eyes still focused on some distant place, Pilar brought it down with full force on the rum barrel, creating such a thud that Dr. Esmeraldo Gloria was shaken out of his stupor and clumsily pulled up his pants and crept farther into the corner of the patio.

"I am going into my room. I expect that you will both be gone when I come out." She picked up her father's belt by its heavy buckle and dragged it beside her, a gesture that offered no comfort to Dr. Esmeraldo Gloria, who blubbered from his spot, begging her not to leave them alone again.

But Pilar could not stay in her room for long, perhaps because as she put back her father's uniform, in a corner of the closet, she remembered the morning that they told her of his death, one of his ragged comrades touching her body with his dirty fingers in the places where they had shot her father. She had always promised herself that no child of hers would ever feel as abandoned as she had felt that morning. When she came back out, one of her old maternity dresses draped over her arm, it was as if she had never been lied to, as if she had cared for her daughter's pregnancy throughout.

"This is how it is," she said to Marcia as she slipped the dress over her, her voice threadbare. "This is how it always is. It is worse than playing with serpents, this playing with love." And then before going to the aid of Dr. Esmeraldo Gloria, whom she would later bathe with almond oil and cure with coconut butter and dress in one of her father's sand-colored Sunday linen suits, she adjusted her own dress and passed her hand through her dark hair and said more assuredly, "Bueno, parece que I have been lied to. I'm going to be a grandmother; we'll need to build a new room for the child."

Única Aveyano never knew her. The morning before Única was born, Pilar suffered a stroke while washing her face over the sink. They found her curled on the cold tiles of the bathroom floor, her loose hair coiled over her cheek, her eyes still open, her face so harmonious and lovely that they knew she had spotted death as it crept up on her, and could not imagine that it had come so soon.

"I think she wanted her soul to be yours," Marcia said to Única during one of her lunatic spells, "to get back at me."

As for Dr. Esmeraldo Gloria, they got to know him very well. After that morning, when he came to Guantánamo to spy on the naked, pregnant Marcia, he never returned to Santiago de Cuba. He established a clinic in Caimanera, a small town near the American naval base. For years after it was established in 1903, the base had been a small operation, but it had since been renovated and expanded. The runways were lengthened, new barracks with shiny tin roofs erected; old officer's shacks were torn down and replaced by modern ranch-style houses. By 1932, the year Única Aveyano was born, the base was a thriving small city, with its own hospital, its own school, a bar, two churches and a synagogue, two radio stations and even its own cemetery. Dr. Esmeraldo Gloria offered his regular services to the yanqui families in the naval base, spreading the word through townspeople who performed menial jobs there. But few yanquis came, till one morning when a woman entered the empty clinic quietly, with a girl in front of her. Dr. Esmeraldo Gloria looked up from the novel he had been reading to pass the time. "I have heard," the woman said, "that you can spare us all a lot of trouble." She was a colonel's wife and this—she pushed the girl towards Dr. Esmeraldo Gloria with the back of her hand—this was her daughter. The child looked directly at Dr. Esmeraldo Gloria, her face devoid of the terror evident in her mother's voice. She had freckles that spilled from the center of her tiny nose towards her cheeks, and marble blue eyes that darted around the room as if she were following the flight of a fretful insect. In a few years, Dr. Esmeraldo Gloria thought, she will be quite a beauty. She was a colonel's wife, the mother repeated, and her little daughter was pregnant. Dr. Esmeraldo Gloria assumed the colonel did not and would not know. The girl's face had suddenly changed, her eyes darkened, her mouth gone slack, as if the mother's saying that she was pregnant had made it so. When the mother said that she could not be by her daughter when it was done, Dr. Esmeraldo Gloria stood from his desk and took the girl's clammy hand. She whispered something in his ear and it was then that Dr. Esmeraldo Gloria understood that her restless eyes had been searching for the instruments with which he would perform his task. But that was something she would never see. It was the doctor's talent that when cases like these left his care, it was as if the blunder and its consequences had been completely rubbed out, as if for a moment the patient had been given the godlike facility to reverse the penal rush of time. After his success with the colonel's daughter, other women from the naval base were added to the many on his patient list from Santiago, who still sought him out in the marshes of Caimanera as if he were a shaman. The yanqui

women grew to trust him so much that soon they started coming to him for other problems, and they brought their mothers
and friends; so with his perfect English and his sympathetic
demeanor, his new practice became a resounding success, and
as he had been welcomed to the marble terraces of the colonial palatial homes of Santiago de Cuba, he was invited into
the homes of officers and given free use of all the facilities at
the naval base.

But he could never forget Marcia, who would not admit him
fully into her life till Pilar's sudden death and Única's birth the
following day, when it was he who arranged the funeral and he
who was the only one there to aid in the delivery. So Marcia
learned to accept his visits every Wednesday with the same
resignation that one accepts a minor disfigurement. He came
still dressed in his surgical scrubs, exactly at eleven o'clock in
the morning, always uninvited, and he brought pastries and
pies that he had baked himself at the base, made of pecans
from Louisiana and sweet pears from Maine and rhubarb from
Georgia, a plant whose cordate leaves, he warned, were as poisonous as unrequited love, and blueberries from California,
dark and lush as an August midnight. When Única was old
enough to understand, he told her that he was glad she did not
resemble her mother, for she would not be able to torture others with her looks. As Única grew older, it was her grandmother Pilar whom she most resembled, her hair lustrous and
funereal, her eyes a burnt tangerine, her skin pinkish and extra
sensitive to the daylight and the touch of others, but most like
Pilar in the everyday expression of her face, which looked a bit
distorted, a bit off, until, that is, you asked her a question she
did not know the answer to, or revealed to her a lie.

Marcia and Dr. Esmeraldo Gloria would share the pastries quietly on the veranda after Única had brewed tea for her mother, till Marcia stood and, with that same hand on which she still wore the thin silver band Christophe Evesque had given her as an engagement ring, brushed any crumbs from her dress and with that quietly dismissed him. It seemed as if Dr. Esmeraldo Gloria learned to take great pleasure not in any hope that Marcia would one day accept his love—that, he knew, was delusional—but in the obvious fact that Marcia would never again accept any man's love. For unfortunately, Única Aveyano writes to her grandson, when you choose to harden the outside to survive some great woe, much of the inside hardens too, or it withers. Marcia would have legions of admirers in her brief life, all but one whom she dismissed without consideration, but it was only with the mention of Christophe Evesque that a glimmer of life would return to her stony dark eyes. And it was on one of their Wednesday afternoons out on the veranda that Dr. Esmeraldo Gloria mentioned in passing that he had heard someone at the base mention something about having seen a certain Frenchman named Christophe who had bought some land near the southern coast. Pues vaya, Marcia couldn't even finish her blueberry cobbler that Wednesday. She went in the house and threw a suitcase together and grabbed Única and led her past the helpless Dr. Esmeraldo Gloria, who was still there seated on their veranda when they returned three Wednesdays later, after a long and fruitless journey took them through the rocky arid land of Costa Sur, where the winds blow hot and fierce as jealousy, through Santiago de Cuba, where Marcia ordered her ten-year-old daughter to look into the eyes of strange young men as they strolled the narrow hilly streets, for perhaps she might recognize the face of her father, to the basilica perched on a hill at El Cobre, where Única heard her mother's rageful prayers to the black Virgin, protesting that she was drowning, drowning just as desperately as the three slaves that the Virgin had saved so long ago; and inside the muggy, windowless sanctuary a chill made Única's skin bristle and she knew that even if the Virgin had heard her mother, She would do nothing to save her.

"¿Y qué?" Dr. Esmeraldo Gloria asked nonchalantly when they returned, weary and sleep-deprived. "¿Qué averiguaron?"

"Get out of here now," Marcia told him, "and I never want to hear that man's name mentioned again in my presence."

Dr. Esmeraldo Gloria, a spotty three-week-old beard on his chin and above his nonexistent lips, obediently stood and gathered all the stale yanqui pastries and pecked Marcia softly on the cheek. He gave Única a longer kiss on the forehead and casually said he was sorry that they had not found what they went looking for. The next day he returned, freshly shaven, his hair combed neatly over his bald spot, with a bagful of fresh pastries, and though it was not Wednesday, Marcia accepted his visit. They sat on the veranda while Única brewed her mother tea, and when he was about to leave that night, Marcia asked him to return the day after, and he did, this time in the same sand-colored linen suit that Pilar had dressed him in years before, after she cured the wounds of Marcia's beating.

At first Única thought that her mother was going to be annoyed that he had chosen such a thing to wear on the first time he had actually been *invited* into their house. Pero al contrario, when Marcia saw him, with that jacket that hung on him like an overcoat and those pants rolled up at the ankles like a fisherman, she burst into a fit of carcajadas that would not stop till much later that night, and she ran into the house and came out swinging her grandfather's wide belt high over her head, but this time Dr. Esmeraldo Gloria was howling with laughter. He dropped his bags of pastries right there on the sidewalk and raised his arms in the air and wiggled his bony little hands and ran into the house screaming, "Ay, ay, me coge," with Marcia right on his tail, her arm cocked in attack position. She chased him twice around the long kitchen table and once on her elbows under it, off one wall and through the narrow dark hallway, into her bedroom and over her bed, batted up against the mahogany armoire and off the dresser, around and around the four-legged bathtub, out to the patio and past the brick oven and up the trellis of bougainvillea to the Spanish tiles of the roof, and down the veranda and into the house again. All afternoon and into the evening, they played this game, boisterous and inexhaustible as schoolchildren at recess.

When Única tried to join in, her mother became serious and shooed her away, even once raising the wide belt over her, though she had never in her life raised a violent hand towards her daughter. Única went and hid in her room, and when she heard all the racket die down, she came out and searched for them all over the house, and they were nowhere. Resigned to spending the night alone, she went to the kitchen to get herself a glass of milk before bed and from the patio heard the familiar sound of her mother's weeping, that distinct and jagged plangent refrain of four halted in-breaths followed by one long bovine ululation on the out-breath that she had come to know so well in her short life. She followed it, and at first could not see her mother but only the dwarfish figure of Dr. Esmeraldo Gloria, curled up next to the outdoor brick oven, facing the southern wall, his pants halfway down his legs, in almost exactly the same position and gesture to which he had been reduced on the afternoon of the beating. Only now, Única saw, as her eyes adjusted to the darkness, he held her mother's small naked body in a taut embrace. Her back was to him, so she could not see her mother's face; in fact, all she could see of her was a portion of her bare shoulder. His chin was pressed tightly in between her wing bones and his hair had fallen to one side to reveal his bald spot. Their bodies swayed together so gently that she could not know then that her mother's crying was not brought on by this great day of child-ish joy but by the dour knowledge that she had finally forsaken all hope of ever again seeing Christophe Evesque, whom Única never knew, and whom Marcia would never see again. From then on, Dr. Esmeraldo Gloria baked all his pastries at their house, and sometimes he had both ovens in the kitchen and the outdoor brick oven all going at once, and the house and its environs were permeated with such a strained sweetness that it became evident to all that some great sorrow was desperately being covered up. As Única grew accustomed to Dr. Esmer-aldo Gloria, she grew fond of him. It was he whom she secretly called her father, and it was not until Modesto took her to the sea in Varadero that she left her little town again, and in the quiet moments when her husband sat beside her after his morning swim, learned to care for someone else as much as she cared for the man she called her father.

There were more stories, Única writes to her grandson, altogether different stories, of Modesto's meticulously planned
courtship, which he prepared with as much fastidiousness and
devotion as he had his most notorious case in the capital,
where he had successfully defended a band of students who
had hijacked three buses in protest of a proposed fare in-
crease. He had argued that since the students had taken the
buses to the hill where the university sat, and since the university was by its charter autonomous and had to answer only
to its own laws, and since the army had violated this charter by
storming the campus, the students should be released to the
chief of police of the university district and he and not the
state should then deal with them. Modesto was the only one in
the courtroom not shocked when the judge had agreed. So he
was not expecting to fail with Única. He always appealed to
Dr. Esmeraldo Gloria's sense of justice, since it was he who
was behind the complicated ruses that would let the young
lovers meet without Marcia's knowledge, one Nochebuena even
begging Marcia to accompany him to midnight mass, though
everyone knew that he had been an adamant atheist all his life.
It all culminated on the morning when Modesto came to ask
Marcia for her daughter's hand in marriage and Marcia chased
him out of the house, threatening him with that same belt that
they then used as their love toy.

      In the end, it was Dr. Esmeraldo Gloria who had to give his
approval, Modesto forced to sit with them on the veranda one
sultry Wednesday afternoon in June of 1951, as he laid out in
detail, and without once daring to look at Marcia but directing
all his words at the proud doctor who acted as father to the
child whose life he had saved for such selfish reasons, of their

future together. Modesto always said it was the worst three
hours of his life. He, who was used to suffering the invectives
of the high-living Havana judges, who had once sat in vigil outside the Miramar villa of one of the most powerful of Havana's
judges, cross-legged beside the marble fountains in the front
courtyard, in his grease-spotted shirt and borrowed sarong and
with a burlap sack full of documents, taunted by cars passing
by on la Quinta Avenida, till the judge reluctantly came out to
him in his leather slippers and silken bathrobe, and so Modesto
was hurriedly able to reach into the burlap sack and show him
the deeds to the homes of hundreds of Havana urban dwellers
he was representing. The government was planning to raze an
entire barrio to build a huge civic square, hundreds of families
evicted from their homes without compensation. The judge,
who had before refused to hear the case, would not touch the
documents, as if somehow they might be unsanitary; he pretended he had forgotten to bring his reading glasses, but he
raised his chin and looked with disdain towards the young
shoddily dressed lawyer.

"Why do you do all this . . ." he asked, and then made a dis-
missive gesture with his hand, ". . . for these people, these
masses? Do you have some sort of political ambition? Is that it?
Do you want a little bit of the power that you so condemn in others?"

Modesto was still busy searching through the deeds and the
question made him pause. It was a rare day when he didn't
look to the near future, a future when he could establish a
credible candidacy in the congressional elections, make a bigger difference than he was making now, and sí, coño, perhaps

own more than one suit, perhaps even find someone to share his life with, and have a nice home of their own. Was there anything wrong with that? Did it tarnish what he was doing? Modesto looked up from his handful of deeds as if he had forgotten what he was doing there and the judge, happy with this small victory, dismissed him. "I will hear the case on Monday," he said, "but it does not mean I will change my mind about anything." In the end, he awarded the inhabitants minimal compensation, enough to find dwelling somewhere else for a month or two. The judge looked with pity at Modesto as he read his judgment and Modesto could not look directly back at him. And in like fashion, Única writes to her grandson, your grandfather had withstood the belittling glare of the most powerful men in the country, and yet was to count those three Wednesday hours with Marcia and her lover (for that is what he called poor Dr. Esmeraldo Gloria, who though he eventually shared her bed and her life, never got any closer to Marcia's heart than the lonesome heavy harvest moon gets to the earth) as the most humiliating and painful moment of his life.

Till now.

Till the Saturday morning a week before when Única went searching for her second death. Simple as that, coño, she writes. She did not want to spend one more fretful night wandering the halls or sitting by the cracked windows of the nursing home, her head bent low to catch the little sea breeze that wavered past the screen, the faint and tinny music that reached her ears as if from a distant boxed-in past; la verdad es que she did not want to spend one more single night there at all. Vaya, chico, not just in the nursing home, but on this earth.

She doesn't remember why she went to the roof first. Ay sí, sí, to look at the sea. The sea, her first companion in mourning. She went up to the roof to look at the sea, thinking that maybe in her precarious state, while she was admiring it, she would just tumble off. Why? She doesn't know why. Not the illness. Not that at all. After she had been diagnosed, her psychiatrist, Dr. Marty, warned her that her illness would do what nothing else had been able to, something finally to make her want to cling to life, to struggle against.

She had heard in the news some weeks before the story of an old married couple that was driving to Orlando to see their new great-grandchild. Something was happening on the road ahead of them; they slowed down so quickly that a big semi smashed into them, sending them into the opposite lane, where another semi, coming the other way, finished them off. Colorín, colorado, este cuento se ha acabado. Whatever suffering there was, must have been cabined in a little box three seconds wide by four seconds long. And somewhere in there, inside that horrible little box, Única imagined, there must have glimmered some speck of peace, as tiny in its confined world as anything might be in the dusty range of eternity. She had heard that there is a moment after a drowning man gives up the struggle, after the limbs have grown torpid, after the urge for breath has abated, where he becomes one with his uninhabitable surroundings, for a brief moment effortlessly a creature of that world to which he must have once belonged but is now a stranger, a foreigner, finally come home. In that moment there is a peace and stillness that passes all understanding for us here above, a peace so treacherously well hidden from us, there in the depths of the sea, tiny and ephemeral as a seahorse. That poor old couple must have felt it, this peace, on their way to see their great-grandchild.

Morning has come, the brazen light beats at the threadbare curtains and Modesto stirs under the sheets. He has not moved all night, and except for the occasional weeping sounds, one might have presumed he had died in his sleep.

It is Sunday. Modesto rises from his bed and walks silently into the bathroom. Única Aveyano comes out of the sleepless night as if from an icy bath, stunned, shivering.

It is a bright Easter morning.

THE WEIGHT OF SMALL STONES

THE RIVER'S CURRENT CHANGES DIRECTION every six hours or so, rushing forth with an igneous fury one way and then the other, as if it were an adulteress running back and forth between her husband and her lover. Única Aveyano likes it best in between, when it is at the point of leaving one to run to the other, when it is gathering its strength. The surface then seems as smooth and dense as freshly laid concrete. She imagines that she can easily walk across it to the glorious city that watches impassively from the other side. Today, at the bar of the restaurant that sits by the water, she learned that the river is technically an estuary, connecting the harbor to the sound.

It is an early Sunday afternoon. She has come alone. In the past she has always brought her husband. At a fair on Montague Street, she had bought him a secondhand corduroy jacket so he could join her at the bar of the restaurant. Jackets required for gentlemen. She liked that. Her husband had his cognac; she had her black tea, sometimes a cigarette, both of which her nurse had forbidden. Today, after dutifully inquiring about her well-being, the bartender asks her where her husband is and she answers simply that she wanted to come alone. The bartender is Cuban, from Cojímar, on the outskirts of Havana—that is why they come and sit at this bar—though he doesn't remember much of it, he says; he left when he was a little boy y ahora es puro neoyorquino. He bunches up his shoulders as if apologizing when he says it. His Spanish is rotten; it exists only in phrases tattered like ropa vieja, in snippets of tangled syntax, so she often speaks to him in her precise English.

Whenever the bar is quiet enough, he makes an effort to come and refill her teapot with hot water and sometimes to refill her husband's brandy glass. He listens to her stories, every one of them up to the morning of her first death. There is little that he questions. Si así lo dice, he says to her, as if the teller of a tale had an absolute right to formulate it any way she pleased. When he is busy, he does not have time to listen to her stories; he runs from one end of the semicircular bar to the other, the city glittering from the panoramic glass windows behind him, the tail of his shirt untucked, the waiters at the service station barking out orders, the customers at the bar jiggling the ice in their glasses to get his attention. Única is afraid for him, that this will be all that he amounts to, that he will be forced to listen to the lunatic tales of old women for the rest of his life. At one point she had suggested to him that such a bright young man shouldn't be so contented in such a futureless job, but he had taken offense. He lowered his charcoal eyes and his arms hung limp at his sides. Única thought about apologizing but did not want to compound her slip-up, so she remained quiet till someone ordered a drink and he was forced to move away.

His name is Eddy.

Eduardo, she corrects him.

Eduardo. Eduardo Caballón. He pronounces the double *l* as if it were a single one. He grew up in Queens. His father worked as a janitor at a small liberal arts college north of the city and drank himself to death. Since then, his mother has rarely set foot outside of their small apartment. They now live on his bartending tips. Así es la maldita vida, he says. She wants to ask him if there are any women in his life besides his mother, but she already suspects the answer. He is like her nurse. Like her grandson. She has gotten good at figuring these things out.

It is a tranquil June afternoon on the Brooklyn side of the river. A southerly makes no mark on the frenzied surface of the water. She is sitting on a makeshift bench that was once one of the bollards on a pier. It is now painted a gaudy silver and there is a quote by Whitman, forged in metal, winding through the shiny railing that surrounds the refurbished wharf, but she has not bothered to walk all the way around to read it in full. Her stepfather, Dr. Esmeraldo Gloria, thought Whitman highly overrated. All huff and puff and no finesse, she hears him from behind her, como cualquier yanqui. He is with her now. He reminds her that he stole a copy of *Leaves of Grass* from the naval base library for her anyway. He never could have guessed, he says, that his stepdaughter would spend her last days on the leafy riverside streets that the lonesome gruff poet once roamed.

The winter coat sits heavily on her shoulder, as if it were absorbing the afternoon heat. She bought it at the same fair on Montague Street. It is the color of the madrugada over the muslin-covered tobacco fields. She cannot take it off, for it would be much harder to drag it along, especially now that she has begun selecting small stones to put in its many pockets—polished ones the color of peeled ginger from the front gardens of the stately town houses on the fruit streets, gray pockmarked ones from the dog park under the overpass, and moss-covered ones from the manicured swamps near the picnic house of the park.

Even out here, she knows that the bartender watches her. He sticks his head out from the side entrance of the restaurant barge. Sometimes he waves at her. During his breaks, they share cigarettes. Perhaps she should not have told him about her collection of stones.

A VISIT

ON EASTER MORNING, Única and Modesto received a lily plant from their daughter-in-law. She couldn't come to the nursing home that day, the note said. She was visiting her boyfriend's family in Tampa, but she wished them all the joys of the Resurrection. Lilies always reminded Única of the sultry mornings when she was a schoolgirl—the gaunt unloved teacher passionately slashing verses on the chalkboard for memorization.

> *Y ella clavando los ojos,*
> *En la pareja ligera,*
> *Deshizo los lirios rojos,*
> *Que le dió la jardinera.*

She still remembered that part, the nailing eyes and the torn red lilies.

Lucas had set the lily plant on the night table, next to the

framed portrait of Patricio. Única stood in front of it, contem-
plating the plant as if it were a strange work of art.

"I'm not going to keep it," she said. "Why should I?" She
turned and looked at her husband. On Sundays, after breakfast,
Lucas always propped a few pillows behind Modesto so that
he could read the Sunday edition of *El Nuevo Herald* in bed.
Modesto did not raise his eyes from the paper. On the doubled-
over front page, there was a picture of the masked marshal pointing his rifle at Elián, his finger creeping up on the trigger. A
colossal headline proclaimed the shame of it all. Elián's face,
she thought, did not look as horrified upside down, and she
despondently tried to find some meaning in this.

She slid an empty wastebasket towards the night table,
picked up the lily plant and put it in, careful not to bruise the
buds, and slid the wastebasket back to its place. The tight
chalky-green buds on the apex of the stalk trembled, fragile as
new-made promises.

"Why should I keep it? ¡Qué hipócrita! Joys of the Resurrection! ¡Ba!"

She looked over again at Modesto, but still it was as if she
were not there. For over a week now he had persisted with this
reticence, as if to punish her. The few times she had tried to
break his silence, addressing him directly, challenging him to
speak to her, he had glared at her, phlegmy tears welling at the
corners of his gray eyes.

The day after Lucas had rescued her from the sea she asked
for him, for her husband. He would not come, Lucas told her,
sitting by her bed in the care unit, tenderly holding on to her
hand as if he were related to her; it may take a while, but even-

tually he would have to accept what had happened and come
to terms with it—he had to (Lucas emphasized by opening
wide his lacquery green eyes), had to be by her side again. It
was normal, though, Lucas continued. To Modesto it was
almost as if, at this late hour, Única had betrayed him with
another. In a way that is exactly what she had done, gone searching for death without him.

"I . . . did not . . ." The inside of her cheeks felt like crumpled paper. The words felt withered and dusty coming out of
her mouth and she had nothing to wash them in. She leaned
forward with great effort and grabbed Lucas's wrist tightly.
". . . go searching . . . for anyone." She wanted to say more,
*Betrayed him with another? Qué tonterías, as if after almost fifty
years . . . what basura do they imagine?* . . . but the wounds in
her mouth and her tongue stung too much and it felt as if they
were parched and cracking and she could not speak.

Modesto never came to see her in the care unit.

When her daughter-in-law came by the nursing home, three
days later, Única was back in the room she shared with
Modesto, sitting up in her bed, her eyes forcibly held open,
fighting off the new barrage of sedatives. The nurses kept a
close watch on her, intruding on her solitude, tormenting her
with questions almost as banal as the ones Dr. Marty asked
her—if she wanted to watch television, read a magazine, listen
to the radio, take a nap—but she shook her head defiantly to
all their suggestions and remained sitting up in the bed, her
weary eyes fixed on the blank wall as if some marvelous film
were projected on it.

Modesto had gathered his reading material and left the
room as soon as they had brought her in that morning. As they

were transferring her from the wheelchair to the bed, she caught him glancing over at her and then casting his eyes downward, just as he had done some fifty years before, when he had clandestinely met her for their first date under a blooming poinciana in the gardens of Parque Martí, exactly as Dr. Esmeraldo Gloria had arranged it. "If you can't ever look directly at me," she had asked him then, "how are we ever to get to know each other?" But it was that, the way he had cast his gray eyes downward, as if he had just been caught in a secret, which she had first loved about him. And that gesture now, so many years later, instantly made her feel better and she wished they had not pumped her so full of drugs so that she could go out in the hallway after him, follow him around the halls of the nursing home, tug at his shirt like a beggar, till he turned around and acknowledged her again. She remained awake waiting for his return. But at about three, Miriam walked in holding hands with her American boyfriend, the artist from Tampa (*ese infeliz, what was his name?*), and Única was glad that she had remained seated upright on the bed, the ruined mask of her face exhibited. Miriam stopped suddenly at the doorway; she backed up into her boyfriend's chest, which was adorned with a whittled rough-hewn crucifix. *Larry? Or Danny? O algo así.* How could she forget something that she had once known so well? Miriam put four fingers to her lips as if she were about to blow a kiss.

"Mamá," she said. And then she rushed to the bed and took Única's hands in hers. "Ay, perdóname, I didn't come earlier, they didn't tell me it was this bad." She put a hand to Única's bruised cheek. "They said you tried to go into the ocean." She laughed and her shoulders shook as if she were weeping. "To the beach, vaya. But now . . . now . . . ." She took Única's hands and pressed them together, flattened them and then pushed them into Única's chest, as if she were teaching her to pray.

She was such an average-looking woman, Única thought, had always been. And the passing time and the harshness of el exilio weren't doing her any favors. Her hair was frizzled from so much dye and too black to match her sagging pockmarked skin, which collected under her chin in a pouchy wattle. The outer corners of her pale tea-colored eyes drooped precipitously, as if they were balanced on the edges of the table of her face and were about to fall off. And recently, she had taken to overapplying her makeup, eyeliner grainy as a van Gogh brushstroke, clownish mascara and a base coat so thick it sometimes seemed her face was made of a defective clay and had been planted on the body, which she did her best to keep in shape, going to the gym or her dance classes twice a week (oh the sight of the poor woman in her leotards in that picture she kept pinned up to a corner of her boyfriend's easel), but which dangerously fluctuated in weight so that she seemed sometimes like a bird too heavy for flight and sometimes like a withered legume. And for all her devoutness, all the rosaries and icons of virgins that hung in the walls of her Coconut Grove home, she had in her middle age been ravaged by the persistent siroccos of a belated lust, changing boyfriends every other year, and sometimes keeping one for the house and one for her travels, business companions as she bald-facedly called them. This artist, this artist from Tampa (the irony of his being a painter was completely lost on Miriam) who was at least a decade younger, as they always had to be, or younger still if she could help it, always seducing them with promises of round-the-world trips gratis from her travel agency, this artist from Tampa (coño, what was his name?) already looked vanquished. Just three years before, he had had a full head of hair, a peachy tint to his skin, his mustache trim and stiff, his posture a dancer's, and to look at him now, ay, to see what she had done to him in so little time, his pale scalp visible through the sugary layer of hair on top, his skin blotchy and scaly, his mustache grown so far over his lips and stained a rust color from coffee and cigarettes, and he stooped now, as if the brief years spent with her were a plank across his shoulders. What number was he in her ghastly parade of boyfriends? And who the hell was she to come and cast her bloodless judgment?

An impertinent smile, soothing as a breeze through curtains, was brought on by this last thought.

"¿De qué te ríes, mamá?" There was fear now in Miriam's voice, mingled with exasperation. She tried to quell it by raising her voice. "It's not funny. We were through this, I thought, all the treatments, the daylong professional care. And"—her voice lowered—"you know what this has cost me—financially and emotionally. And we're almost there, casi casi. Soon you'll be as healthy as you have ever been. You're coming out of it. Why this, then? Díme, Única. ¿Por qué? Why all the heartache, why all the drama, why put us through all this"— she frowned—"if, that is, all you ever wanted to do was die?"

"Miriam," the boyfriend finally spoke. He put a cautious hand on her shoulder and she pressed her cheek to it and sobbed, making noises, Única thought, like a sow giving birth.

"No, no, Lenny, es que I don't know what to do anymore."

Ay sí, Lenny, that was his name, pobre Lenny. How could she live in the same house with someone for more than two years and so easily forget his name? Pobre Lenny, who had had the misfortune to have really fallen in love, not like the others, not lured in by the big vacation packages, the extravagant never-finished house, the unrestricted use of the Mercedes and the Jaguar, but simply fallen in love. How devastatingly ordinary.

Lucas walked into the room sideways, leading Modesto in by the hand. Miriam stood up and wiped her tears spasmodically with the back of her hands. Modesto kept his eyes downcast, that morning's reading material tucked under one arm. Everyone waited for Lucas to say something, but it was Única who spoke first.

"My kidneys are failing, they say. That's how I am coming out." She stressed the final two words.

"Ay mamá, I know, I know. But soon they can start the treatments again." She looked to Lucas for approval, "Sí?" Lucas twisted his mouth and nodded unconvincingly.

Miriam lifted the collar of her blouse and this time dried her tears with a corner of the bedsheet, leaving two moth-shaped smudges. Lenny searched his pockets for a handkerchief but only found one of his stained paint rags, which he did not dare offer Miriam. She stood and went around the edge of the bed and gave Modesto a hug and a kiss. Modesto kept his arms at his side. With her knees bent, Miriam lowered her face till it was in his line of vision. She smiled wretchedly.

"Pero bueno, aren't you glad we've come? Mira, saluda a Lenny. Do you remember Lenny?" Modesto did not look up, but he nodded. Of course he remembered Lenny, Única thought. What a stupid question. He probably remembered his first, last and middle names. It was from all the reading, that's how his mind stayed so strong. And from the brandy he had every night. Helped preserve things, clean up the veins. What would happen to her mind? She hadn't been able to read much after the treatments had started. The words shuddered on the snowy field of the page. And if she persisted, the point between her eyes felt as if some blade were being sharpened there. The letters she wrote to her grandson had become a struggle. It was all that happened around the illness that disturbed her the most, the smaller ground she was losing on a daily basis. Her kidneys had been mildly damaged by the chemo. The second phase had been stopped temporarily. It happened, the doctors said. But that's why she had been feeling so listless, so expended, so gloomy lately. She wanted to say that she had been gloomy a long time before this, but she just stared at their filmy faces and tried not to follow the grisly logic of their *when*s and their *if*s.

"But you look good, mamá." Miriam was still beside Modesto. "Doesn't she, papá?"

"*You* look terrible," Única said.

Miriam straightened her back. She instantly stopped crying. She looked back at Lenny, admonishing him for failing to come to her defense. "Terrible? I look terrible, she says." She laughed, throwing her hands in the air and then pressing them to her mouth, and in that moment seemed to make a quick decision, a calculation of how much she would have to tolerate from her ill mother-in-law.

"I am leaving," Única said.

"Leaving?" Lucas asked.

"I am leaving this country where daughters throw away their parents."

Modesto went to the window and stood with his back to them. He did not part the curtains.

Miriam went to the bed and took Única's hands. "No hables boberías, mi amor. No one has thrown you away."

"I am leaving this country, then," Única said, a note of agitation raising her voice, "where mothers throw away their sons." She pointed to the portrait of Patricio on her nightstand. "There. You won't deny that, will you? You did chase him from his own home."

"Ay, Única, qué mala eres," Miriam said, "qué injusta. After all I have done for you."

"To end here, having my ass wiped by strangers."

Modesto turned. He took quick shallow breaths. He was fighting back tears. "Cállate, Única, cállate ya. ¿Para dónde carajo es que te vas?" He then turned to Lucas and asked him for what purpose he was brought into this room. Lucas went to him. He put a hand on his shoulder and whispered in his ear.

"He says that I should shut up," Única spoke to Lenny. "He wants to know where the hell I think I would be leaving to." She hunched her shoulders and smoothed the bedsheet. "Sorry, as you know, my husband doesn't speak English so well. I don't want you to be lost."

"Señora Única, por favor," Lucas said, keeping one hand on Modesto's shoulder, "both of you, this is not the way to work through this."

Miriam turned to Única, trying to defuse the situation. "Are you still seeing Dr. Marty? What does he say about all this?"

"I told him that I had wanted to go for a morning swim," Única said sharply. "Nothing so mentally troubling about that, right? Then . . . then he read me some poetry."

"Oh," Miriam said, and twisted her mouth. She tapped her lips, making a mental note. "Maybe . . ." Then she put a hand on Lenny, looking to end her visit. "Maybe after a few weeks, maybe you can come spend some time with us." She nodded vigorously and sought Lucas's eyes and his approval. Única had known the invitation would come. It was the easiest way out for her, an invitation like that. She and Modesto would spend a week or two in Coconut Grove and then Miriam would ship them back to the nursing home, her conscience eased.

"What about the kidneys?" she said as an afterthought.

"They'll be closely monitoring her," Lucas said. "She's a healthy woman, they'll recover and then the treatments can continue. But maybe, maybe you ought to give some thought to Patricio's plan, to the place in New York, if his friend can work something out that's, vaya, financially feasible."

"Ay, Patricio . . ." Miriam squished her eyes and groaned. Some thought seemed to be grounded between breath and voice, beating its pinioned wings. "Well, if that's what's best . . . and if he can do it, claro. But he will. It's in his nature, el santo, to give of himself. Sometimes too much. That is why so many have taken advantage of him. Vaya, he's so easily influenced. He's tormented, sad sometimes." She had begun by speaking to Lucas, but had ended up as if speaking to herself, mumbling the last words.

"What the hell are you talking about?" Única said. "That boy is happier and more alive than all of us. It's you who torment him! You who chased him from this city."

"Ay, mamá, why does it have to come to this? Why do we always end up fighting?" Her tone was more genial now. She walked over to Modesto, kissed him lightly on the cheek and put a cautious arm around him. "Mira, we're going to go now. I think mamá needs her rest. That is why she is so cranky." She wrinkled her nose and moved to the other side of the room and planted the same kiss on Única's cheek. A few black streaks ran down her face.

"Fix yourself up, niña," Única said. "You look like a sad paya-sona." Miriam kept her face pressed to Única's, not letting go.

"I love you, mamá," she said loud enough so every one in the room could hear her. "I hope you haven't forgotten that."

Única let a moment pass but then relented, and spoke as if Miriam had suffocated all her anger. "Thank you, thank you for coming to see us. Maybe we can go spend some time with you for Patricio's birthday."

Miriam nodded and patted her cheeks. "Sí, sí, maybe we can talk to him about this plan of his." She went into the bath-room and no one spoke or moved till she came out some min-utes later.

They waited in silence. At one point, one of the residents, an ancient drooling woman strapped into a walker, wandered past Lenny into the room, raised her arms and yelped. The neckline of her blouse was soaked in spit. Lucas led her out, answering all her mad questions consolingly, and Miriam, just coming out of the bathroom as Lucas was leading the old woman out, found this a convenient excuse for leaving. She promised Única and Modesto that she would take them to Coconut Grove for the week of Patricio's birthday in May, and though Única would tell Lucas the moment they had left that if there was any place where she would less rather die than in the nursing home it was in Miriam's Virgin Mary–infested home, she agreed, as if heartily, to go.

"At least she offers that," Lucas said when Única had made her comment. "Vaya, to be honest, señora Única, there are women in Miriam's situation who would not be there for you at all, not at all." He signaled to the ancient drooling woman he had led out of the room. "Do you know how many of the residents here are completely abandoned by their families? Completely."

At about one o'clock, after he had finished reading the entire Sunday edition of *El Nuevo Herald* and had eaten his lunch, Modesto finally spoke to Única again. She was in the room watching a tawdry dramatization of the Magdalene and the Galilee women coming upon the rolled-over boulder at the Savior's tomb, the only thing on television that didn't have to do with Elián. Modesto broke into the room speaking, holding his reading glasses aloft, as if they had just been having a conversation a few minutes before. He said that he didn't understand it either way, why they had wanted to keep that boy away from his father, nor why the father hadn't had the cojones to come to Miami and get his son on his own.

"If it were our boy," he said, and then stopped. He waited for Única to come to him. He took her hands, wrapped them in his and pressed them to his cheeks. "If it were our boy, coño, who would have stopped you? Who would have stopped you from knocking down that door with your bare little hands?"

She waited.

"Why?" he said. "My Única, my Única doesn't jump into the sea just because she is sick." He swallowed a breath. "Can you still miss him that much?"

His words passed like shadows on the periphery of her vision. They barely registered. She wanted to say that she missed him tanto, mi amor. More now than ever. But she remained silent and waited again. He kissed her hands. "Don't leave me," he said. "Don't leave me."

She felt the sinews of his anger tearing, till its limbs and its body lay in pieces before her.

"I wasn't leaving you, chico. It was a crazy morning. Maybe all the drugs. I was going for a swim."

"Única, no jodas. Yo te conozco," he said. *I know you.* And it was true. He was the only one who did know her.

And then he said that if she ever tried it again, to take him with her, for they were one, weren't they? Remember? They would never leave each other. Isn't that the promise that he had whispered in her ear the night after the fire that took her stepfather's life, those disquieting days after they had returned from their dismal honeymoon, that they would never suffer like Dr. Esmeraldo Gloria had suffered in that brief month he had spent apart from her mother. Isn't that why they stayed in Guantánamo? Isn't that why they did not return to the capital and to his career, because nothing else compared to the life they were going to build together?

Remember?

Y ya, ya, that's all he would say.

She didn't answer. She let go of him and found a nail clipper and quietly began to trim his nails, collecting the crescent-shaped pieces in one hand as if they were fragments of seashells.

THE HOUSE UNDER THE WORLD
OR THE THIEF OF DREAMS

IF ONLY YOU COULD HAVE SEEN your mother on the day you were born, Única wrote to her grandson.

When Patricio came out of the womb, on a rainy May day in 1972, he reached his little hand for his cheek and stretched his fingers to cover his yet unopened eyes, as if the habit of modesty were something he had learned in other lives, brought with him to safeguard him from the shames of this world, as determinedly as he dragged that variegated plasma behind him like a shorn coat. But he brought nothing into this world more decidedly than that auspicious thing that was hanging, no, pero que no, pero que réqueteno, not hanging, vaya, for already as he came out of his mother and they placed him in her cradled arms, already he was too much like his father, unwilling to shed a tear and with that husky thing pointing straight to the heavens, at the accursed gods who had just given him life. Miriam at first didn't notice, but then she saw the astonishment on their faces (all of them in that makeshift operating room), even on old Sariol, who had delivered a million babies in their town, but whose lazy eye now fluttered like an open book hit by a blast of wind, as if he were searching in the pages of his life when on earth he had seen this before. Miriam looked down below her newborn's modesty, the hand covering the face, and saw it, that fat skin-drooping finger now pointing at her, bouncing urgently on the wound in Patricio's belly as if it wanted to say something, as if its pursed lips were holding back a hundred stories of the world it had just come from.

She almost threw her son off her own body.

"Ay, ay," she screamed. "¿Qué es eso?"

Good thing Única was there, because old Sariol, by then almost eighty, was in no shape to catch the boy (his role there more as an overseer, giving orders to the nurses like a great theater director: *Gently now, put your heart into it*), and the nurses had all given a little gasp and taken a big pace back as one does in the presence of a great painting that the eyes cannot fully comprehend, so it was left to Única to take the child from his mother and swaddle him in blankets, up to Única to explain to Miriam there was nothing wrong with the boy, and that his father had been born in very much the same condition (though not as heartily endowed, she didn't add), which prompted old Sariol to start mumbling behind Única, *Ay sí, sí, now I remember.*

"Que Dios lo proteja, entonces, a mi pobre hijito," Miriam said, reaching out for her son again. "That's not a good sign."

And to Miriam's credit, from that day on, till the morning they left Cuba, even though Modesto and Única's son, Cándido, had abandoned her for the umpteenth time just a few months before only to return those last days of her pregnancy, she never spoke a base word about her husband, as if she were afraid that whatever ill she would speak to Patricio about his father she would brand him with it and condemn him to fulfill it in his own life.

Cándido, for all his good looks, all his charm, all his wisdom, all his courage and all the love that he had in his heart and gave out freely, in great meaty ladlefuls, as if he were feeding the very very hungry, as if he knew that he was going to die far too young to ever be rid of it all, Cándido made an awful lot of people suffer. Even Única knew this, though she would never say it outright.

She had tried once to measure the manner in which she had lost Cándido, as if the steps could be traced from the very moment they took his bloody newborn body from her because he would not breathe. It had been a severe birth—feetfirst like royalty, Sariol had announced—and for over eight hours Única struggled to push him out of her body, but he seemed not to want to leave the comfort of the womb, and it felt as if he were grasping at its walls with his little hands. So it was surprising when he turned out to be such a peripatetic child, who one moment would be playing tranquilly beside his mother and the next be found in the neighbor's yard, perched precariously on a brittle branch, peering into the insides of a rotted tree. He would go anywhere, escaping his playpen and crossing main streets, chasing frogs into the swift currents of the Bano River, sitting with eyes closed on railroad tracks, listening to the rumble of an approaching train until just the last minute. He wandered carefree through his early years, farther and farther from whoever was watching him, as if his only mission were to extend the boundaries of his childhood. Yet Única was able to tame him somehow, for even before he hit puberty he began to shed some of these childish instincts; there were moments when he mimicked the adults so fluently in their docility, even to the way he greased and parted his unruly dark hair, to the restrained patterns of his speech, that at times he seemed a perfectly proportioned little man. And it might have stayed that way, Única thought, he might have matured harmlessly towards insignificance. ¿Y qué? Don't we all? But by the time Cándido had grown into himself, as a young man, Única heard others say that he made them believe when he spoke to them—by the intense glare of his midnight eyes, by the way he reached out and grazed with the ends of his fingers significant spots on your person, by the manner he pretended that any space that was his was yours as well—that no one else had ever commanded his attention so devotedly. And yet, Única wrote to her grandson, who that ever laid a claim to him, to that fleeting moment of absolute attention, did not suffer greatly for it?

When Cándido's son, Patricio, was born, on that rainy spring day of 1972—such a beautiful boy, but the result of such an ill-conceived marriage—it was Única who considered herself responsible for all of it. So it was she who had to be there for Miriam and her grandson every time Cándido left Guantánamo on one of his adventures in a meandering path towards the capital, his legion of lovers trailing after him like leaves in a windstorm, so that at times during his absences their flat little town became desolate, and it seemed that there were no young or middle-aged people left, only the old and the children—mothers and fathers, husbands and wives, all chasing after Cándido like the throng that followed Jesucristo into Jerusalem.

He had started young.

When he was eleven, during the weeks when the world came to a stop because of the Soviet missiles, Cándido would disappear into the field adjacent to their house every afternoon to work on what he said would be their new house. He began to dig a hole in the ground. At first his parents let him; it was a little boy's way of dealing with the terror that was in everybody's heart. What harm could come out of digging a little hole? He went out to the field at two every afternoon, wearing only his shorts, and a campesino hat and pair of work boots that Modesto had needed when he was forced to volunteer in the cane fields of Camagüey the year before, which reached halfway up to Cándido's knees. He did not return till dusk, his skinny body smeared in mud, each day with some new treasure in his blistered hands that he had found under the earth: a shard from a clay pot, or an old cola bottle, or the dismembered head of a plastic doll, with little bits of hair sticking in patches to its crown and its eyes wide open, or the bones of a small bird, delicate as the fingers of the unborn. Each day they would ask him how the new house was progressing and he would answer, "Bien, bien, ya casi," and bathe and eat and fall into a deep undisturbed sleep. He was probably the only one who slept well at all in those very disturbing days. One afternoon, after it was all over, Modesto went out to tell him that they would no longer need the house under the earth. But he soon came running back into the kitchen through the back gate and grabbed Única by the wrist and led her out to the field. In the center of the field, there was a mound of earth taller than Modesto, being made taller yet by the little spits of dirt coming from below. They approached the hole cautiously, Modesto's hand still tight around his wife's wrist, treading gently, as if they were afraid of what they might find at the precipice of the first great work of art their son had created, which would end up not just a monstrous hole in the ground, but what Cándido called his house under the world, where he would live out all his explosive desires, and heal those whose love lives were festering. When they reached the edge of the hole, Cándido was some six feet below, digging in neat lines. Clumps of packed earth from the high walls, dark and streaked with orange like a sunset, fell on his familiar back and into the space between his shorts and his tailbone.

"It's over, mi'jo," Modesto said gently. "Khrushchev has shipped all the missiles back. We don't need a new home anymore." And then in almost a whisper, as if he knew that his words would have no effect, "It's over, mi'jo."

Cándido waited until he had finished digging one perfect row from wall to wall and then turned and looked up at his parents. He stood erect, shirtless, his chest puffed out like a rooster. New long muscles, taut as guitar strings, reached out from his neck and made two small fists around his shoulders. It was as if he had willed the beginning of his journey into manhood. His black eyes shone with his newly discovered powers and he planted the shovel into the dirt as if it were a flag.

"I'll keep going," he said, his slim boyish body twitching with fatigue. "I'll keep on going deep enough so that nothing that happens up above"—at this he pointed with a pout to the ground on which his parents were standing, on which their home and all the other homes stood—"can ever affect us."

They knew that he meant it, that he would have kept on going till his little not-yet-a-man's body collapsed.

Modesto then spoke: "No, no, that is not possible, mi cielo. There is no well deep enough or mountain high enough for that. You have gone as far as possible."

But looking into his son's feverish eyes, Modesto remembered his days in the capital not as if they had happened some twenty years before, but as if they were all a new story and he had not told anyone yet. He remembered the rush of huddling with his fellow law students atop the escalinata, the steps that led to the highest point on the university hill. There they would gather to protest uninvestigated assassinations, election fraud or any of the other corruption that was as commonplace in the capital as the night itself. From this spot they could easily watch the approach of university riot police, and Modesto remembered a brave young man who had started law school during Modesto's last year. During one of the gatherings atop the escalinata, as the riot police took the first steps up, clubs in hand, helmets in place, this foolish young man raced wildly down the steps, arms in the air, screaming injustice as if he had just invented the word. The police easily subdued him, encircling him and beating him with their clubs, before they moved up the steps to round up the other students. It was not until the next day when they went to visit him at Calixto García Hospital that they found the new student's name was Fidel Castro.

And though he had no patience for any of his old schoolmate's policies those days, it was that image that came into
Modesto's mind—of that foolhardy young man racing down
the steps to take a beating—as he forgot that Khrushchev had
shipped all his missiles back to Russia, let go of Única's hand,
sat on his rump and jumped into his son's hole. He would help
Cándido build his house under the world, he announced.

Única stood above them. There was a pot of pork-filled
tamales steaming on the stove for that night's dinner, which
had taken her all afternoon to prepare. She had to finish hanging the bedsheets she had washed that morning and then go
stand in two separate *colas* at the bodega and the butcher for
their weekly milk and coffee rations, for chuleticas de puerco
or flank steak for ropa vieja if there was any left. Afterward, she
had to finagle for the week's fruits and vegetables through
someone she knew in la bolsa, who got them direct from a fin-
quero nearby. Sí, perhaps Khrushchev had shipped back all his
missiles and the globe wasn't going to explode like a piñata,
but life still had to be toiled for, here *above,* as her son put it;
so when Modesto reached out a hand for her to join them in
their house under the world, his gray eyes now lit with as
much exhilaration as his son's, she said:

"Mira, no estoy para estas loquerías. I'll be up here keeping
your lives together until you get tired of playing your little
games."

The next day, Modesto hired an engineer (who moonlighted
as a truant patrol) to help them. They poured cement to hold
back the walls during the rains and made a roof out of a
pitched trellis that could be draped over with a thick canvas
but that was usually left open and eventually became thickly

entwined with the branches of a wisteria that Modesto planted nearby. They dug channels for drainage to protect the underground house from floods.

But the house became for Cándido something his parents could have never imagined.

After it was built, there were days when they didn't see Cándido at all. By the time he was eleven, it was as if he were living on his own, and he came to his parents' house only to get ready for school and to have dinner and to sleep. Única complained to her husband. Their house felt unlived in without their son there, the rooms too spacious, the spotless terrazzo floors unwelcoming. The mahogany-framed mirrors free of streaks and handprints. The chairs in the dining room too neatly set around the table, undisturbed, stiff, as if in perpetual wait for some very important guests. The spring afternoon rain fell in the central courtyard languorously, no longer a reason for joyous splashing. Even the morning light in the upper gallery seemed forlorn; it shifted over the frescoed walls, barely bothering to brighten the sylvan figures there, and through the brightly colored wood balustrade as if disheartened by its duties.

"And it's not just that," Única told Modesto. "I miss my son, carajo. I miss him asking me for things. I miss him needing me." Y mira, she also missed watching him fall asleep from just beyond the doorway of his room, missed watching him sprawled with his drawings on the kitchen floor, watching him stumble through life as if he were doing it all on his own.

Modesto told her that she should let the boy work things out on his own, that she should be glad that he was different and hadn't built his playhouse in the trees like other children.

There were a couple of years during his childhood where Modesto had feared this, that his son would grow up to be just like the other sons, so when the boy became less adventurous in his wanderings, when he seemed to cling to his mother too much, he invented new games for him. One of the most popular was based on Hansel and Gretel. He would take Cándido to certain spots in and around town—to the poinciana grove near the yellow church, to the movie theater on Calixto García Street, to the open-air market near the railroad tracks, and farther out, to the hills overlooking the naval base, to the aqueduct near the Yateras River—and leave him there, to see if the boy could make his way back alone. Hidden, from a distance, Modesto would watch as the boy, undaunted, oriented himself by looking at the height of the sun, or at the arrangement of the stars if it was dark, as if he had been a sailor in a previous life, before he chose the quickest route home. He grew so good at the game that he began to play it by himself. He would wander thoughtlessly from their house on Narciso López Street and walk and walk till he had no idea where he was and then figure out his way back. More than once, he hid himself in the papaya gardens of the Jewish doctor Sara Zimmerman and the old woman, at the end of the day, would show up on their doorstep with Cándido by the scruff of the neck as if he were a stray cat that had followed her home. One day, Cándido went as far as the arid scorched coast of Costa Sur, and when he had reached a pebbly beach, a kaleidoscopic carpet of seashells leading to the sea, he thought he had reached the very rim of the earth. He did not return for three days, and for three nights Única and Modesto, hand in hand, crisscrossed

the streets of Guantánamo calling out his name simultaneously, *"Caaaaaaan-dee-do,"* and imbuing it with such longing
that those who heard them would later tell them that they
thought their son had died and that they were searching for
the ghost. Modesto never doubted that his son would find his
way back, wherever it was he had wandered off to this time,
and when he showed up at their door, his skin blistering from
the torrid sun of the desert-like coast, his eyes glittering from
having seen the brink of our world, Única went into a rage.
Anything she could get her hands on, she threw at Modesto—
a porcelain vase, the leaky cafetera, a cast-iron pan, three
chunky bars of laundry soap, the mop bucket still half-full of
dirty water and even an electrical fan, which she lifted over her
head with both hands and hurled so violently towards her husband that it flew over his head.

"Así es," she screamed, "así es that you teach him how to be
a man, by abandoning his family!"

As she cured Cándido that night, with cocoa butter and cold
compresses, she made her son promise never to roam off again.

So now, Modesto said to his wife some years later, now she
had finally gotten what she wanted: the boy was right next door,
building a little playhouse under the earth.

"It's not a playhouse, Modesto," Única answered. "The boy
lives there. It's not even our property."

"Pero bueno," Modesto said, dismissing her with a flick of
his hand, "isn't all the land the people's, the workers'? Isn't that
what Fidel says?"

In less than four years, he had grown disheartened with la
Revolución that he had fervently supported. He had rooted for

his old schoolmate and his band of rebels so devotedly that on the days after the guerrilleros descended from the mountains into Guantánamo and Santiago, Modesto had opened his house to them. Makeshift hammocks were strung across the courtyard. Four pigs were slaughtered and pit-roasted in the vacant field next door, and a full cask of rum was emptied before the rebels left town on their march towards the capital. But it was not long before Modesto started thinking that the insane boy who had run head-on into a phalanx of riot police had mellowed into the most common kind of criminal, a petty autocrat no better than the one he had replaced. By October of 1962, Modesto spoke of Fidel with the derision one might reserve for an ex-wife who had run away with another man.

"If our son is afraid of something," Única said, trying not to let the conversation turn political, "we should help him. We are his parents. We love him."

"Sometimes, Única," he answered, sounding as philosophical as Única's grandmother Pilar, "you just have to let others figure things out on their own. No matter how much you think you love them. Go, go if you want to, if you want so much to help him, go out and spend a night with him, and then maybe he will tell you what he is afraid of. And you, maybe you will tell him the same."

Única had never forgiven her husband those three days Cándido had disappeared, and from the moment her son had returned she had decided that the responsibility of his upbringing had fallen to her and her alone.

So, one night after Modesto had fallen asleep, she went out

through the courtyard, past the chicken house and the old wooden gate to the abandoned field that was said to be the future site of one of those boxy Soviet housing units, those upright coffins that were sprouting up all over the Island, so characterless and indistinct, with their stark cinder facades and tiny prison-like windows, that often tenants could not tell one from the other and wandered into apartments in which they did not live. Única waited for her eyes to adjust to the darkness, till she saw the shadow of the wooden structure suspended above the hole. The wisteria had by then only begun its winding journey around the trellis that served as a roof for Cándido's underground home. Coming from beneath, she could see the flickering of a candle that danced in the moonless night. As she approached, she heard a low voice, so she crouched and, leaning on her hands for support, ambled closer till she heard another voice. There was someone else in there with their child. She leaned in so she could peer into the hole. And what did she see there but the candlelit craggy face of old Miguel Rulfo, his flinty weasel eyes wide open and looking on her shirtless child and murmuring to himself. Her breath quickened and she became frightened, for Miguel Rulfo had become legendary in their town for his ways with young girls and unmarried women. Had he become even more degenerate? Had he turned to boys? Did that happen to decrepit old men?

He owned a magnificent finca up towards the mountain, and bred horses and had always ridden into town on a horse he called Sangre de Cristo, for on its left side streaking down from its mount there was a spattered crimson stain. Some said that it was onto this very horse that he lured young unmarried women and on its very back that he would rape them, so many, so often, that the poor horse had become permanently marked. After the triumph of la Revolución, they didn't see much of him. It was said that with each successive Agrarian Reform Act, his lands shrunk by half and he was desperately trying to keep hold of whatever little plot the government left him. And then, one summer they heard that Sangre de Cristo had died; one morning he had bolted from the stables and had dashed about without a rider, back and forth from the town to the mountains, tracing each place where Miguel Rulfo had taken him to commit his depravities, looking, they said, for Miguel Rulfo's countless sons and daughters, till eventually the old horse's heart had ruptured and it tumbled to the earth. No one understood why, one morning, the beast had burst away— some said it was to avenge the sins of his master. And they hadn't seen Miguel Rulfo since. But there he was, this pervert, in the middle of the night, in a hole with her child. She leaned farther over the hole and was about to call out for help when she noticed, in one corner of the underground chamber, the bare shoulder of a woman, and when she let her face be touched by the candlelight, Única saw it was the pleasant face of Minerva, Miguel Rulfo's long-suffering wife. She had a rap-turous expression on her face (as if encountering that kind of bliss that can only be felt after much misery), like the one in those icons of the Virgin where she turns and finds the bare-foot angel in her hovel. She was surprised that Minerva was still alive, for no one had seen her in town since the days of the war against the Germans—which Cuba had participated in only economically, selling sugar and coffee cheap to the yanquis—since the days when her husband began to prey on unmarried women. And now Única's child, her young innocent child, went to Minerva and put his little index finger under her chin and lifted her face and kissed her on the forehead and then on her moistened eyes and then on her parched lips, as if trying to teach the old man how, after all these sinful years, to love his wife anew. And Miguel Rulfo dropped to his knees like a penitent, clasped his hands in front of him and wept. Hypocrite! Única wanted to call out. ¡Canalla! It's a marvel she hasn't murdered you in your sleep, cut off those old overused cojones. But Única was distracted by the sight of her young son passing his yet boyish hands, dirt deeply encrusted under each fingernail, through the old woman's long gray hair and then sneaking them under her blouse and caressing her breasts, making her sigh with twenty years of lost pleasures, causing Miguel Rulfo's groans to grow more anguished, as if he were suffering from the opposite of all his wife was finally reveling in; and, as Cándido pushed the old lady back into the darkness and lifted up her long multicolored Indian dress and spread open her legs and jumped on top of her, determined but awkward as a young colt, the only thing visible to Única from above was the undulating small of his back and the only thing audible was the heavy exhalations of the old woman, like a hot wind sucked out of a stove, and the mongrel whimpering of her delinquent husband. Aghast and full of shame as she was for being present there, for witnessing, Única felt stuck in her spot crouched by the trellis for the six different times that Cándido showed Miguel Rulfo how to make love to his forgotten wife.

Everyone has their little sins. That one was hers. Night after night, Única went to the back gate of their house and waited till she saw a pair of shadows move quickly across the wide field adjacent to their property and creep towards the meager light coming from her son's house under the world. Every night she promised herself that this would be her last, that she wasn't doing it because she felt a thrill in it, because she hadn't felt alive since her son had abandoned their house. She would not admit that only now as she was anticipating the act of spying on him would her blood course unrestrainedly, would a warmth return to the ends of her fingers. She told herself that she was doing it rather for the same reason she had done almost everything since the child had been born, to make his life—no matter how outlandish or mysterious it might become—as real to her as her own, to do for him what her mother, Marcia, had never done for her. But as she moved quietly to the flickering light in the center of the vacant field, her hands clasped in front of her, her steps measured and tiny, so that her approach would have been almost imperceptible, she already felt in the weakness of her knees, the rush of lurid thoughts at her temple, that she would surely return the night after, and the one after that, to watch, from just beyond the shadows, as her naked son made love to strangers.

There would be many others after it all began with Minerva, for Miguel Rulfo learned his lesson well. He and Minerva were seen hand in hand in town for the first time in over twenty years: touring the gardens of Parque Martí, with their bare feet dunked in the pebbly shores of the Bano River, at midnight mass the following Christmas, and even once, were spotted in the papaya gardens of the Jewish doctor Sara Zimmerman, doing there what Cándido had taught them. Tales of their implausible bliss abounded. Y bueno, that rainy season, as the woody trunk of the wisteria began to wind its way around the trellis that was the ceiling of Cándido's new underground home, at least one new estranged couple came to see him every night, at first from their town only, but soon news spread throughout Oriente of Cándido's successes, of his magic in reuniting the most unhitched of duos through his carnal expertise—that he had learned where? with the chickens in the henhouse? the stray dogs in Parque Martí?

Or more likely, Única thought, in the gardens of the healer Sara Zimmerman. Única knew Sara Zimmerman well. She had visited her gardens on Perdido Street after it had become evident that she could not have another child, that Cándido's violent birth had taken its toll on her womb, as Sariol explained it, as if the child had been envious of any future sibling who might thrive in *his* haven. Sariol said it was beyond him, and then he recommended Sara Zimmerman. The old woman was known to have mysterious powers that she had learned from the great-great-grandmother of her late husband, a prune of an anciana who had carried nightlong conversations with the bald prophet Elijah. Sara Zimmerman's lush gardens spread from the center of a mossy fountain at whose edge she always sat her clients and told them a little about herself and about the healing powers of the juice of the papaya stalks, so nutrient rich that she used it to treat anything from meningitis to wrinkled skin. Though apparently not her own. She was an almost bald rail of a woman with pouchy worn skin, and though almost all her front teeth were missing, she was always laughing.

"What else to do after so much sorrow?" she explained to Única as she led her into her examining room.

She had lost six brothers in the Nazi nightmare and had narrowly escaped herself when a wise aunt smuggled her to a kibbutz in Palestine, where she met her husband, a poet. She had lost him and a young daughter, both to malaria, in the same month, and the year the state of Israel was established had left for Cuba, running from grief, as she now understood it.

"You have heard the story, no?" she said as she pressed papaya leaves, large as elephant ears and soaked in the milky sap of the stalks, one over the other on Única's exposed belly. "Of the shipload of Jews that were turned away from almost every major American port by that bastard Roosevelt, and floated on the sea for days, homeless, nationless, till they were welcomed in the port of Havana, where at least some were allowed to unboard. Bueno, that's why I came here and not there."

Única thought that after her visits to Sara Zimmerman she would soon conceive again. But the treatments had an unexpected effect: the more she recalled the unbearable weight of the giant soaked leaves on her belly, the less she craved the prospect of other children, till she had forgotten about this future almost entirely, as simply as she had forgotten any inconsequential moment in her past.

"We can never foresee," Sara Zimmerman had explained to her on her last visit, "the manner in which we will be healed."

And it was these words more than anything that made Única suspect that Cándido could have learned his new art only from the forgiving nature of the bald laughing old woman, there in her gardens, where lovers went when they had nowhere else to go.

In search of Cándido, couples started arriving from as far away as Baracoa and Holguín, and then Camagüey and Matanzas, and finally the most metropolitan pairs from the capital itself, the women with their faces veiled and the men with the brim of their panamas pulled down to their noses, and the most rustic guajiros came from the Viñales region, their faces exposed as the afternoon sun. They wandered around the ill-lit perimeter of the vacant field like souls in purgatory, chain-smoking cigarettes and bickering in hushed voices as if embarrassed of their disdain for each other, as they waited for their turn to enter the house under the world. Sometimes Cándido would not go to bed till two or three in the morning and went to school the following day with his eyelids barely open and with the stupefied shuffle of someone who has been endlessly traveling around the globe in his nightmares and is no longer sure whether it is day or night. But somehow, every evening, after he had completed his homework, he was up to his task, and besides, he told his parents, he was doing good, couldn't they all see that?

"Pero, niño," his mother once said to him, exasperated, "what kind of good? Are you going to fuck every unhappy wife on the Island?"

To which he formulated an answer whose truth she never wanted to investigate. It was an answer that stopped her nightly visits to his underground home for over a month.

"Sometimes," he said, blushing a little at his mother's use of such a vulgarity, smiling just wide enough so that his dimples closed his response in parentheses, "I have to do it with the husbands."

And so he continued, with the support, surprisingly, of Modesto, who pleaded with his wife at night, pacing from one corner of their bedroom to the other, slapping the palm of one hand with the back of the other as if he were in a courtroom trying to convince a judge, trying to persuade her that it was every soul's right and privilege to find its own way in this world.

Imagínate, Única thought, though she couldn't agree more.

As the months went by, the wisteria whorled itself around the trellis over Cándido's underground nest, securing its privacy, though it would not bloom, as if flowers would have marked Cándido's serious enterprise with too flighty a symbol. For, even his permissive father had to admit, Cándido seemed far too unhappy for someone who was doing others so much good. He had lost much of his sense of innocence and guilelessness that had first driven him to create his house under the world. And when he spoke of his endeavors now, raising his voice, signaling with his finger to the heavens—when they were fortunate enough to have him sit down with them for dinner or on the way out to school—his voice took on the seriousness of a politician, or what to Modesto was even worse, a revolutionary, a comunista.

And then four rainy seasons later, when Cándido was already growing bored with his mission, Miriam appeared. She was a bony girl with sunken cheeks, who seemed too much the unfortunate offspring of any of those miserable couples waiting in line. Though even they, who were languishing in so much wretchedness, knew enough not to stand too near her. She waited by herself. She was unmarried, only a year younger than Cándido. When her turn came, she descended the wooden ladder alone into that underground house of wrongdoing and forgiveness.

Cándido sat shirtless and cross-legged in his hole as usual. He had stuck his head out from under the wisteria and said that the girl would be the last one for the night, the rest would have to come back the following night, to which responded a chorus of groans, the prelude to one more afflicted night of matrimony, beds unshared, mornings ungreeted.

"Where is your husband?" was, naturally, the first thing Cándido said to the girl.

Miriam shook her head. She could not look at him.

"Niña," Cándido said, as if he were a messenger from the heavens, which so many by this time believed him to be, "do you know who I am? Why won't you look at me? Do you know where you've come?"

Cándido was sixteen then. A faint shadow of a beard grew in only on the line of his jaw and on the tip of his chin. His torso was hairless except for dark tufts around his nipples. But perhaps because of so many nights spent with the most luckless in love, or because of the erect posture of a prophet, even as he sat cross-legged on his thin mattress, he seemed much older.

Miriam nodded. She was a plain girl, barefoot and flat-chested, with a boy's narrow build, lanky black hair that fell on her cheekbones and on her round caramel eyes, which were far too big for her face. She wore a filthy man's T-shirt that reached halfway down her thighs. It's a testament to Cándido's character, Única wrote to her grandson, that of all the people to whom your father revealed the secrets of love, he himself was to fall in love only once, with this sad homely girl.

"My parents are dead," she said.

Cándido waited before he answered. He shrugged dismissively: "I don't bring souls back from the dead, niña."

"Oh," Miriam said, still not looking at him. "But isn't it possible that my parents can still be out of love in the other world? I still hear them going on with their nightly fights in my dreams as if nothing extraordinary had happened to them at all, as if I were still a little girl sleeping in a room beside them, and they were still alive. What about the possibility of this?"

"Anything is possible. But there's nothing I can do for them. For you. Mira, not that I—"

"Oh." And she got up and turned to climb up the ladder. "Gracias."

And Cándido would have let her go. But for one small thing: as she was climbing the steps, he noticed a soil mark on her undergarments, and it stirred something in him. He did not know why exactly. Perhaps he saw her for the first time as the helpless child that she was.

"Wait. I wish there was something I could do. Something I could teach the dead to make them more cheerful, more contented with each other, vaya, with their situation. Pero, mira"—and here Cándido, too, turned into a child, his shoulders slumping, his eyes wide with curiosity once more—"I don't yet know anything about the dead."

At this Miriam turned and smiled. Her teeth were unevenly spaced, but it was a handsome smile, Cándido thought. "That's funny," she said, "that you say *yet*. Maybe that's why you're so good at your work, coño, because you are so ambitious." And again, she gestured as if to leave, turning and continuing up the ladder.

"Wait. Maybe if you stay here tonight, maybe you'll hear them from here . . . and maybe . . . pues, maybe I can learn something."

He stood up, went to her and guided her down the ladder to the chicken-feather mattress thrown in one corner of the chamber for his demonstrations with the distressed couples. And he laid her down to sleep, and rested his head on her chest, hoping to hear the shouting of her parents, hoping to steal her dreams for one night. But though she fell asleep almost instantly, the girl writhed and growled like a wounded tomcat all night. When Cándido wrapped his arms around her and held her close to him, her face would grow calm momentarily, and then, just as he dozed off, her seizures started again with a renewed ferociousness. She slobbered and bit into him and her moans grew more guttural. But the more she struggled, the closer Cándido held her and the more he set his mind to make her well. Near dawn, clammy as someone's who has broken a high fever, Miriam's body softened and she rested.

The following day, Cándido offered her one of his great secrets. It was the thing that had made him such a success, this boy who was not yet an adult and already the greatest marriage counselor on the entire Island. It wasn't just about carnal love, he told her, although that was a big part. (The girl blushed.) The problem with most lovers was that although they knew perfectly well how to be happy together and successfully, they knew very little about how to suffer propitiously, how to suffer with each other.

"And, let's face it," he said, "in this world, it is much better, it is more useful, to know the latter than the former."

Miriam looked at him as if he had just told a riddle. He was going to ask her what she had dreamt about the night before, but he decided that he did not want to know. That it did not matter anymore.

He led Miriam by the hand out of the house under the world, across the vacant field, past the wooden gate, through a narrow corridor that led into his parents' courtyard, where Modesto and Única were having their breakfast. When Cándido crossed through the courtyard with the girl in tow, Única stood and followed them.

"Where did you find that?" she called.

She stood and watched silently from the other side of the bathroom door. Her son filled the bathtub halfway and commanded the girl to step into it and the girl did, still in her dirty shirt.

"No, chica, así no," Cándido said. He stripped her of the shirt and her underwear and folded them neatly, as if they had just been taken down from the clothesline. He had her sit in the tub and poured water over her and washed her hair and her face and under her arms; with a toothbrush he scrubbed her fingernails, then he handed her the soap so that she could wash on her own down below.

"Go ahead," he said. The girl held the soap in her cupped hands as if it were a living thing.

"I can help," Única said from the doorway.

The girl looked up and smiled at her through the suds on her face.

"Careful with her eyes," Única said.

"Estamos bien," Cándido answered irritably, and then took the soap from the girl and washed her below himself. The water had turned so murky that he could not see his hand.

"Perhaps you can find her something to wear, por favor," he called to his mother.

The girl giggled when she stepped into one of Única's child-hood dresses, a loose-fitting linen one that had been a gift from Dr. Esmeraldo Gloria and which Única had always saved along with others, tucked mindfully inside a pale walnut chest, just in case she should have a daughter. As Única tied elegant bows with the three straps in the back, Miriam pressed her nose to her shoulder.

"It smells like it was dried in the rain," she announced.

Única sat Miriam on her lap and brushed her hair, which was so maniacally entangled that clumps of it came out on the brush.

Miriam was as hungry as the bearded guerrilleros must have been on the morning they descended from the mountains. She ate three servings of breakfast, huevos revueltos, and slices of chorizo and even the empanadas de carne that Única reheated from dinner the night before. And just as Única started ques-tioning where this wild girl had come from, Cándido grabbed her again and took her out to the house under the world.

They spent the afternoon talking. When the girl said that she did not feel comfortable in his mother's old dress, he stepped behind her and untied the three bows. When the dress fell from her, he was able to look at her as he could not when he was bathing her, with his mother watching from the doorway. He passed his hands over her bare shoulders. And then left her there alone, and went about lighting the hundreds of candles that lined the walls of his house. Figures appeared on the walls.

She had not noticed them the night before. She pointed. "What are those?"

"Those are my paintings. Do you like them?"

Miriam laughed. "They're strange!"

On one wall there was a drawing of a man with three faces, one looking distractedly at the heavens, the other one dismayingly at the horizon and the last one with its eyes shut as if in prayer; in his hands he held the battered pieces of some sort of stringed musical instrument. On another wall there was a rushing white river out of which mermaids swam doggedly upstream like salmon. On another, the disemboweled figure of a handsome young prince on his throne, his entrails spilling down his inner thighs, a quiet resigned look on his face, as if he had been expecting this all along—the dark walls of the throne room seeming at once to be closing in on him and extending somewhere just beyond the darkness. On the last wall an ancient muddy village of adobe huts was seen as if by a vengeful angel flying high above. And from behind these paintings there seemed to be others struggling to get out, seeping from the very earth that surrounded them. As the candles flickered, the outline of a doubled-over figure would appear in the sugary foam of the river of mermaids, and when the light moved a different way, it would detonate tiny explosions of color in the darkness around the disemboweled prince.

Miriam approached each wall, passing her hands over the surface. "What do they mean? Is this what you dream?"

The hundreds of shadows cast by the candlelight now danced around her like schoolchildren and made her, for a moment, beautiful.

"They are dreams that I have stolen from others," Cándido said. He guided her to the chicken-feather mattress. "I can do it with yours too. If you will let me. I can make them beautiful and strange. I can do it as simply as I can become one of these drawings, estos garabatos."

Then, as if to prove this, she heard his voice as it emanated from the depths of the white river, from the fathomless gray skies over the muddy village or from the darkness of the throne room with the disemboweled prince, the voice as ephemeral as those little explosions of color. Then a kiss passed over the side of Miriam's face and settled as a sigh in the hollow between her breasts. It was as if he were returning from the world of his paintings for her. So when she reached out in the darkness and found Cándido, now ready as she was, naked, aroused, she bequeathed him all her ghosts, all her dreams, in the fury with which she assaulted his body, leaving bite marks in the shape of walnuts on his cheeks and neck, rotted-plum bruises on his limbs, so many scratches on his torso she might have flogged him with a branch of thorns, and a rawness throughout, as if an old skin had been forcibly ripped from him.

Beside his sacrificial body, she slept as sound a sleep as she would all her days.

With that, his brief and miraculous career as the Island's greatest marriage counselor was over. He bonded himself to this girl, whose dreams he had stolen, and whom later he would make most unhappy. And Miriam bonded herself to the memory of that night and she would spend the rest of her life looking for that fragile peace she had found in Cándido's house under the world. Yet, to this day, so many years after his untimely death, Única wrote to her grandson, Miriam had not yet learned how to suffer at all.

Anyone who knew her son could have foreseen what was to come next. The girl could certainly not be blamed.

Vaya, it didn't take long for the restless Cándido to grow tired of spending his nights with the poor lonely orphan. By the time he turned seventeen in 1969, about a year after Miriam had arrived, he began to miss school, to disappear for days and weeks, running from her, searching perhaps for one who would teach him what he had taught others, but more likely, Modesto explained to his wife, just running from the flatbed trucks that would round up young men in those days to take them out to the cane fields, to *volunteer* in the great national goal of ten millions tons for the upcoming sugar harvest. And when Cándido disappeared, guess who was left to take care of Miriam, to drag her from the chicken-feather mattress and feed her and hold her till she fell into her dreamless sleep, because the brothers at the orphanage wanted nothing to do with her after they found out what she, puta, had been doing every night since she ran away? It was during those days that Única got to know Miriam, during those days that they learned the uneasy love with which to approach each other. Única sat Miriam at the dinner table with them and corrected her table manners as if she were their daughter. Única by herself took charge of the education that the brothers had refused to finish, and with the books that Dr. Esmeraldo Gloria had given her, even began to teach Miriam a little English, not really imagining how much use it would be to the girl one day.

THE LOSS OF A FAMOUS SMILE

THE BOY HAS LOST HIS TWO FRONT TEETH. He is afraid to smile. So when he arrives at the airport in La Habana in late June of the year 2000 and his grandmothers and cousins and uncles and aunts surround him, he pinches tight his mouth, as if he were bathing in dirty water. In Miami, Única is sure that they will say that he does not smile because he has been forced to return. But here, in the basement of Dr. Abdel Alirkan's town house in Brooklyn Heights, the newscasters, who have interrupted the afternoon soap operas, repeat again and again that the boy has lost his two front teeth and that that is why he is afraid to smile.

Única translates for her husband and he shakes his head as if he does not want to understand her. She looks over the pictures that her grandson took of Elián during his visit to the National Zoo and the boy does not smile in any of them.

Later, at the restaurant by the river, after Eduardo has

poured him his second cognac, her husband will murmur that they will never see the boy's famous smile again. When Eduardo points out the rabid enthusiasm with which the family greeted the boy at the airport as proof that that is where the boy belongs, Única is about to agree with him, but she notices her husband as he stares silently at the buildings across the way, lit like a forest of giant Christmas trees. He mildly shakes his head and Única says nothing. She keeps her apostate thoughts to herself.

TO LAUGH LIKE A BLACKBIRD

THEY HAD DONE IT TOGETHER, one after the other, as if it had been carefully plotted. A one-two combination to Miriam's psyche, fiercer than that of Teófilo Stevenson, the great Cuban Olympic champion. First, Única's diagnosis in the summer of 1999 and then, less than a month later, Patricio's coming-out letter. It had left Miriam reeling.

That's how you say it, no? Única wrote to her grandson, *coming out,* como si fueras una quinceañera. But regardless, we have to work on this, the timing with which we bring calamity to this family. Miriam says that we are better than Cándido at inventing monsters, a phrase that she stole from him long ago.

She was writing her letter, partly to answer the one Patricio had written them (which had been addressed to Única as well as to Miriam—though Única was able only to peek at it before Miriam ripped it from her hands and set it afire), and partly because Miriam had put a code on all the phones so that she could not call out, y avergonzarnos por ahí, by telling everyone about the contents of Patricio's letter. As if there was anyone she could call. Except him. Her chiquito. There was so much to tell him. Even the things Miriam had forbidden her to tell. *Forbidden*. Her daughter-in-law had the vocabulary of a dictator.

She had written the letter because it was the only way she could tell him.

She had been feeling tired lately, not rising till well after Miriam had gone off to work, sometimes neglecting all her chores at Miriam's house, leaving the night before's dishes in the sink till late in the afternoon, letting Modesto's shirts and trousers and Miriam's blouses and skirts (and even Lenny's paint-splattered jeans, which she used to iron when he let her) collect in a mound in the laundry room. She had even lost all her passion for cooking, imagine that. Patricio had once told her that she should open her own little restaurant on Calle Ocho, had vowed to help her do it. Not that Miriam forced her to do any of those things. That's what dishwashers, dry cleaners and private chefs are for, she said. It's not like we are starving! She was very proud of that, the fact that they were not starving.

Miriam, who with three different loans had taken over the bankrupt travel agency she worked for in South Miami. She had emptied the place of boxes and boxes of old paper, useless travel histories from deceased customers, ancient receipts and tax documents, and outdated brochures that seemed now to offer travel to other times as well as other places. She gutted the two small rooms, painted each a yolk-yellow, the Virgencita's color, bought three used computers and spent an entire week ordering new pamphlets and glossy travel magazines from the four corners of the earth. She changed the name of the agency from Odyssey to Paradiso, suggestive not only of the dream destination of any traveler, but hinting also at the lost paradise to where hundreds of boxes a week went out from her doors, full of American jeans, priceless toiletries, toys with extra batteries inserted into every crevice, bars of chocolate and boxes of hard-shelled gum, all kept safe and in place by wads and wads of cotton, of which everyone knew there was a such a great shortage on the Island that dentists had to pilfer pill bottles and sometimes slash open pillows. And as the agency began more and more to specialize in sending aid packages to Cuba and in arranging tours of the Island for homesick exiles, el período de sacrificio and the legalization of the dollar in Cuba were a great boon for Miriam. She was doing very well. She had purchased a house with a pool in Coconut Grove, and the moment her son had moved out began refashioning it with its many extensions.

"Let it be," Miriam said to Única when she first brought them into her home. "Relax and enjoy your old age. That is why I brought you here to live with us."

She had redecorated a room overlooking the pool, on the second floor, for Única and Modesto. It was furnished with new pieces from the Burdines collection, made of cherry. There was an antique quilt, patterned with watermelon slices, draped over the bed with a meditated carelessness, as if to give the impression that the new bed had been slept in already.

Única never felt comfortable in the room. At night, she climbed out of bed and lumbered to Patricio's old room on the first floor, by the kitchen. It was furnished still with a school-boy-sized desk (which he had so rarely used), a small black-and-white TV, and his old toys and dolls, which lined the upper shelves of the near-empty bookcase like sentinels.

One morning Miriam found her asleep in Patricio's narrow bed, and she sat on the bed beside her and tucked her tangled hair behind an ear. Única pretended to sleep. That night when she returned to the room, Única found the bed laid out with new sheets and with the watermelon quilt. From then on, she would not even bother to go up to her room. And after the evening news, Modesto made his way up the stairs by himself, gripping the banister for support, and she finished washing that night's dishes alone.

At least that, Única wrote Patricio, at least she hadn't been a burden, she had made herself useful, even if it was with something as inconsequential as cooking and ironing and doing the dishes.

But lately she felt useless. Lenny ran her bundle of clothes to the dry cleaner's in the morning before he started to paint, and afterward early in the afternoon, he went to pick up their dinner from the caterer, and when they were finished with it, he put all the dishes in the dishwasher himself. And then he put them away while Miriam took the first of her two nightly strolls in the garden. It was obvious. He took pains to be a good partner.

A good thing. For Única just wasn't up to her old tasks; there were days when she never even made it out of Patricio's old bed, too weary even to hit the buttons on the remote to change TV stations, so that she watched the boring gushy telenovelas on the Spanish station that Modesto put on for her. Some days Modesto would accompany Miriam to the agency and help her in arranging documents. Other days, he would bring a chair into Lenny's studio and watch him paint.

"What are his paintings like?" Única asked him one night while they watched a telenovela in Patricio's old room, Modesto in a chair beside her bed. She had never dared to go into Lenny's studio, too afraid that she would glimpse, in the very action of his art, the way he applied paint to the canvas, images of her son.

"Crazy. Paint all over the place," he said. "But he's passionate about all that craziness, and it shows, vaya, it shows in the work."

Modesto lowered the volume on the television, but he did not take his eyes off the silent images. She sensed that he wanted to say more. How, after all, could they talk about painting without thinking about their son, about his phantasmagoric canvases? She wanted to say more also, but she couldn't.

This is exactly why Miriam said that she wanted to put Única back in therapy. She should have someone to talk to, that's all, someone outside of the family. During the day, when Miriam was at the agency, she had Lenny take breaks from his studio and make periodic checks on her mother-in-law. Lenny dutifully complied, came quietly into the room, drops of bright colors clinging to his thinning hair like psychedelic fleas. He sat on the floor by the bed, not wanting to stain Miriam's precious sheets, and watched the telenovelas with Única for fifteen or twenty minutes, aunque, el pobre, no hablaba ni gota de español. And then he left her alone, normal as can be, even though they had not exchanged a single word. Única thought he was a smart boy. He knew better than to ask her if she was all right.

Única was not going back to therapy. What a grand waste of time that had been, as if with all that had happened to her, she didn't have a right to a little depression now and then! At least she was able to stand firm on that. No more therapy. So Miriam relented when Única agreed to go to a regular doctor for a checkup.

After a few weeks of tests (one in which they poked a dagger-like needle into her spine) they got their answer. She had an acute form of leukemia. The doctor had Miriam come sit with them to discuss their options. He was a red-faced man with bad skin and closely cropped gray hair. He wore jeans under his white robe and white sneakers. His whole demeanor seemed to Única disrespectful to his present role, to the news he conveyed. On the street, one might have guessed he was a comedian or a character actor. He put Única in a foul mood.

"What options," she asked, "aside from a quick death?"

"Ay, mamá," Miriam said, and went on to explain to the doctor some of Única's psychological history as she understood it, from her absent father, to the death of her mother and stepfather that sandwiched her wedding day like poisoned bread.

"Pardon me," the doctor interrupted. "I don't see what all this has to do with her present condition."

This infuriated Miriam. So before she lectured Única on the manner with which she took the news of her cancer, on how selfish she was being, not even thinking about Modesto, she lectured the doctor on everything from his unprofession- alism to the lines of dirt under his fingernails, and boldly asserted that they were off to get a second opinion and that he was fired. Única hadn't known doctors could be fired.

"Cuidado," she said to her grandson in the letter, "I think she thinks sons and grandsons can be fired too. After she got your letter, she went around for a couple of days carrying a rolled-up copy of her will telling Lenny, your grandfather and me how she was going to scratch you right out of it."

So they went and got a second opinion. Another series of needle stabs in the back. Única wrote to her grandson that she felt like Caesar surrounded by the murderous senators. Tests that offered exactly the same results, except that this doctor was much better dressed and much more somber during the meeting to discuss their options—yes, he used exactly the same word. Única said nothing this time, let Miriam handle it all, simply because she did not want to go through the third opinion process with her.

The somber doctor thought that she was all-around healthy enough to withstand a few rounds of chemotherapy. He said that she was in excellent health for a sixty-seven-year-old. I guess that means not counting the cancer, Única thought. The chances were excellent for five- to ten-year survivals, he said. He showed them graphs and jabbered like a bookmaker.

"The earlier we start any treatment, the better," he said. "The odds are good for someone your age."

He put Única in a foul mood also. She felt like starting the tale that Miriam had called her psychological history so that he would interrupt her and Miriam could fire him too. But she held her tongue.

Miriam had wanted her to wait for the second opinion before she told Modesto. Just to make sure. And now she wanted her to wait again.

"Wait for what this time?" Única said.

They were sitting at the kitchen table, Modesto no more than ten feet from them, sitting out by the pool on the other side of the sliding glass doors.

"No sé," Miriam answered. She was frantic, drinking cup after cup of cafecito even though it was past ten at night. She got up to brew a fresh pot and spoke with her back to Única. "Maybe we should come to terms with this ourselves first. So that we can tell him calmly. This is going to devastate him."

"Ourselves?"

"Sí, ourselves. This affects me too."

"I'm telling him tonight."

Miriam turned around. "He doesn't deserve this. Not now."

Única had to smile. "Pero ven acá. You really think that if we don't tell him that he is not going to have to live through it? You really think that?" She shook her head. "Ay, niña, so many triumphs here in el maldito exilio, and it is almost as if you were still that ignorant little orphan girl that wandered into our lives."

Única looked out at her husband by the pool and then caught a reflection of herself on the sliding glass door, and it was as if her face were hovering behind him, ready to whisper some dire secret.

Sometimes Única thought that that afternoon when Modesto passed her house on Narciso López Street and saw her sitting there on the veranda was the unluckiest day of his life. There had been moments, little moments in all their years here in Miami when she saw him laugh at something, at an old Cantin-flas movie, or at Tres Patines on the radio, moments when he raised both his arms after Marino had thrown another touch-down, moments when his soul leapt at joy like old man Saturn, that she wondered how all may have been different for him if he had never met her, or if he had been more loyal to his first love, the law, whose calling had become more and more faint with each passing year, with each revolutionary decree passed down by the Central Committee, with each land reform en-acted, till it was nothing but a murmur by the time they had paid their way into the rickety lancha at the port of Mariel. In Miami, he had tried to work as a paralegal in a few agencies, but it was at a time when the children of an earlier wave of immigrants were coming of age and they had little patience with the older generation's unwillingness to blend in, to even learn the language properly. When Modesto turned of age to collect the meager helpings from the government, he retired altogether and they lived on that. Gracias a Dios, he always said, for the generosity of the United States government. They, who had hardly worked a day in this country and yet every month came the check, the stamps, the medical benefits. Gra-cias a Dios for these strange kindnesses. (But what Única Ave-yano found truly strange was that in this country she had been made to take her husband's surname, so that all her checks and government papers belonged to a certain one named Única Duarte, a certain one she was sure did not exist.)

Modesto did not know about Patricio's letter, and *that* Única would not tell him about. If Patricio wanted to talk to his grandfather about whom he chose to sleep with, that was up to him. It was enough to have watched Miriam's reaction. Enraged, fuming. For an entire afternoon she stomped from room to room of her oversized house, all those rooms that she did not need except for moments like this—her stomping ritual when she got upset.

You should see the house now, Única wrote to Patricio, there are staircases that lead nowhere, rooms that have no floors, roofs that have no rooms under them, that seem to float in the air as if by magic, doors that open to other doors and then to brick walls. ¿No me crees? You'll see when you come visit. Don't put anything past your mother.

When Miriam tired of stomping on the day she got her son's letter, she went out to garden and in her fancy business suit got down on her knees and began furiously pulling out the weeds from her flower beds, all the time holding the crumpled letter in her hand, as if she wanted to bury it there in her garden, entomb all its irreversible truths.

"Unfathomable," she said when she came back into the house. Her rose Donna Karan outfit was ruined, streaked with mud and makeup, her necklace had snapped and little precious pearls fell from the crevices of her body and onto the kitchen tiles like petrified tears, and when Única went to her, to hold her, to console her (because again, Única saw her as that helpless dirty bony girl her son had led by the hand into their house so long ago), that's when she reached out the soiled letter—keeping her mother-in-law at arm's length— which Única only got to peruse before Miriam snatched it out of her hands again and set it afire.

"It's you," she said as the little bonfire burned out on the kitchen floor, "you and that son of yours that Patricio gets all his ways from."

It never ceased to amaze Única how often Miriam had the gall to speak ill of the dead. At that moment, Única vowed that every time Miriam did it to her when she was dead and gone, Única was going to return and so disturb Miriam's nights, so frazzle her days that she would never speak ill of the dead again. Her psychiatrist, Dr. Marty, once read Única a poem by John Donne about a rejected lover who comes back to haunt his beloved. She is in the bed of another lover, who has just denied her advances for more sex. Única remembered the ending, and thought it one of the most satisfying ghost stories in all of literature.

> . . . And then poor Aspen wretch, neglected thou,
> Bathed in a cold quicksilver wilt lie
> A verier ghost than I.
> What I will say, I will not let thee know,
> Lest that preserve thee; and since my love is spent,
> I'd rather thou should'st painfully repent
> Than by my threatenings rest still innocent.

Every time Miriam tarnished Cándido's name, she pictured Miriam in that bed, the ghost's cold fingers reaching under the covers for the warmth of her sex.

■

After her diagnosis, she had gone back to Dr. Marty. She had specifically told Miriam that she did not want a Cuban shrink, that she wanted an American, and, remembering Sara Zimmerman and the mystery of her healing, someone Jewish if possible. And here he was again, good old Martin Perlman, his hands gesticulating with the brashness of the curlicues of the embossed script of his Harvard degree. He spoke to her of the human legacy of sorrow. He had not changed, still he spoke of poets and characters in literature as if they were intimates, of Hamlet as if he had gone drinking with him the previous night. At first she had just sat there and listened as Martin Perlman scribbled on his pad and she let him quote Hamlet and Whitman and the songs of David, as if any man, no matter how great a poet, how sweet a prince, how mighty a king, could ever fathom the pain a mother feels when she loses her only son. But after a while she had started to bring in her own selections of poetry, to introduce him to some of her stuff, Neruda and Lezama Lima and Sor Juana. He understood her language perfectly, he said, but still, she often had to translate for him and this made it more fun. Sometimes now, the night before one of her sessions, she would sit at Patricio's schoolboy desk and translate lengthy passages, copying them out in her neat script. Poor Miriam. If she had ever found out that she was again paying two hundred dollars an hour for this poor Harvard schmuck (that's what he called himself), her Dr. Marty (that's what she called him), to read to her and to get himself an education in Hispanic poetry, she would have killed Única herself.

And then, Única thought mischievously, everything would be solved.

The last time she had seen him, he had read her a darling little story by Rubén Darío that she brought in called, let's see, how did she translate it, ay sí, "The Death of the Empress of China." It was about a man who forsakes his wife for the porcelain bust of an empress and eventually she gets so mad that she shatters it on the floor and they kiss madly, and their pet blackbird dies laughing at all the nonsense. And so they too laughed, Dr. Marty and Única laughed like the blackbird at all the nonsense, and so he thought he was making her better.

About her son, he rarely asked after her diagnosis. Única wondered what they taught him at that fancy medical school.

She could see them all in their well-lit laboratory, with their white coats and sanguine faces, holding on to monstrous fig-urines (these all the awful manifestations of human sorrow, this is its legacy, they are told), which they will be taught to take apart, limb by limb, and bury in a hundred different places so that they may never be put together again, so that they may crumble to harmless dust. When she talked to Dr. Marty about her son it was as if she were talking about someone who should never have existed at all, whose memory was some malignant tumor that had to be dislodged from her bowels. When she got really exasperated, when there were twenty minutes left and nothing for Dr. Marty to read, no verses left for him to quote, she screamed at him, a tempest of words assuring him that the memory of her son could no more be excised from her body than her own blood, than the fluids in her spinal cord, than the marrow in her bones. He answered that that's not what he meant, that's not what he meant at all. And they sat quietly for the rest of the time, like a husband and wife who have just quarreled.

All of them, Única Aveyano thought, Dr. Marty, Modesto, Miriam, shrouded in silence against the memory of Cándido.

Gracias a todos los santos, she finished the letter to her grandson, now that we know what was wrong with me I seem to be back to my old self. She hoped it would stay that way till the treatments started. She got up early, at three at the latest, brewed cafecito, scrubbed pots and pans from the previous night's dinner before sunrise, laundry and ironing in the morning, the housecleaning late morning, which she had to compartmentalize, the kitchen with its endless white oak cupboards and industrial stainless-steel appliances for one afternoon, the bedrooms and linen closets for another, the gallery on the second floor and inner courtyard, both lined with colorful Mexican tile that needed gentle scrubbing for an entire morning, trips to the grocery store in the early afternoon on Monday, Wednesday and Friday, on which days she would have to hurry back to start dinner, which she timed to the precise minute when Lenny would come out of his studio and Miriam would arrive from the gym or dance classes.

Sometimes, after ironing, she would come out and sit by the pool till the sun rose.

It was a Saturday morning. She was alone. The light fell softly yet, discreet as a servant. Miriam and Modesto wouldn't be up till later, but she already heard Lenny fumbling in the kitchen. He'd hasten to his studio soon and they wouldn't see him till the afternoon. Weekends were like any other working day for him.

She wished Cándido had been so diligent about his work. Pero el pobre, en Cuba no era fácil. Paint that goes on walls was scarce enough, the one that goes on canvas was almost nonexistent, so he made his own mixtures, with motor oil and crushed flowers, with egg yolks and pollen, or with the crushed shells of polymites as the great Catalan surrealist had taught him when he visited Guantánamo; sometimes Cándido used mud as paint, once he even used pale dog shit for the color of the Virgin of Cobre's cheeks. Volatile combinations that not long after the paintings were finished fell off in flakes and clumps, like hair and skin from a disinterred skeleton. Sí, coño, he was being scandalous and foolish long before it was in vogue. And to find a proper canvas, that was another story. By the time they left Cuba their little house was stripped of curtains, her linen closet left with only the most threadbare sheets. She wondered what happened to all his paintings. Unlike Lenny, Cándido was never very cunning about his work: for him his art was never any more than a thing of the present; if he ever did think about his posterity, he never showed it. He used to look at Patricio, hold his son close to his chest and dab his nose with his makeshift paint and proclaim that here was his posterity, here his most beautiful creation. She wondered if her grandson remembered any of it at all.

Cándido should have been a poet. Única would have memorized all his poems and recited them to Modesto in bed and to Miriam and Lenny over dinner, and written them out for her grandson in a neat script, and maybe then they could not force her to forget him.

LIKE THE AMAZONAS

MEMORY IS LIKE THE AMAZONAS, Única Aveyano thought, the way it fissures into the landscape of time, the way it ravenously collects the rains of all the days and the years.

In 1980, when they applied for permission to leave Cuba, after the crowd had stormed the Peruvian embassy, and others had spent days figuring out ways to force their way in, even though there were rumors that food and water were in very short supply and people were shitting on the marble floors and pissing on the Cuban mahogany furniture like dogs, Miriam, knowing that Cándido would not go with them, had convinced Modesto that for their grandson, the benefits of growing up in a free society would far outweigh the disadvantages of losing a father who was only around for one or two months a year de todos modos. It was difficult to disagree with her, though Única tried, at first confronting Miriam outright: How dare she imagine a life for this child without his father? To which

Miriam responded with the simplest truth—Patricio's father was never there.

He spent most of his days in the capital, not working or anything (bueno, no es verdad, working on his art whenever he could find any material, but certainly not helping financially or emotionally with his son's upbringing). Cándido tenía complejo de van Gogh, Miriam said—because he had never sold a painting in his life, he took this as a sign of his irrefutable greatness. At nights, he roamed the cobblestoned streets of La Habana Vieja during the apagones, torches planted outside many of the tenement houses. He always said he liked the warm evenings best, when no one stayed inside their homes. The narrow streets were crowded with people then, many who took the balmy night and the apagón (¿por qué no?) as cause for a celebration, and music was invented from upturned barrels and garbage can lids and from the loose bricks of walls, and from broken sticks used for percussion. In contrast, the buildings themselves bent in on each other, as if wary with the heat and frightened of the darkness; some were literally supported by large pieces of timber that jutted out into the street. But for Cándido it was as if he were strolling through the great boulevards of Europe; and that is why, Miriam knew, he would never leave, not for her, not for his parents, not even for his son.

When Cándido did show up in Guantánamo it was either to ask Modesto for money or to swindle some old lover out of it.

It was difficult not to agree with Miriam. In the course of Cándido's many disappearances Modesto had slowly grown fond of her. At first she accompanied him silently on his long afternoon walks when the law offices would close down for the siesta hour. Then she began to bring Patricio along and they would venture into Parque Martí and sit under the poinciana trees and listen to the street musicians, and when Patricio would wander away from them, to the steps of the yellow church where men hovered over makeshift chessboards, it was Modesto who would go after him and take him by the hand and it was Miriam who became like his own child. Years later, they were still very close, Única thought, at least there was that. And once Miriam had convinced Modesto of the advantages of leaving, it was only a matter of time before Única fell in line. Though, again, she tried to ignore them. Not to discuss the topic, she avoided both Miriam and Modesto, would not sit at the dinner table with them and pretended instead to be reading in a hidden corner of the parlor till all of them had fallen asleep in their communal bed.

Later, Única begged Cándido to join them. Some nights she wanted to get down on her knees and weep at his feet, like the Magdalene. She even threatened to give the house to the government so that Cándido would have nothing once they were gone. He replied only that if she cared so much she would make sure that none of them would leave him. And then he made a deal with Modesto: If they would give him the house, he promised to follow soon behind.

How long had they lived with that hope, all of them, even after the port of Mariel had been closed? Cándido could have gotten out any time he wanted. He knew so many people, in the cities and in the country, bigwigs in the Party and wealthy Europeans, and of course many in Miami. They had imagined

that Cándido could travel from one world into another with
the ease of that sort of afternoon rainstorm that is kindled in
the steamy waters of the Gulf of Batabanó, south of the big
Island, and crosses through the southern coastal swamps and
past the shantytowns of Havana, veering west, as if it wants to
go sightseeing, towards the dilapidated mansions in the
Vedado district and then capriciously east again through the
old city towards the beaches and across the Florida Straits to
the capital del exilio. There were some afternoons in Miami,
after a particularly rowdy thunderstorm, when it was most
quiet there, as if all the clamor needed a time to settle in, that
Única swore she could hear the cry of certain ferocious birds
from the Zapata swamps, of street vendors in narrow streets of
Santiago de Cuba, of the swish of machetes in the cane fields
of Camagüey, and of Cándido's ghost pinned under painted
rocks on the rocky northern key where his boat was shipwrecked, never even making it out of Cuban waters.

Pero bueno, they figured that Cándido didn't ask for permission to leave because he didn't need to, because he could
follow behind them anytime he well pleased. There were times
in the years between the last freedom flight and the morning
the crowd stormed the Peruvian embassy demanding freedom,
those many times that Cándido disappeared, that they thought
he had already left and was safe in Miami or in Paris or in
Barcelona under the patronage of a bounteous supporter of the
arts. But then he would appear again, disheveled, unshaven,
thin as a stray dog, some friend or lover in tow, and sheepishly
ask Modesto if he could stay in his old apartment in the
storage house. When Miriam heard that he had returned and

that he had company, she would set off on a daylong tirade, addressed sotto voce to no one in particular, but always beginning and ending with *ese maricón* and at some point cursing the day that she had ever wandered away from the kind brothers who had given her a home. Some nights Cándido would even sneak Patricio back into the storage house and lay a blanket on the hard dirt floor and abandon his friend or lover to the thin chicken-feather mattress and sleep with his son cuddled in his arms. Única was the one always sent by Modesto to fetch Patricio before Miriam noticed where her son was, and when Única wrested him from Cándido's sleeping grasp, both of them hissed softly, as if some flame were being snuffed with two wet fingers. Could her grandson remember? How he whimpered all night long after Única set him beside his grandfather and Miriam and herself, in that wide island-sized bed where they all slept together? Did he remember how he decided to take his revenge on them by nightly soaking that giant mattress to its springs, every time he was ripped from his father's arms; so that eventually Miriam and Modesto went grumbling to a still-damp bed, which not even the torrid summer days could dry all the way through. And nights later, when Única asked them if she needed to go fetch Patricio from his father, they both pretended they were already asleep and they waited patiently till Cándido had fled again to have the child back with them.

In his letters from Cuba, Cándido said he could not sleep in that wide bed after they had left. He said that those he brought to sleep there with him awoke in the morning with their bodies soaked in a pestilential sweat, as if Patricio's old boy self

were still there, wetting that bed, punishing them for abandoning him, awoke as if all night long they had been thrashed
and whipped by their guiltiest thoughts. Cándido himself awoke
with numbed limbs, dragged helplessly in a trail of dreams of
being buried among withered torsos and caved-in skulls and of
being forced back headfirst as he was into the small dark cav-
ern of his birth. In Miami, Modesto read these letters first and
shook his head and took off his glasses and pressed hard on the
bony ridge between his eyes, before he passed the pages on to
Única as if they were soiled napkins, but that's the way Cándido was, as free then with his words and his thoughts as if his
parents were his school chums. As time went by, his letters
became more graphic, as he began to recount in lurid and
grotesque detail his dreams and his sexual liaisons and how
he planned to work them both into the fabric of his obscene
art. Modesto forced himself to read every single one of those
letters, and often Única would awake in the middle of the
night to catch Modesto huddled over a tiny light on the kitchen
table, their son's letters spread out before him as he attempted
to compose some response, to make some logical sense of them
as if his son's life were no more complicated than one of his old
court cases. She still had Cándido's grim letters, still carried
them with her from place to place in the lining of her wicker
suitcase, like a miser carries his stash of counted bills. She had
never dared show them to Miriam or Patricio, though she
imagined that Cándido's absence prowled like a pack of wolves
in the nether regions of her grandson's heart, preying on his
every fleeting joy.

THIS SQUALID GARDEN

HE IS WITH HER NOW AS HE HAS NEVER BEEN. Única Aveyano follows the figure of her stepfather across the ancient bridge to the shores of the island city. When he tells her the island's name, as he reads it on a placard in the bridge, he breaks it into three words. Man. Ha-a. Tan. Barefoot, in her great-grandfather's oversized linen suit, with a frayed panama to protect his bald spot from the almost tropical July sun, he leads her as if he were a tour guide, as if this strange eternal city were now his. She follows the blackened soles of his feet.

She is hungry, she calls out to him, and he stops in front of a bakery on Canal Street. Old Chinese men huddle against the tables near the walls, and if they notice her, it is only glancingly, as if she had long been a part of their world. She orders two pork buns and pays in coins, unwittingly giving up one of her small moss-covered stones. The cashier puts it up to the fluorescent light, pinched between two fingers, and examines it as if it were jade, then slips it into her bra and thanks her. She sits by the men near the wall. They slide their chairs to make room for her and then a little extra room, as if they know she is not alone. Too hot, one of them says, grabbing the sleeve of her midnight-colored coat, too hot. Then she bites into the sweet center of her bun and forgets about them. By the time she is finished with the second pork bun her stepfather is gone. She hurries out to the street without saying her good-byes and sees him about a block away, his baggy suit rippling among the throng. She follows him till he turns into a crowded side street, an open-air market where the pedestrians spill from the sidewalk, where no car, only delivery trucks, dares enter. She looks up at the street sign.

There is Mott, she says.

And she is dragged forward into the pulsing current of the market. Passersby bump into her and she feels their hands digging into the pockets of her coat, stealing her polished stones. Frightened, she steps into one of the markets, the stalls ponderous with still-living creatures, glistening striped bass flopping in shallow pans of murky water, skittish blue-shelled crabs mounted one on top of the other, hundreds of bullfrogs peeking dolefully out of the infernal lake of garbage pails, giant severed fish heads in pans of crushed ice, the engorged gills speckled with ruby droplets. She looks one way and then the other for the fluttering linen suit of her stepfather, but she knows that she will not see him, that he will have left her here in this squalid garden of the living.

AFTER ELIÁN

ÚNICA HAD DRIVEN THE MERCEDES BEFORE. Back and forth to the grocery, to the dry cleaner's, to personally deliver travel packets to the homes of VIP clients as if she were Miriam's assistant. In fact, for two of the three years that they had lived with Miriam, after Miriam bought the Jaguar, the old Mercedes had come to be her car. She had her own set of keys, the seat was precisely adjusted to her frame, and the little plastic statuette of the Virgin of Cobre had been removed from the dashboard and replaced by a much bigger piece of the Child of Antioch. She was a natural. In her mid sixties, she had passed the driver's test without making a single mistake. Miriam had driven the Mercedes only when the Jaguar was in the shop. And once, she had spent an entire afternoon with solvents and turpentine trying to remove the oversized statuette of the Child of Antioch from the dashboard. She had bathed the thing in chemicals, bleaching his silvery robes, purging his cheeks of their primrose vigor, his eyes of their Prussian steeliness to no avail. The thing, its staff firmly planted on the ground, was stuck there as if by its saintly will. Miriam had protested that it was a hazard, that it obstructed her peripheral view, but Única knew that Miriam was just as afraid of saints as she was of the specter of death and that the only likeness that was allowed in her house was that of the Virgin, albeit in her hundred incarnations. No crucifixions. (The crosses were snipped from all her rosaries.) No bloody sacred hearts. No lesion-infested Saint Lazarus. The Virgin had been spared any damage to her earthly body; all her wounds were invisible. This proved very attractive to Miriam. Once, Única had bought her daughter-in-law a framed copy of Caravaggio's *Death of the Virgin,* in which the lady's pale barefoot corpse, dressed in regal crimson robes, is watched over by her followers, simply to frighten Miriam, to show her that she too, this undeathly one, went the way of all others. Miriam had thrown the thing aside as if it were a sacrilege, eventually buried it under the long unused, carefully hidden Christmas ornaments in the attic, and called Única a degenerate and a santera. Another time, Única had repeated a story she had read in *Newsweek,* the apocryphal tale of how the Virgin had been raped by a Roman soldier named Panthera and the bastard child had grown up to be the King of the Jews. This pleased Única, that the Savior was as much a bastard as she was.

"Desfachatada," Miriam had said. "It's easy to see who your son got his character from."

That evening, in late May of 2000, when they got into the Mercedes, Única noticed that the Child of Antioch had been sawn off from the dashboard at the ankles; his perfect little feet in their golden sandals and the lowest segment of his humble staff were all that remained, and yet it was enough to endow Única with a sense of daring, knowing the saint had not completely abandoned her, had in Única's absence made Miriam's Mercedes his own.

She touched the air above it and with a wiggling of her fingers, like a bruja, re-created his irremovable presence.

Modesto was slow getting into the car. She had awakened him and dressed him herself and on their way out to the cul-de-sac where the Mercedes was parked, in front of Miriam's house, Única had walked behind him, dragging her own suitcase-like box that held the inflatable raft she had ordered on the Internet. She lifted it by herself into the trunk.

Modesto asked only once where they were going.

"We're going to see Patricio for his birthday."

"I thought he was coming here."

"No," Única had said, kneeling in the dim lamplight of the upstairs room, tying his shoelaces. "We're going to see him."

He grimaced. "They are too tight, too tight." And he never asked where they were going again.

He sat in the passenger seat, fiddling with the buttons of his Walkman and a handful of tapes. The rest of his tapes were in the nursing home, he said. Única whispered to him to close the door slowly, not to shut it. It would make too much noise. It wouldn't be a long trip, she said. She readjusted the driver's seat to its old setting and leaned over Modesto and helped him pull the passenger door closed enough so that the inside light went off. They sat in darkness and waited, Única hoping that Modesto would fall asleep, but he was fidgeting with his shirt, sticking his fingers under the collar.

"The buttons are wrong," he said. "There is an extra one up top." He held it away from his neckline for Única to see, stretching the collar tight around the soft skin under his Adam's apple. Única nodded. "We'll fix it . . . don't worry." She did not look at him. She couldn't. She had her window rolled down and was listening to the sounds from Miriam's room, watching the shadows flutter in the hundred candles that Miriam lit every night as if her bedroom were some sort of chapel. This is what happens when you are raised by monks and priests, Única thought. She wondered how many of the perverts had had their way with the little girl Miriam.

The bedroom window was cracked open. A genial breeze blew in and stirred the candle flames, as if it were a melody egging on dancers.

One more time. They would do it at least one more time. They had done it twice already and were whispering now, or Miriam was whispering, cajolingly, perhaps trying to convince him, to enliven Lenny one last time. Única waited, rooting for him as she had all night. She had used the first two times to make it this far, to dig through Miriam's purse for the keys to the Mercedes and a handful of bills, to turn on the dimmest light in the upstairs bedroom so she could dress Modesto (herself wearing nothing but an old housedress and slippers), to make it out through the patio door where the alarm had not yet been set (that one Miriam did last, after she had left Lenny exhausted upstairs, after she had taken her last naked stroll through the garden), to sneak into the Mercedes and leave the doors closed but unshut. Past the shrill throes of her insatiable lust, they were two-thirds of the way out. All they needed was one last time and she could turn on the ignition, slam the doors shut and they would be gone, and Miriam would not know till the following morning, if then, for often she was so harried in the morning, so busy painting her face, coercing her body into her designer costumes, that she might not even notice the Mercedes missing from its spot. But even if she noticed, it would not matter. She would not send the hapless Lenny after them. His energies were reserved for the candlelit nights. She would wait for Patricio to arrive, let him handle it.

But it would not matter then.

Wide shadows undulated on the wall, like something from the original *Night of the Living Dead,* which she had watched with Modesto years before at the theater on Calixto García, giggling so uncontrollably that the theater manager had asked them to leave. That night, they had left the theater and snuck into the gardens of Sara Zimmerman, and made love on the muddy grounds of the papaya patch, as if they had nowhere else to do it, as if their passion were as forbidden as that of the many others who visited those gardens.

Única heard Miriam hum and the shadow tightened in on itself and grew darker and rocked to and fro, like a prehistoric egg stirred from within. Miriam moaned and soon groaned and before long was weeping uncontrollably and lamentably as she always did during the act, for she knew how brief it would prove and how long the torment before the next one. She wailed from the pitched ceiling of her throat as if each time she did it, she were becoming a widow all over again.

Única turned the key. The Mercedes's motor switched on measuredly as a sleeper's breath and blended in with the hum of the night. She reached over Modesto and pushed open the passenger door, then slammed it shut. She did the same with the driver's side. The light inside the car blinked on and off, on and off, like a beacon. Above, in Miriam's bedroom, the noises had settled into a more rhythmic pattern—her shrill cries, his fatigued groans, like the rusty noise of flamingos. Única cut the wheel all the way to the left and lifted her foot from the brake to set it gently on the gas. The tread of the tires on the rocky dirt beneath was louder than the motor, but no match for the noises above. She circled the cul-de-sac, her aching foot just barely resting on the pedal, and waited till she was on the main street to turn on the lights.

"There," she said.

"There," Modesto repeated. Then, "Now what?"

"Now we go."

And she pressed her foot farther down, and as soon as the car began to move at a steady pace through the empty unlit street, she felt comfortable, in control, her old mastery of the wheel naturally reasserting itself, and what lay ahead seemed no more unreachable or daunting than any faraway spot that you could get into a Mercedes and drive to.

■

The familiar-looking man had helped them fill the raft with air and drag it to the pebbly beach and had sat with them awhile. When she had made it through the struggle of sitting down, half folding her legs in front of her with her hands, she and Modesto inside the raft, the man outside of it, Única searched in the bundle of money that she had taken from Miriam and handed the man a twenty-dollar bill. He took it surreptitiously, closed his dirty fingers over his palm as if his hand were eating it and then slipped it in his pocket.

"Gra-see-ass," he said. Única had never seen someone so young in such a distraught condition. He had not shaved in days and his dark blond hair was greasy and lanky and hung over his ears like flaps. There were flaky patches on his cheeks as if someone had rubbed egg whites on them and they had dried there. His teeth were chipped and broken off at various places and dulled by cigarette stains. He wore crusty jeans cut off below the knee and a bedraggled floral print shirt unbuttoned down to his navel, so that his large womanly nipples and pale hairless belly, which looked like giant honeydew, were exposed. He was barefoot and his feet were calloused underneath like a hobbit and dirt was crudded under the toenails like old sins. He reminded Única of one of the many yellow dogs that used to roam Parque Martí. But when Única looked closer, into his wide-open eyes, which were the color of papaya flesh, she saw a sorrow that made him her comrade.

"So, where are you going with this thing?" He pushed out a long breath of cigarette smoke. He lit another cigarette with the previous one.

"After Elián," Única said. She felt Modesto giving her an incredulous stare, even though she had her side to him.

The man put his index finger to the tip of his chin and looked out to the sea. He wasn't surprised. He passed his tongue over his lower lip and nodded. It seemed for a moment that he was trying to look over the horizon to see how near Cuba was and how perilous a journey it might be before he gave his approval. Even the destitute, Única thought, had a strong opinion on matters pertaining to Elián González.

The raft was spread on a rocky beach on the south side of Lower Matecumbe Key, halfway between Miami and Key West. It was a narrow strip of land, with room for not much more than the highway and a few restaurants and motels and bungalows on each side. These key towns existed, Única thought, as if hanging on to the highway for dear life. They had come here once, and it had not been difficult to find again. Just a little remembering. It was the exact location where Cándido's friend Dagoberto Masa's balsa had landed. He had drawn a map of the spot in the silent months after he told them about Cándido's last days, and Patricio had driven them here one Sunday afternoon. This exact spot. They had found it. What better way to begin their trip back? This morning, Única and Modesto had stopped and eaten at a fish restaurant in Isla Morada. They had lingered at their table without speaking, playing with the sludge of sugar at the bottom of their coffee cups, as Única tried to remember the details of Dagoberto Masa's map, until they had been asked to leave. They had left the Mercedes parked on the side of a road a few hundred yards away. It was there that the man had first approached them and offered to help them fill the raft with air. He had walked it to a gas station and brought it to them, carrying it upside down over his head.

After some consideration, the man nodded.

"He's not there yet, is he? Elián?" he said, and when no one answered him, he answered himself. "But he will be." He nodded again and stretched his vision farther out into the sea. "Yup, he will be. So it's good that you're getting a head start."

Having considered the risks and approved the journey, he sat there with them till dusk and said or did very little else, except that for every third cigarette that he lit he offered one to Única. He asked once if she wanted him to help them drag the raft out into the water, but Única said no, and then she assured him that the tide would rise up and come get them. She didn't want to say anything about the wild boys she was expecting to rise out of the sea with the tide. He nodded and took up a handful of the pebbly dry sand and let it run through the dirty fingers of his free hand. He pulled out a switchblade and dug into his fingernails, examining them scrupulously till he was sure they were clean. Then he folded the switchblade but held on to it in one hand. Modesto glanced over once and put his hand on Única's purse. The young man grunted and shook his head. When he ran out of cigarettes, he stood up and walked to the shore, again surveying the treacherous watery route towards Elián. The twilight was draped over the dark tranquil waters, the fallen fluttering banners of a defeated day. He walked ankle-deep into the water, but because of the cut of his jeans it seemed that he was walking right on the stained surface and could have just kept on walking as far as he pleased. But when he flicked his last cigarette aside, he came back towards them.

"Good luck," he said. Then he went about examining them coarsely with his eyes as if they were worthless animals at a fair. "To tell you the truth, he looks in much better shape to complete this trip than you do, ma'am." He nodded and registered her expression. "I'm sorry, I'm just calling it as I see it. Are you sick?" Única did not answer. She wanted Modesto to step in for her, to tell this brash dirty young man that he was being rude, but Modesto could not understand anything that the man had said and she wasn't about to translate. So the man tapped the pocket in which he had slipped the twenty-dollar bill and winked and pointed at them with the closed switch-blade. "Whatever," he said. He sat down beside them again, and since he couldn't smoke, he just stared out into the water. Única heard him clicking the switchblade open and shut, open and shut, till he grew tired of this and without saying anything else stood up and left Única and Modesto sitting on the raft, the gurgling tide rising towards them.

"Good luck anyway," he said.

Modesto sat cross-legged beside her, his spine stubbornly erect. She had made him take one of her sedatives after they left the restaurant in Isla Morada, but it wasn't having any effect. He had forgotten his Walkman in the car. Única lifted her hand and was going to reach out and touch him but, no-ticing the proud lift of his chin as he looked out to the sea, thought better of it and let her hand sink back down beside her gently so he wouldn't notice. She remembered that gesture, that cocksureness of his in the face of impending adversity. She had first seen it on the afternoon when he came to ask her mother and Dr. Esmeraldo Gloria for her hand in marriage. Her mother, Marcia, as if in dire need of replaying some drama from her earlier life, had thrown him out of her house only two weeks before, had sworn in a fit of dementia that she would use her lover's contacts at the yanqui naval base to have him murdered if he ever again came near her daughter, had pro-claimed, as her fragile lover sat beside her on the veranda,

holding his plate of freshly baked pastries, reaching out a fee-
ble hand to her, her intense hatred of all men, of their unre-
liability, their deceitfulness, their treachery. And still, there
Modesto was, two weeks later, one foot on the lowest step
of their stoop, the other on the sidewalk, his hand wrapped
tightly around the rusty unpainted rail of the balustrade, his
grizzly chin lifted so high in the air that it seemed that his body
was drowning in the rising tide of his smugness and only his
face remained afloat.

It was near the middle of the siesta hour and the shadows were short and desolate. A lone horse-drawn carriage clip-
clopped on the river cobblestone street behind them. The screech
of a bicycle followed close behind. Then a long silence.

"What do you want?" Marcia finally said, surprisingly ami-
cable. "I thought I told you never to show your face in this
house again."

It was the last thing that Única heard clearly. Her mother
turned around and saw her peeking through the curtain, so
Única drew back from the window and for the next three
hours—as she stood with her back to the opposite corner of
the room, her hands clasped in front of her lips, wanting to
pray but knowing that no one had ever taught her how—heard
only the echo of their voices and was sure she would never see
Modesto again, certain that her mother would never let this
rag-doll lawyer take her away, certain that after all these years
her mother had not learned, even though she had undeniable
proof in the devotion of her lover right there beside her every
morning, noon and night, that not all men were like Christophe Evesque.

How could she then foretell that less than six weeks later, she would wake up in Modesto's cramped two-room apartment above his half sister's house, vomiting, sitting on the edge of the bidet, her body twisted and crouched over the rust-stained toilet, elated though, for she knew this meant that a life was laboring into existence inside her. And even then, Modesto, as he stood by her in the cramped bathroom that offered not an inch of room between the tub, sink, bidet, toilet, naked, so that when she looked up—any time she thought she was finished, that she had squeezed her stomach empty and peeled off its insides as if it were a half orange—at the pale bush of his crotch, at that turtle-headed thing hanging there, half-engorged with a thick vein on its brow as if it were angry, always at least half-engorged when in her presence in those first weeks of their life as husband and wife, with his hand on the back of her neck, rubbing generously, and even then, as he tried to console his orphaned wife, before he went to work in the law offices of the great poet-lawyer Reginaldo Botero, with that chin raised above the horizon, as if even the most incidental strife of this world, even this, even morning sickness, were some great punishment meted out by a corrupt Havana judge that he had to face with that stony pride.

So Única, now, many years later, laughed from her side of the raft, laughed uncontrollably. Though none of it shook Modesto. He remained still as a yogi, his eyelids half-shut, his mouth half-open, the backs of his long spotted hands resting on his knees. And when he spoke to her, his voice papery but unruffled, he did it as if he had finally found something within him to match the abysmal well of her grief, something that was quite the opposite of that defiantly destitute gesture he had brought with him when he came to ask for her hand so long ago.

He asked her if this was how. If this was why they had stolen Miriam's Mercedes and come out here to the middle of nowhere. If this was why she had bought Patricio such a ludicrous birthday present—Patricio, who since their perilous trip across the Florida Straits had been so afraid of the water that he had probably forgotten how to swim. (Who could blame Patricio? Única thought. Pobrecito. She had held him, his face buried in her chest, for the first three days of the trip. It was supposed to have taken only a handful of hours, but the flimsy lancha had run out of fuel and they had drifted westward with the Gulf Stream, their Maydays ignored. And Única had been careless that afternoon during the rush for the daily water ration. She had put him down, and the next thing she knew, Modesto was shouting at her, begging her to tell him that she still held the boy in her arms, and then she shoved her way to the prow and saw it, his clump of dark hair floating in the silvery water.)

Única stopped laughing. She was silent for a great while, and as the last light was dragged under, and the tide approached them methodically as a sniffing hound, Modesto murmured beside her, so low and rhythmic that it seemed he was reciting a rosary.

She wanted to break the mold of his serenity, for him to rail against their little excursion, but he had never railed against anything before, and he wasn't about to start now, now that he had finally made peace with her lunacy by refusing to stand against it anymore—for *that* he had done all these years, stood unyieldingly against the onslaught of her madness as if he were a seawall—by letting it wash over both of them, finally over both of them, for they were one, weren't they, they were one at last. Isn't that the promise that she had whispered back? Remember? As if any of it mattered now.

Única set her hand in Modesto's open palm and he closed his fingers tightly around it—more a gesture of solidarity than forgiveness, Única thought. He wasn't going to stop her, stop them. The tide stretched towards them, oblivious. A bright half moon rose in between two clusters of dark clouds, lit up their edges, and then coyly hid its face again. But it gave Única a brief moment to catch the expression in Modesto's eyes, some wish that his resignation had not yet extinguished. A kiss? Something else? It had been so long. Before the diagnosis, way before that, but she could not remember it. It had been so infrequent since they had left Cuba, since the news of Cándido, since the early morning on which she sat at her kitchen table while he still slept and pretended to eat her last breakfast, his attempts at love always bungled somehow, by her unwillingness to participate (to touch him, to kiss him, to do anything but lie there as he pulled her bloomers down below her knees, unfastened her bra, and smothered her with feverish sloppy kisses as if he were washing her corpse), by her anger at his gruesome ability to keep any fire burning within him after all that had happened to them. And now, here, during the brief burst of moonlight, she saw it in his eyes, that glow still, and still murmuring, as if she were the answer to all his unheard prayers.

She moved closer to him and kissed him on the cheek and

then on the ridge where his fleshy ears joined his face. Long
ago, during the early years of their marriage, she had found out
that this was his favorite spot to be kissed, when he would turn
his face away from her till her lips finally rested there, and she
could kiss him and whisper to him at the same time, whisper
to him anything she desired, anything she wanted done, any
promise, for after a few minutes of kissing this spot he was
hers. She let her hand rest on his inner thigh and continued
kissing him, pushing up with her other hand from behind her,
her body aching towards him, as if this could answer his sense-
less murmurings; and just as the moon stuck a sliver of its face
out again from behind the mantle of the clouds, like a child
timorously watching the goings-on in some forbidden and
remote place, Modesto tilted his head towards her acquiesc-
ingly and pressed against her, and his body collapsed. His head
rested on her lap. She removed his glasses and made to dry his
tears with the brittle sensitive skin of her palms, but there
were no tears there, so she traced her fingers over his lips. And
for the first time since that indelible afternoon Dagoberto
Masa had shown up on their doorstep with his irreversible
truths, she yearned for his sloppy kisses.

CÁNDIDO'S DREAM

ON THE NIGHT BEFORE PATRICIO was born, Cándido dreamt of giraffes, a horde of giraffes on fire streaking across a barren plain. He told Patricio that story often, but Patricio remembered it only from that one time, in the summer of 1980, when he was eight and they were about to leave. Maybe it was the only way Cándido knew how to say good-bye. He carried Patricio in his arms and held him close while Miriam hastened to get away. The boy pressed his cheek to his father's face and Cándido wet him with kisses. Patricio was growing more and more into the image of his father, Única thought, in the impenetrable black eyes, the coiled unruly hair, the coppery skin and that tantalizing half pout at which both their lips were almost always set. She was halfway between Cándido and Miriam, one hand on his back and the other stretched out towards the open door of the bus that was taking them to the port of Mariel. Cándido had not asked for permission to leave, even though, according to the government, Única said, he was as undesirable as any of the others they were letting leave. He had separated from Miriam two years before and moved out of Única's house, but after they had applied for permission to leave he had moved back in with them so the government wouldn't take it. He was with another man. A socio, a buddy, he called him. They slept in a storage shack next to the chicken house, the same place where Cándido and Miriam had spent the first few months of their marriage together, so that it was still set up like a makeshift apartment, with a freestanding cast-iron stove, a tiny refrigerator, a narrow bed with a prickly chicken-feather mattress, and under it, a tin bedpan that Cándido and his socio rarely used, preferring to relieve themselves in the fragrant field next door where the wisteria choked the rubble of the fallen Soviet housing building. Cándido wasn't leaving, he had said. He wasn't going to be floated to Miami on a garbage barge. En Norteamérica no se le había perdido nada. But when it came to it, he couldn't let go of Patricio, and Única was caught between them, with Miriam—one hand reaching back and holding on the pant legs of the gold-toothed bus driver, screaming at Cándido from the steps of the bus: sinvergüenza, así que ahora no puedes, now you love him, now you want to hold him, mira, carajo, your time to love or hold anyone in this maldita family passed you by a long time ago, degenerado, where were you when that child really needed you, y que me perdone tu madre, but what cojones were you coddling in that cavernous mouth of yours while your child cried for you at night, mira, gran cacho de maricón, let him go, let us all go now! The bus lurched forward and Miriam turned around and beat the bus driver with her open hands and warned him she would rip open his face with her nails if he left without them and Única stretched her arm farther towards the open door, screaming at Miriam, at Cándido, at Fidel, at Dios Santo, not sure who to blame for the fact that she was losing her one and only son to take her grandson to a better place, and Cándido held Patricio tighter, kissing him and whispering in his ear all the things he had dreamt about on the night before Patricio was born, of the giraffes on fire, of translucent angels with tiny blue wings and arms of marble, of priestesses with two faces and three arms and fingers so delicate that they could hold, without shattering, the fragile glass of time, the powdery wings of orange butterflies, of contorted men and women, who scoop by scoop molded themselves into pale sandy flesh, under the bright waterfall of a dark lake, and of the mist-like ghosts of blue-haired dogs, all this he told his son he had dreamt about before he let him go forever. And then, when they had finally dragged Patricio into the bus, and Miriam had kissed the gold-toothed bus driver on his greasy head, and the boy told her what Cándido had whispered in his ear, she burst into laughter, a discordant noise in that sweaty bus packed with frightened souls.

"Ay, niño," she said, "haven't you learned by now that your father is a liar! That's not *his* dream, that's some painting he saw once in an exhibition in Santiago, the one that he says changed his life! Do you want to know what he really dreamt about on the night before you were born? ¡Cucarachas! Hundreds and hundreds of cucarachas streaking out of the old oven door, through the stove tops, from the cracks in the walls, from the abysmal depth of that cheap pisspot, and him trying to beat them all down with a wooden kitchen spoon, cucarachas even coming out of his ass and his pipi, thousands and thousands of cucarachas, niño, that's what he dreamt about on the night before you were born, and he woke up beating himself on his breast and his cheeks like a penitent, and in such a sweat that I thought my water had broken. Imagínate, yo, nueve y pico months pregnant, had to wake up in the middle of the night to calm down this no-good husband who was frightened by a dream like a child. But I did, I calmed him down, I pushed the hair out of his eyes and told him it sounded like a good-luck dream, that it probably meant that his child would be as hardy and indestructible as the cockroach, and that his child would need such qualities in this world he was being born into, and I kept passing my hand through his hair till he was able to fall asleep again, and minutes after he awoke, late that morning, my water really did break."

Miriam patted her son's head, and the gold-toothed bus driver, whose seat they were pressed against, turned around and gave Miriam a leery smile, till Única, who was still standing on the steps, since there was no other room on the bus, told him to watch the road please, lest he get them all killed before they got a chance to drown.

Later on, Cándido would say in his letters that Miriam stole his only son from him, that she took off with him under the cover of night without even letting him say good-bye, that if he would have known that she was taking his only son from him, he would never have allowed it, that it was she and not he who was una degenerada, una malagradecida, una frígida, that he would never have done this to her, taken her greatest joy away from her, that he sometimes awoke in a sweat, with his arms wrapped around himself, knowing that he would never see his son again.

During those first few months, when they all lived together in the two-room apartment on Meridian Street, Miriam read her son his father's angry letters when Única was at the market and Modesto was taking his daily stroll in Flamingo Park. The letters were written on paper so thin that all the colors of the world passed through it, so delicate that as she read them Miriam daintily held each sheet out before her with its corners pressed between her fingertips as if she were holding it up to dry, and Cándido's childish block letters seemed to float in the air. Única kept the letters hidden between the pages of her old *Réplicas* and *Vanidades,* which she stacked behind the sofa bed, inside the old wicker suitcase where she also kept her three antique Christmas ornaments and the portrait of her father, the French sailor, and Miriam always put them back, in between the exact pages where she had found them. And then one day, the letters stopped coming. At night, while the house slept, the boy crawled under the folded-out bed and looked for them in vain between the pages of the magazines; but there were never any new ones. Miriam explained to him that it was because Castro had set up letter catchers all throughout the perimeter of the Island, who went up in hot-air balloons and employed gigantic butterfly nets, and whose only job was to ensnare the flocks of letters migrating out of the country. His father's colorful angry love letters were among the many caught and were probably trapped in a glass box somewhere, buried in the bowels of the Palace of the Revolution. And so Patricio imagined them there, their flaky iridescent wings pinioned in some dark room.

Única was the only one who could bring him the same kind of joy that his father's letters did, for it seemed that she knew so many stories about his father's life, it was as if she had lived it always alongside him. When Miriam was out cleaning the palatial houses of other Cubans in Coral Gables and Coco-Plum, Única pleased Patricio by telling him how from the beginning, from his very birth, he was too much like his father, no, no, es verdad, way too much like him.

TENDING HIS GARDEN

IN THE GARDEN WHERE SHE SPENDS HER NIGHTS, no one comes looking for her, not her husband, not her nurse, not her grandson, not the doctor. They have granted this space to her. She has never seen Dr. Abdel Alirkan out here, so she has begun taking care of his flowers. There's a gardener, he says. Fire him, she says. What good is having a garden if you can't take care of it on your own? On Mott Street, she bought a bullfrog and set it loose on the retaining wall to patrol for slugs and snails; she removed black-spotted leaves from the rosebushes and made tea from compost to spray on the roots and they are now in their full August bloom. At night, she sits on the wrought-iron bench and watches the house fall asleep, the doctor last in his upstairs room, his reading light on till it is almost time for him to go to the hospital. Some mornings she has to go with him so they can draw her blood and perform their tests, take their opaline photographs of her innards. There is a pink scar on her breast from where they removed the old catheter. Every other

Tuesday, he drives her to the dentist, where they are fitting her for new dentures. He is reading a biography of the Buddha, and he carries it with him everywhere, sets it on the dashboard of his Lexus, so he can look up a quote if he needs to as he is driving. He wonders out loud if he could ever have the courage of such a man, to leave his wife and young son to go searching for the forgetful truth. A vile courage, he says, a vile courage to so abandon the smaller parts of life.

She sleeps in spurts, nodding off on the wrought-iron bench. When she awakes and she thinks the bronze horse in the center of the garden is snorting, its head reared backwards, its front hoof tap-tapping on the terra-cotta floor, she knows it is near dawn and she goes to her bed so her husband will not be frightened when he awakes. He sleeps on his back, with the duvet folded over just below his waist, his hands clasped on his chest. She takes off her midnight-colored coat and folds it on the back of a chair, careful not to let stones spill from its pockets, and settles herself down beside her husband, on her back as well, as if they were already resting on the twin plots that her daughter-in-law bought for them in the cemetery in Miami where Jackie Gleason is buried. In bed, she cannot sleep. She listens to her husband and wonders what might happen if she touched him, if she reached over and passed the back of her hand over his grizzled cheeks, if she leaned over him to feel his breath on her brow, if she put her fingers under his nightshirt and left them there till he awoke. But she does not. She waits for the morning atop the covers, in her housedress, her soiled bare feet hanging off the side of the bed.

Sometimes, she hears Patricio and Lucas go out into the garden after she has left it, to wait for the morning together.

THE SANDY GUEST

IN 1992, ALMOST TEN YEARS after the torrent of Cándido's increasingly delusional and obscene letters stopped headlong, and calls to their Guantánamo neighbors revealed that their old house had long been abandoned and occupied by some government apparatchik, a man came to see them at their little apartment on Meridian Street. Única was in the back, in the narrow concrete patio outside the kitchen, aprovechando the two hours of direct sunlight they got in the early afternoon to hang their laundry. She heard Modesto calling anxiously as if something had just caught on fire, and when she hurried to the front of the apartment she saw her husband standing there in his undershirt and slippers, stooped over and holding the door open wide like a servant, signaling with his chin to a young man standing on the threshold. The visitor stood tall and slender, gaunt almost; he was wearing a pair of threadbare jeans, faded almost to the pale weave of the fabric, and a crisp oversized guayabera that contrasted sharply against the old jeans. He was barefoot and there was sand between his filthy toes and his hands were clasped in front of him in a gesture of forced meekness.

"He says he knows Cándido," Modesto said. And immediately Única's heart lightened.

Knows. Knows. In the present tense.

"Pero, coño," she said, ignoring the visitor's dirty feet, his demeanor of a petty thief, "have you lost your manners? Ask him in."

Modesto gestured with his chin again and the young man stepped into the tiny space that was their living room during the day and their bedroom at night. He left two thin trails of sand behind, which they would leave there for many weeks, stepping around them as if they were the evidence of a brutal crime. He sat on the very edge of the sofa bed, keeping his hands clasped in front in him and his eyes cast downward. He mumbled something: an apology for his dirty feet. He said he had just come from the beach, where he was forced to bathe every day. He gave off a strong brackish odor, of hidden marshes near a sea. Única offered him coffee, a sandwich. He shook his head and still would not look at them. He was unsettled. And though he sat, he rested his weight forward on the balls of his feet, as if he were a fat seagull about to take flight. A breeze passed through the back kitchen door that Única had left wide open and slipped out the front door and must have warned off others because in a matter of minutes it became intolerably muggy inside the apartment. Modesto made a move to open some windows, but she stopped him, afraid that the young man might become more uncomfortable than he already was and leave. Somehow she knew what he could not give voice to.

"¿Cándido Duarte Aveyano," he said in a crusty voice, "es su hijo?" It did not matter anymore that he was still using the present tense.

Modesto was half-turned towards the window, as if he'd rather watch the remote goings-on of the placid afternoon outside than what was transpiring inside their home. He nodded slowly, yes, Cándido is his son, has always been his son more than he has been anybody's anything.

The young man raised his chin and then cocked his head to one side, like a parrot that is about to squawk. "Vaya," he said. Then he looked once directly at Modesto and once directly at Única and then back down. "Vaya, ha muerto."

And then he shook his head vigorously when he heard Modesto fall to his knees and curse their own son, their homeland and the tiny little prison that was their home, though Única was not sure if he meant their apartment or the whole city of Miami. She let Modesto have all the emotions that afternoon. She went stiff and had not the strength to go over to him and help him bear the burden of it, could not offer simple solace, could not tolerate the thought of even touching him; on the contrary, she was overcome by a shocking sense of social shame at having this stranger see Modesto broken down like a widow. Amazing, isn't it, she would think later, what a mind does in these moments. She was calm. She went and made the cafecito and sandwich that she had first offered the stranger, set the cafetera on the flame and layered the ham and Swiss cheese and slices of chorizo on the buttered toast as if nothing extraordinary at all had happened, as if this dirty bird of a stranger stopped by every afternoon for his cafecito and sandwich. When Modesto tired of weeping and cursing, he made his way out of their apartment, leaning on the walls, in his undershirt and slippers as he was, and they did not see him or hear him till much later that night, out back on their tiny patio, hanging the wet laundry that Única had left in the basket.

After he had gulped down that first sandwich, the stranger stayed.

His name was Dagoberto Masa. He had known Cándido. And this he said with an exaggerated opening of his hand, as if Única were to infer from this in what manner he had known Cándido. And others, others who went with them knew him too. Again the gesture of his dirty hand. None of them would have dared without Cándido. Some, in fact, were pretty well off, artists entrenched in the government bureaucracy like pigeons roosting in the abandoned rooms of a ruined house. They had been planning it for over a year. Cándido had befriended an old Spaniard (he did not have to gesture with his hands this time) who owned a sailing boat and kept it docked in an abandoned marina near Cojímar.

"And why then?" she interrupted Dagoberto Masa. "Why couldn't he have dared this ten years earlier? With his own maldita family? That way we could all have drowned together."

Dagoberto Masa hunched his shoulders: "Things were getting difficult, señora," he mumbled. "El período de sacrificio was just closing in. We were losing all our freedoms."

"You had lost all your freedoms ages ago, idiota!"

Dagoberto Masa grew silent. He gave her an exasperated look and asked if she could bring him another sandwich, to which Única quickly obliged, again afraid that she had offended him and that he would leave with his story, their story, untold. When she returned, he eagerly took the plate from her hands and corrected her:

"We were artists, señora, all of us . . . and in that kind of society, usted sabe, sometimes we artists lose our freedoms before anybody else, pero a veces, vaya, if we play our cards right, flatter the right people, give in a little to one's principles, one can keep them a lot longer."

"Artists? All of you used him, you were vagabonds, hangers-on! And—"

He raised a finger before she could protest that Cándido had never flattered a soul in his life, and would not abandon his principles even for the sake of the son he so loved.

"And . . . not drowned, señora. That's not how your son perished." A tone of indignation had seeped into his voice, perhaps occasioned by having been called an idiot, perhaps by her error in predicting the course of his narrative, as if this were some tale he were inventing and not the story of the death of her only son.

Then he ate his whole sandwich, methodically, with much more care than that with which he had devoured the first, daintily pinching it with his fingers and taking little bites with his horselike incisors, as if in the space of a few minutes he had been enlightened. He nodded, either to compliment her on the tastiness of the meal or to get some signal from her, and when he spoke again it was with the presumed agreement that she would not interrupt him.

"I came to speak to you," he said, his voice now gurgly with sentiment, "because I promised Cándido. Y vaya, a man doesn't break his promise."

And he went on with his story, and she dared not interrupt him, though most of it seemed as much outlandish and impossible as made-up.

He said that one moonless night, when the forecast called for calm seas, Cándido and twelve others had stolen into the abandoned marina and all piled into the old Spaniard's sailing vessel. They had sputtered out of the bay into the sea and shut off all the power on the boat till they had made their way past the patrol ships of the Cuban coast guard, gliding on the jib like the ghost of a sunken galleon over the dark waters. When they had thought it safe, after the green lights of the last patrol boat glimmered behind them as harmless as fireflies, as forgettable as a dull summer night, they had erupted into cheers and turned on the motor full throttle and no more than minutes later, Dagoberto Masa said, pursing his lips, their troubles had begun, as if the sea had taken notice of this ghost gliding on its belly. It erupted around them; the little sailing vessel suddenly felt as if it had been swallowed by some horrible sea monster with mythical stomach problems. The stars disappeared. The air became charged with morsels of electricity tangible as horseflies. And the night sky was sundered and a curtain of rain and seawater enveloped them.

"False forecasts," Dagoberto Masa claimed, raising his fingers to the heavens, becoming angry for the first time, "for not even that we could get straight from the government. They lied even about the weather. We should have listened to Radio Martí, but Cándido was adamant about not listening to anything that originated from Miami. Vaya, in a way it was a mystery that he was going with us at all, because as you know he never had a good thing to say about los Estados Unidos. Quién sabe why he came with us. According to him, we had enough fuel and food to set sail on the Spaniard's vessel all the way to the harbor in New York City, where we were to dock in a marina under the Brooklyn Bridge. There, he said, the old Spaniard had saved a space for us! And we believed him, ese maricón, we believed all his crazy inventions. Vaya, una pena, señora, for like I said, I think your son just saw it as a kind of adventure. Otra locura que se le había ocurrido. Nothing more."

They never even made it out of Cuban waters. Floating on debris from the wrecked ship, six of them made it to a barren rocky key from which in the clear light of morning they could still see a gray sliver of the mainland. Four times during the next two weeks, Cuban patrol boats passed by near enough to see them and hear them, but recognizing what they were and where they were, left them there to perish. They ate what little they could find in that hellish strip of land, crabs dug out of their dark homes, algae and seaweed stripped from the surface of stones like old paint, and once, an old mouse-colored pelican that came and settled amongst their huddled group and folded its wings underneath him as if offering itself as sacrifice. They collected rainwater haphazardly, in their old sneakers and in rough-hewn containers fashioned from the flotsam of the sunken vessel, but drank it too eagerly afterwards, thinking that the patrol boats were just playing with them, that they would soon be removed from the rocky key and taken to a Havana jail, where, at least, there would be food and water aplenty. By the second week, one of the men tried to swim to the mainland, and the day after, one of the soldiers in the patrol boats told them with great howls of laughter that his body had washed ashore. Another of the men tried to swim towards the patrol boat, but when he got close enough they fixed a firehose on him and it was as if he'd been shot with a rifle, his body went limp and disappeared. On the tenth day, Cándido began coughing up blood, and the color of it on that colorless island thrilled him. With the feathers of the old pelican as brush and his own blood and the innards of the sacrificed bird as paint, he began drawing wing-like shapes onto the canvas of the hard gray rocks, and when he was done, when he had run out of material, he escaped to one end of the key and out of sight he drank handfuls of seawater and soon after died. Dagoberto Masa and the others buried him under a pile of his painted rocks. Two days later, the patrol boats finally approached the strip of rocky land and the men there gratefully surrendered, in their delirium leaving Cándido's body behind. Two years later, listening this time to the weather reports on Radio Martí, Dagoberto Masa boarded a much more flimsy vessel than he had that night with Cándido and the others, but a mild west wind accompanied them and they made it ashore the sands of a rocky key halfway between Miami Beach and Key West. He was surprised that when the Americans had found them, they too had firehoses that they aimed mercilessly at their rough-hewn raft as if it were a vessel of war.

By the time he had finished with his story, which he embellished with many more scenes and details that Única chose not to remember (of an orgiastic feast two mornings after they had been shipwrecked, por ejemplo, where they drank each other's urine and so on, thinking for sure that the soldiers in the patrol boats would soon come to get them and that they should enjoy their last few hours of freedom), Modesto was already out in the back, hanging the bundle of wet clothes she had left behind. When Única went out to see him, all he said to her was that she should ask their visitor to stay for dinner, to spend the night if he had nowhere else to go. And he continued hanging the clothes in the brisk dusk air while she made dinner. When he came into the house, he played Glenn Gould's recording of the *Goldberg Variations,* over and over, for days.

Miriam had never believed any part of this story. And for that, Única had never blamed her. Why give more credence to this foul-mouthed stranger's story than to the ones that they had been telling themselves, that Cándido was as Cándido had always been, as forgetful of his dear ones as of the faces one might encounter on the Malecón during a careless afternoon stroll, that he was still roaming the streets of his Havana, his adopted city, sleeping with anyone whose sorrow matched his own (a habit he fell into while very young), and cursing God (as he imagined van Gogh might have) for not giving enough texture to the sunflower, enough color to the gray stones of a barren key. And then, Única thought, Miriam might not have given much credence to Dagoberto Masa's fantastical tale, perhaps because she had so long ago begun to think of Cándido as dead, that this second death of his meant nothing to her.

Dagoberto Masa stayed with Única and Modesto for many months. He never repeated his story and no one ever asked him to, though he drew childlike drawings of the rocky beach where Cándido was buried and treasure-hunt maps of the spot in the Florida Keys where he himself had washed up two years later.

Modesto found it necessary to sleep on the spot by the window where he had fallen with the shock of the news. She did not fight him. She laid sheets on the floor for him, a soft pillow for his head, and did the same for Dagoberto Masa on the other side of the sofa bed. He stayed with them, eating at the table with them, trailing behind them on their walks around Flamingo Park, like a pet dog. He wore Modesto's shirts, his pants, his underwear. His feet were too big, so he always went barefoot. They never spoke to him, hardly ever spoke to each other in those days. For a while, though, they had considered looking around for a one-bedroom apartment so that their unexpected visitor would be more comfortable. Miriam could not tolerate the sight of him, and during those months she grew accustomed to visiting in the early afternoon, while Dagoberto Masa roamed the beaches and bathed in the sea. He returned near dinnertime, his feet tracking sand. At night, Única could hear both men weeping into their soft pillows.

And then, one afternoon, Dagoberto Masa did not return. He had taken all his drawings with him. They waited for him till their dinners congealed with the evening breeze. It had felt as if he were going to be with them forever. They missed him. For many days Modesto wandered the streets of Miami Beach looking for him, leaving at dawn and returning at dusk, and then one night he announced that the sea must have devoured their visitor while he was bathing. Única swept all the sand from the house and scattered it in the backyard as if it were someone's ashes. That night, Modesto returned to their makeshift marriage bed and spoke to her at length for the first time in ages. He told her in detail the story of how he had saved their grandson when he fell overboard on their trip over from Mariel. He told her the story as if she had not been there watching in horror, how the boy had been caught in that flood of thirsty souls, all surging forward for their daily water ration—some with tin cups in the air, others with cups they had made with the innards of their shoes, others simply with one palm cupped under the other—that no one noticed the child pushed aside and aside till he was pushed over the port side. And the boy, voiceless with the shock, struggled for only a bit and then laid his head down in the sea as if it were a pillow. No one would have noticed had Modesto not been watching. He yelled her name, te acuerdas, screamed her name across the mass of thirsty souls: "¿Única, Única, el niño está ahí? El niño, is he with you?" As if his eyes were fooling him, as if the intolerable thirst were making him imagine his grandchild drifting hurriedly away from them, facedown in the sea. "No! No!" Única screamed back. He could not remember making the decision to jump in. All he remembered was thinking: Somebody, somebody will jump in and save the boy, and then being in the warm sea, trying to keep the boy's head above his shoulders, shaking him to make sure that he would not stop breathing, the overcrowded lancha an impossible distance away, as if it were about to fall off the edge of the world. The American coast guard cutter found them first, te acuerdas, finally answering the endless Mayday calls from the lancha's captain, but they found *them* first, imagínate eso, just a boy and his grandfather floating for so many hours in the measureless sea. Modesto said it was the only worthy thing he had ever done in his whole life, and then he fell into a deep sleep, and for the first time since Dagoberto Masa had come to their door, he did not weep through his dreams. Única Aveyano remained awake the entire night.

It was her turn, she knew, to begin mourning.

INVENTION OF THE MONSTERS

EVENTUALLY, EARLY IN 1970, THE LONG-DELAYED PLANS for the housing unit were put into action. One afternoon, during one of Cándido's disappearances, they surrounded the field with concertina wire. They cut the wisteria at the root, filled Cándido's hole with earth, and Soviet engineers in red helmets and brown uniforms set to work on the skeleton of their building. On the day he returned, Cándido hopped over the concertina wire and nearly strangled one of the men in the red helmets. He spent four months in a Santiago prison convicted of assault and they had no word of him until after he was released. Cuban workers erected the building in less than three months. A six-story abomination painted battleship gray (its only attempt at ornamentation the Moorish-style latticework that served as the outer walls for certain terrace spaces on the upper floors), it cut off all afternoon light from their backyard and its windows peered directly into Única and Modesto's bedroom and over the wrought-iron grill of their courtyard, into their dining room and kitchen. Families moved in and out with great frequency, mostly transitory workers in the alfalfa fields near the yanqui naval base, or others, enmeshed in el castigo, those duties that they had to fulfill in order to obtain permission to leave during the Freedom Flights of the late sixties and early seventies, who volunteered their labor at the sugar mill or the rum distillery or in the revolutionary hospital north of the town.

In the spring of 1971, Father Gonzalo married Cándido and Miriam in a small ceremony at Saint Catalina de Ricis Church in Parque Martí, and they were to mark some of the watershed moments in their marriage in relation to that drab building. The wedding itself was something that should have never happened, Única would later admit to herself, although it was something that she had then openly encouraged, thinking it would settle Cándido down. Y no sólo eso, that ratty girl had turned into something else. Each time she took Miriam into their home after one of Cándido's disappearances, she noticed some other quality about her—the way her cheeks had filled in and her acne disappeared, leaving only faint scars that Única showed Miriam how to disguise with a little blush, the manner with which the curves of womanhood gave a new mystery to her every move and gesture, the subtle slow tone in which her voice deepened, so that by the time she became a bride it was rich and mellow as a jazz singer's—that reminded Única what a decent-looking young woman she was becoming, as if she were feeding on the nutrients of Cándido's presence, and without him would have always remained that wretched little girl in soiled undergarments, the way the cacao tree remains barren and sickly without the shadows and aliments provided by mother-of-cacao. So it was not just for him, for her son, but for Miriam also that Única had arranged the wedding, forsaken the thin silver band that Christophe Evesque had given her mother and given it to her son and told him what to do, y sin refunfuñar, coño, it's what is best for everyone here, she was tired of playing mother every time that he disappeared.

On the day of their wedding, about a year after the building had gone up, they noticed that the wisteria Modesto had planted years before had somehow survived in the dark underpinnings of the housing unit. It had crawled out from under the square of the building and had begun to creep up its outer walls. "This is a good sign," Única said, "a good sign for this union." Soon, nourished by the light of day, the wisteria began to grow at a fantastic rate, as if it were sugarcane. Its branches thickened into trunks, broad as human legs, which crept higher and higher, rooting themselves into the sills and flimsy framework of the perennially open windows, into cracks in the mortar and into the very shell of the building, effortlessly, as if the walls were a spongy cake, and finally around the Moorish-style latticework of the upper terraces. The authorities soon took note and faint efforts were made to cut the thing down again, but the wisteria had by then become indistinguishable from the wall itself, and besides, the building had now acquired a sophisticated look. The thick leafy vines made it seem as if it were a thing made by nature and not jury-rigged by a bunch of men in red helmets. It became a desired address.

The storage room next to the henhouse in which the newlyweds lived made for cramped and moldy living quarters; and

perhaps it was partly this, Única thought, that was making
Cándido so restless. So they filed a lease application for one of
the small apartments with the aid of an old university friend of
Modesto who then sat in the National Assembly. He was surprised to hear from Modesto and taunted him for wasting his
life away in Reginaldo Botero's office, dealing with petty civil
cases, instead of sharing the glory that was the process of la
Revolución. Modesto answered curtly that he called to inquire
about the lease application and not for career advice. Ah, bien,
his friend said, and then told him that he would help, but that
it was a very long shot, for even some Party honchos had
moved in and torn down walls between the smaller units to
make room for their extended families. The building seemed
one of those by-then-very-rare phenomena, a revolutionary
project that had become a resounding success. The town police
captain, Camilo Suárez, a wretch of a man with womanly
blond curls, proclaimed it a shining example of how Mother
Nature endorses and blesses la Revolución.

The building's fame grew. Cándido, who had somehow convinced Miriam that they should hawk Christophe Evesque's
old engagement ring so that he could buy paints and canvases
in Santiago, had attended there the opening of the much-
heralded Surrealist exhibition and fallen in love with one of
the paintings by the great Catalan surrealist, titled *Invention
of the Monsters*. Even though he never spoke about it, would
never speak about it until his son was old enough to listen to
stories, the painting transformed him; he was smitten. He
stood in front of it, memorizing all the stories that he would later
invent and reinvent for his only son, of giraffes on fire streak-

ing across a barren plain, of large-breasted women with faces
like horses, of lovers so joyful with each other that their cheeks
had fused together one night. It was, he would say later, as if
someone had entered the small dark room that had been his
universe and picked him up from where he was crouched in a
corner and led him by the hand out of that little room, out of
that tiny house, out into a world he could have never imagined.

Somehow, too, the painting made him more daring in his
escapades; and from then on, any time Modesto or Miriam or
Única would chastise him about his notorious ways, about the
ruinous course of his life, he would tell them to leave him
alone, pues, better to invent his own monsters than to live with
anyone else's. It became his favorite catchphrase, which his
wife would later steal from him and use for her own purposes.
Cándido befriended the Catalan painter as he befriended everyone, with a mere glance and that halfhearted smile, and told
him about the Soviet housing unit and brought him for a week
to Guantánamo. The Catalan sat, in his bone-colored guayabera and silken swimming shorts and rope sandals, on a canvas
beach chair across the street from the Soviet housing unit,
twirling and twirling his obscene mustache, forcing himself
not to blink those bullfrog eyes of his, but still not quite being
able to pinpoint what seemed monstrous, incongruous about
the whole scene. He stayed in his chair for two whole days,
Cándido crouched on the ground beside him like his Sancho
Panza. No one ever saw the Catalan get up once to use the
bathroom or eat or drink or sleep. Polymites, strange snails
with rainbow-colored shells native to that part of the world,
took a liking to the reek of the Catalan's fame and slowly began

to invade his unmovable presence. They casually surrounded him, increasing their numbers day by day, even infinitesimally crawling up his feet and towards his ankles till, when the artist finally stood, it seemed as if he were suspended over the surface of a kaleidoscopic pond. He looked around him, at so much color, and then pointed at the Soviet building and made the most obvious proclamation.

"There are no flowers on that damn plant!" And then, with all the confidence of a world-famous artist, he added, "But there will be."

He asked for canvas, he asked for paintbrushes, he asked for paint, but of course this was Guantánamo in the early 1970s, where you had to stand in a two-hour *cola* for coffee and milk and rice, and suffer the humiliation of having your weekly food marked off on a ration card, not Paris or Barcelona or New York, so there was no canvas, no paint, no brushes.

Cándido showed the Catalan the bundle of American dollars that he had taken with him to Santiago in search of paints and canvases.

"Things are not so good por aquí, sabes. Es difícil resolver."

The Catalan didn't want to be bothered with such mundane details, and with five words he taught Cándido as great a lesson as anyone could teach an artist in revolutionary Cuba.

"Then invent me some, carajo!" he said, and sat back down on his beach chair.

Cándido followed the Catalan's instructions flawlessly. He invented. He stole one of his mother's bedsheets and bound it tightly around the branches of a chestnut, then broke into Camilo Suárez's stables and snipped the tail of one of the police horses, and, carefully calibrating the colors, he expertly mixed lard with the crushed shells of the polymites, which he collected from around the beach chair on which the Catalan still sat, staring intently at the subject of his next masterpiece. Like any true master, when he started working on his painting, nothing else mattered. It was well-known that for all his self-promotion and high jinks and phantasmagoric imagery, the Catalan was a draftsman of the caliber the world hadn't seen since Raphael or Dürer, a classical painter in his heart of hearts; and in that brief week in Guantánamo he proved it. With his horsetail brushes, with his lard and snail-shell paints, the tropical noons searing his delicate skin, he made a portrait of the housing unit covered in wisteria blooms so lifelike and exact that you could almost smell them, the buds dangling so daintily, it seemed as if they could be lifted off with a light breeze, the branches so masterfully rendered they gave the illusion that they perforated the canvas and existed on the back side. And he displayed it there across the street from the Soviet housing unit, and the painting became an even bigger attraction than the building.

And then the wisteria, as if life for a moment envied art, bloomed for the first time.

Thick creamy clusters appeared first in the uppermost branches and poured down over the whole building, dusk-colored clouds falling on it in frothy clumps. At first their fragrance hung in the air, mysterious and pleasing as a lovely face behind a veil. The little disappointments of the day, a coffee stain on a just-ironed tablecloth, empty shelves at the bakery, too many Xs on the ration card, a nick on the end of a finger while gutting a hen, a wasted afternoon, a son's unpleasant look, seemed more tolerable in the intoxicating air emanating from the Soviet housing unit. Nightmares all but vanished. Modesto stopped snoring. And the common late-night shouting from the storage room was silenced, replaced by an opposite kind of noise. Cándido and Miriam began to get along, holding hands under the dinner table, listening to each other's every word and behaving like lovers in public for the first time since he had first started disappearing. Única once found them in her bathroom, Cándido knelt outside his grandmother's old tub, bathing Miriam as he had on the day she'd arrived. Única did not dare to repeat the request to help as she had that day and hastily excused herself.

Soon, after the Catalan had left with his painting, devout throngs began to gather around the blooming Soviet building. They reached and pulled the twilight clusters to set them in vases inside their homes, and when every flower at hand's reach had been plucked so that it looked as though the building were lifting its dress to reveal its ankles, people started climbing up the vines to reach the higher clusters. Eventually, Camilo Suárez got news of the wisteria's hold on the populace and he sent his ragtag crew of sandaled and barefoot officers to keep guard on the building and the throng was dispersed and when, days later, the wisteria bloomed again in all the sections where it had been stripped, many were sure it was miraculous and they began to see a shadow of the mutilated handless corpse of Che Guevara made by the thick protruding vines on the west side and the anguished bodiless head of Santa Bárbara in the drooping of the clusters on the east side. (Though to Father Gonzalo's credit, he discouraged all these delusions in his weekly sermons. But who ever listened to his lonely voice?) The throng grew. It was said that those who managed to get into the building would be rewarded with everlasting happiness, stomachs that would not hunger, feet that would not wander, hands that would not clench, hearts that would not long or envy, minds that would not remember affliction. Busloads of pilgrims from as far away as Havana and Pinar del Río arrived in Guantánamo again, to see the miraculous vine, to force their way into the little paradise that had once been a Soviet housing unit, and Camilo Suárez's ragtag band of soldiers was no match for them. Some even joined the pilgrims as they walked into the building and set up house inside its narrow hallways and its boxy lobbies, and when they became too many, they forced open doors and settled their belongings in the living rooms, kitchens and bedrooms of the renovated apartments and by the sheer number of their presence evicted the Party honchos and all their families. In retaliation, Camilo Suárez cut off power and water to the building.

Cándido and Miriam, perhaps because of lack of a better thing to do with their newfound affections (and because they, for a moment, so much resembled what was promised of life inside the wisteria cage), left the storage room and with their chicken-feather mattress established their new home in a spare bedroom of one of the Party honcho units on the upper floor. And although they could not leave their spot or else they would lose it, and they were forced to subsist on the meager provisions that the newest pilgrims brought into the building, or those Única could sneak up to them without being attacked

on her way (for it seemed true, once inside the building their
bodies yearned for less and less), and although there was no
water for them to bathe with and the toilets ran dry and were
clogged with excrement, giving off a stench that even the
miraculous wisteria could not disguise, and although after
sundown there was barely enough candlelight to go around, so
that they were forced in these dark hours, with the ends of
their fingers, to get to know each curve, each mark, each crevice, each swelling in the other's body (by then more out of
curiosity than desire), Miriam huddled beside her husband,
peaceful as that first night when he had stolen all her childhood dreams. And it must have been on one of these unlit
madrugadas on the sixth floor of the Soviet housing unit, when
they must have searched each other in their most secret corners, when the hunger and deprivation that they were under-
going must have caused each morsel of bread that they had
eaten to be transubstantiated into a part of each other's body,
that you, Única wrote to her grandson, were conceived, for a
few months later when the building collapsed, Miriam walked
out of the rubble with clusters of wisteria clinging to her hair
and so skeletal that no flesh could hide the swelling in her
belly. And the building was bound to collapse, weakened as it
was by the invasive wisteria and by the intolerable weight of so
many occupants, and shoddily designed, as it must have been,
by the Soviet engineers.

It began its death cry about a week before it collapsed,
deep turbulent groans, as if a great mountain were buckling
to its knees. Father Gonzalo took it upon himself to visit the
building every day and convinced many to leave its dangerous

grounds, and when some left, all the deprivation that they had endured but not felt in their long weeks there came upon them at once: children wailed with hunger, young men and women were struck rabid with desire and the elderly with the heavy burden of all their years. But this was better, Father Gonzalo screamed, as he lost control over them and they wandered the town like packs of wild curs, better this than not to feel anything at all. This, the road to a better paradise. Fewer and fewer were convinced by him, and on the hazy morning that the building collapsed there were over two hundred souls trapped inside, Miriam and Cándido among them. Very few survived, Miriam, Cándido and a handful of others who had been residing on the top floor and whose fall was cushioned by the million flowers that had been the chopped-off head of Santa Bárbara and protected by the woody branches that had been the shadow of el Che's desecrated corpse. Many bodies were never found and when the wisteria began to wrap itself again around the ruins of the building and bloom again, this time in a more natural cycle, producing its elongate poisonous pods, not even Camilo Suárez dared to cut it down, for it would have been as useless as stabbing a ghost.

It was said that when the Catalan heard of the building's collapse and of the many deaths that it had caused, he covered the canvas he had painted in their town in the whitest gesso and shredded it into a thousand pieces, tiny as wisteria petals. And as if in repentance, he made a pilgrimage to New York and rented the entire top floor of the Plaza Hotel and daily would walk barefoot to the Metropolitan Museum, some twenty blocks north, to sit humbly in front of his muscular and acrobatic

Crucifixion, where he was kept on close watch, for it was rumored that the Catalan, condemned by the current art critics as crass and overly commercial, had in those days been expelled from his own artistic movement, and wanted all his other paintings destroyed as well.

And there the story ends for now, Única wrote to her grandson, with the barefoot penitent Catalan and the rubble of the Soviet housing unit covered in fragrant flowers, which for many years thereafter was guarded by soldiers against curious children, who had no idea why it was necessary to guard the frontiers of a garden. If left to their own devices, in such dearth, the children would have feasted on the deadly pods.

PART TWO

HER FIRST DEATH

ÚNICA AVEYANO WENT SEARCHING for her first death by eating the crushed glass of three antique Christmas ornaments. Aside from the portrait of her father and some of Modesto's favorite albums, which she had slipped into the lining of the pale wicker suitcase, they were the only things of value that she had tried to smuggle out of Cuba. When they disembarked from the bus near the port of Mariel, a mulatto soldier poked the suitcase with his Belgian rifle and made her open it. He said in a loud voice, as if announcing it to everyone leaving the bus, that it was las viejas who were most responsible for trying to strip the country of its natural resources. Patricio stood to the side holding Miriam's hand, imagining a horde of bent-over old women toting suitcases filled with sugar. He knew from Fidel's Sunday speeches that this was their country's most precious resource. Though on Sundays, Modesto spoke back to the television, as if it could hear him, and told it that the country's most precious resource was actually the Russian ruble; then he dismissed the rest of the speech with a flick of his hand as if el Líder were a feckless servant. The mulatto pointed again with his rifle, this time at a pair of cardboard boxes on a make-shift table behind him, brimming with confiscated booty, mostly silver plates and flatware that glimmered tawdrily in the hazy sunshine. This must have been the resource he meant, each family's past as inherited from weddings to weddings, from funerals to funerals. Clouds of hungry mosquitoes buzzed over the family mementos, as if they still retained the scent and the flush of the living.

Única knelt on the muddy ground and opened her suitcase. The antique Christmas ornaments were wrapped individually in Modesto's old undershirts and she unwrapped each one and held it up with both hands towards the soldier. The first one was shaped like the head of the magus Balthazar, the one who brought frankincense to the baby Jesus and whose skin was as dark as a mamey seed. A ribbon of gold was entwined under-neath his turban. The second one was shaped like an engorged rooster. Its feathers were five shades of blue, its tail fanned out. Its crest was a fiery orange. The third piece was the sim-plest. It was a silver tear the size of a large plum. It glimmered with a more delicate élan than the pieces in the cardboard box. The soldier looked at each piece with distaste and each time glanced down at the suitcase hoping there might be something of greater value hidden under the bundle of housedresses and bloomers and hosiery. He poked the end of his rifle into the suitcase. Then he took the silver tear and threw it high in the air and shot at it. He missed and the silver tear landed in the mud with a soft thud. The shot garnered the attention of the horde of pilgrims moving from the muddy mosquito-infested field towards the port and they began to rush headlong towards the sea. Patricio thought of the stories from the Bible that Única often read to him, of the herd of possessed swine stampeding off the steep bank into the lake. A portly, concerned sergeant came over to them and chastised the mulatto soldier for firing his weapon and sent him off somewhere else, threatening to put him in a boat and send him to drown with the gusanos, and he himself began to check everyone's documents. Única stood up and took back the silver tear from where it had fallen unharmed. The slip under her dress was showing and its lacy hem was stained with mud. After their papers were checked, they went off to look for Modesto, who had left for the port of Mariel a day earlier with a bundle of yanqui dollars sewn into the band of his boxer shorts, for it was only with yanqui money, he had heard, that spots on the safest boats were secured. His law partner, Reginaldo Botero, had risked his license by finding the illegal dollars for Modesto, though he could not come with them. And without being asked why, Reginaldo Botero had said of the land that all of his poetry dealt with, that it would be like a husband abandoning his terminally ill wife. Still, he had found them the dollars by selling some of his rare leather-bound books through la bolsa. So it was a good thing that Modesto had not been with Única. He would have been very upset that she had endangered their passage out, after so much had been risked, for the sake of three Christmas ornaments, his albums and an old photograph.

As it were, they could see that most of the boats that they were allowing into the port were not seaworthy. Their captains, they had heard, had rented or borrowed whatever vessel they could to come pick up relatives, only to be told that they would have to make three or four trips with boatloads of complete strangers first, before they were allowed even to see their relatives. Some boats were so badly weathered and overcrowded that they listed dangerously, even before leaving port.

It would be a long time before they used the wicker suitcase again. It was kept under the sofa bed, and later in a high spot on the top shelf of the closet. It was a storage place for the ornaments and for Única's copies of old magazines and for Cándido's increasingly demented letters. Every so often, when they were alone, Modesto would take down the suitcase so she could store a new bundle of magazines and during the holidays so she could hang the ornaments on a dwarf Christmas tree that was no taller than the boy Patricio. Modesto never failed to remind her about the mulatto soldier and about the fact that the ornaments had almost cost all of them their freedom.

"And for that they are more valuable, coño," she answered him, though she did not think much of the freedom for which they had paid such a drastic price.

Some four years after the afternoon on which Dagoberto Masa disappeared, Única was stealthy as a predator. Modesto was in a very deep sleep, perhaps because he had returned to his habit of sleeping on the floor, where he was more comfortable, perhaps because he was searching for both his dead son and their long departed visitor in the caverns of his dreams. Única pulled down the wicker suitcase (heavy with old magazines) out of its high spot on the top shelf of the closet all by herself, took out the antique ornaments, each bundled in one of Modesto's old nightshirts, and set the cafetera over the flame as she did every morning before sunrise. She sat at their dining table less than ten feet from her sleeping husband, unwrapped the precious ornaments and unceremoniously cracked each open like an egg and primly, taking each lustrous jagged piece as if it were a wafer and placing it on the end of her tongue, ate all three of them.

When Modesto awoke, the house reeked of burnt coffee and Única was slouched over her breakfast plate, a thin mahogany streak of blood down the side of her chin. He shook her by the shoulder and she lifted her head as if she merely had been taking a nap.

"Perdóname," she said, "I forgot about your coffee."

She stood up to turn off the flame under the scorched cafetera, but made it only halfway to the stove, collapsing on the kitchen floor, almost with the same violence with which her grandmother Pilar had collapsed while washing her face on the day before Única was born. Modesto huddled over her and took her in his arms, and when she began convulsing, he pried his fingers into her mouth. "¿Dime, dime qué has hecho, muchacha?" When Única's body went clammy and still, he remembered thinking the same thing he had thought when Patricio had fallen into the sea: Somebody, somebody will come to save her.

It was not until early that afternoon that Miriam appeared. The fire squad and the paramedics were already there. A neighbor had smelled the smoke from the scorched cafetera. They had found Modesto still seated on the linoleum floor, his wife's limp body in his arms. A small, patient fire reached up from the stove to the cupboards.

Única survived, the doctors said, only because the glass of
the antique ornaments was so delicate and thin that much of
it dissolved in her stomach acids.

During his consultation with Miriam, the young doctor who
had attended to Única in the emergency room held up a sliver
of blue glass to the severe white light of the hospital.

"We found this piece lodged in her cheeks. See, you can
almost see through it."

Miriam perfunctorily looked through the glass. The young
man's fingers were long and elegant and she imagined the ease
with which they had searched the inside of Única's mouth.

"Very beautiful," the doctor said, "they must have been very
beautiful ornaments. What a shame."

"Mira, what about the patient, doctor? Is she going to be OK?"

He continued to hold the piece of blue glass aloft, turning it
from side to side as if he were trying to divine something from
the way it let the light pass through.

"Oh, yes, yes, the patient is going to be fine, perhaps a little
bruised by the trauma." He brought the piece of glass down and
looked at Miriam. "Though that's not really what I would be
worried about. I would be concerned with the future, if I were
you. The patient's future, of course, but also that poor man, her
husband, who did nothing, nothing at all, just held her there as
if she were already dead. So in that sense she was lucky, she
escaped tragedy. Most of us are not quite so fortunate."

He held out the sliver of blue glass to Miriam and placed it
in her palm. Miriam stood there with it at arm's length, as if
she were holding something radioactive.

"A memento for the patient, señora. Like I said, most of us
are not quite so fortunate."

Miriam waited till she had been left alone and wrapped the piece of glass in tissue paper and crushed it to dust with the heel of her shoe.

After that, she took her in-laws in, partly because she must have felt sorry for Modesto, who had confessed to Miriam that he was afraid to live with Única by himself, afraid that the next time it would happen, again he wouldn't know what to do. So off they went to Miriam's house, a whole room was redone for them, though Única soon found that she could not use it, sneaking instead into Patricio's old room. Modesto worked part-time at the travel agency arranging files and looking over the books for Miriam, and Única, after reluctantly agreeing to see a psychiatrist, maniacally took on all of the household chores, the maintenance of that gigantic, largely uninhabited house; so much so that Miriam got rid of her Guatemalan maid and of the private chef that came and cooked for her and the current boyfriend three times a week. It was good, she said to her son when she finally called him in Key West to tell him what had happened, good for Única to keep herself occupied.

As if she had been driven to eat old glass for lack of a better thing to do, Patricio thought.

"Has anyone asked her why?" he said. "Why she would do something so absurd?"

They had asked her once, Miriam said, while Única was still in the hospital. She and Modesto had stood on separate sides of the bed, each taking one of Única's hands. "And do you know what she said? Mira, coño, la pobre." She looked at Miriam and then at Modesto and she said that she had read that in La Habana there now were entire families that lived solely on the nourishment of stolen streetlights. They scavenged the city for them, sending their youngest and most nimble up the poles, stealing all the bulbs. At home, they would crack them open as if they were spiny lobsters. Así están las cosas en Cuba. The article said that whole swaths of the city were now lit only by gas lamps, because all the lights had been eaten.

After that, they left her to Dr. Marty. They did not ask her again.

PART THREE

ABUELA AS CUPID

MIRIAM WAS FRANTIC.

"They are gone, gone, gone," she said.

Única had stolen her Mercedes, had taken over three hundred dollars from her purse, and if Patricio didn't find them before nightfall, she was going to call the cops.

"You're not going to call the cops," Patricio said, lowering his chin and glaring at her. "I'll find them." She remained silent, looking straight back at him. "OK?" Patricio found it necessary to repeat himself. "Do not call the cops." Finally Miriam nodded. Some things at least they could still agree upon. They had both developed a strong dislike for police officers during Patricio's years in high school. The way they walked into their living room and sat down without being asked, the way they talked in hushed patronizing tones and scribbled almost everything you said in their thick notepads.

"Canalla que es," Miriam said, clenching a ragged tissue to

her lips, "after all I've done for her. It's that blood, that blood that all of you have."

She was still wearing her flowery silk bathrobe that smelled most like her, a sweaty blend of old desires and tangy soap and stale perfume, pacing barefoot from room to room, Lenny following her around like a butler, passing tissues to her from the endless supply he had balled up in his hands. She had been crying all morning. There were tissues strewn in every room of the house leading to the living room, where they now stood in front of her most valued work of art, a hallucinatory landscape of the Cuban countryside that featured three giant royal palms in the forefront, their woody trunks rendered in globs of coffee and sepia paint. The artist was an old exile who had been one of Lenny's mentors. He had recently passed away, inflating the painting's worth. Patricio always referred to the painting as "The Three Penises."

"And she took him, she took poor Modesto." Miriam pointed towards the adjoining room, to a few prescription bottles sitting on the dining room table. "Didn't even take his medication. Coño, always the most innocent ones who get trapped in her wiles."

She was running nonstop through one of her trademark arguments, the lineage of degeneracy that Patricio had inherited from Cándido, who in turn had inherited it from Única. They were the tormentors, it followed, she and Modesto the innocents, the martyrs.

Patricio listened, as he knew he must if he wanted to get any information out of her. At what time did she notice them gone? Had Única said anything the night before? How the hell do two old infirm people make it out of your house and steal a car from right out front without you hearing a damn thing?

"No te atrevas," she pointed at him with a fistful of tissues, "don't you dare blame this on me! Where would all of you be if I had not kept this family together with mis propios cojones? Y mira, don't you curse in front of me!"

Patricio sighed. He gazed at the three giant royal palms to calm himself. "Mamá, can we just talk for a moment without screaming at each other?"

Miriam grabbed a new bundle of tissues from Lenny and resumed her roaming.

Patricio looked at Lenny for the first time, poor emaciated Lenny, his cheeks sunken like a beggar. "Did you see anything?"

He shook his head.

"Twenty-four hours!" Miriam called from another room. "One day! And if you don't find them I am calling all the cops, all the cops that ever came into this house looking for you! We'll see if they don't find out what you're up to these days, degenerado!"

Patricio grabbed Modesto's medication and left. He had a plan.

There weren't too many sixty-eight-year-old Cuban abuelas who had tried to play Cupid for their gay grandsons. Recently, every time he talked to his grandmother, she brought the conversation around to one of the nurses in the home, a boy whose family was from Guantánamo, like theirs. During one of those calls, she whispered conspiringly that she had found out his phone number, and Patricio absentmindedly wrote it down and stuffed it into his wallet, where he kept so many other phone numbers that he had to carry his money and credit cards in a silver clip in his front pocket. Patricio had always imagined this nurse (what was his name?) to be some pasty pimply queen (though once Única had mentioned he looked like a young Brando!) who had endeared himself to Única just because he happened to take a liking to the portrait of Patricio that he knew she kept on her nightstand. After driving for a few minutes, to get himself out of the range of Miriam's hollering, he pulled over to the side of the road and dug through his wallet till he found Lucas's number. It had always proved a saving grace, this practice of keeping every phone number he was given in the perplexing order of his bulging wallet. Often, when clients noticed the disarray of the wallet, they gave him expensive leather phone books as parting gifts, or electronic organizers, all of which lay unused in a cardboard box in some corner of Patricio's mostly unfurnished home near Key West.

Crossing the bridge to the island of Miami Beach, Patricio pulled out his cell phone and then a small pink cellophane bag with pellet-sized Ecstasy pills; before he punched in Lucas's number, he dropped his first hit of the day. He threw the pink bag on the passenger seat, where it settled among all the brown bottles of his grandfather's medication.

Lucas let his machine pick up (a lispy voice), but as soon as Patricio said his name, he picked up.

"What? What's wrong?"

"This is Patricio. I'm Única's and—"

"I know, I know who you are." And then a pause. How did he know that something was wrong? "It's your birthday, isn't it?

Have they come to see you? Where are you?" When Patricio told him he was in South Beach, Lucas gave him his address, Michigan and Ninth, and told him to drop over, and before Patricio got a chance to ask what he knew about his grandparents, he hung up.

The two-story property on Michigan and Ninth had a neglected wraparound yard of dried lawn the color of potatoes and weeds that had been ignored for so long that they had grown woody and tall as sunflowers and were advancing like an encroaching army on the war-ravaged structure that was the house. It was hard to believe that a gay man lived there, hard to believe that this prime address hadn't been snatched by some real estate mogul and renovated back to its old art deco charm like the houses behind it and across the street. It stood out there on the corner of Michigan and Ninth like a dried scabby lesion on a smooth cheek. Patricio approached the rusty gate and was about to go onto the front porch, which was crowded with stacks of dismembered patio furniture, and knock on the door, when he heard someone calling him from the balcony above. He stepped out onto the cracked, weed-covered walkway, shielded his eyes with one hand—for the light was already becoming too bright—and tried to reconcile the half-naked figure leaning forward on the balcony railing with the effeminate acne-infested boy he had imagined.

Lucas was wearing green Christmas boxers sprinkled with snowflakes. And that's it. Nothing else. He was flat-bellied and muscular, especially his legs, whose muscles quivered like plucked chords as he swayed back and forth on the railing, his bare feet wrapped around the lower rail like an acrobat. He had wide eyes and a strong chin and thick black hair, closely cropped on the sides and tousled up top, and he smiled as if the day had been made for him.

"Around the side," he said, motioning with his arm, "around the side."

Patricio had no idea what this meant. He had inadvertently stepped all the way back to the rusty gate to try to get a better look, and felt a tinge of shame behind his ears as he stood there, rubbing off some of the rust on the gate with a fingernail and looking up at the balcony, not thinking about Única, or of her grave illness, or of the danger into which she was leading Modesto, or of his hysterical mother and her pathetically devoted lover, or of the fact that the hit of Ecstasy he had just taken was just about to take effect (where he could always feel it first, that tingling on the tip of his coccyx), but of the chances that he could soon sneak his long pointy tongue under those loose-hanging snowflake boxer shorts.

"Around the side," Lucas repeated, a little perplexed, it seemed, at the dumbstruck presence beneath him. He shook his head and leaned forward on the railing and opened his arms wide.

"¿Hablas inglés, coño?" he said, slapping his hands down to his sides.

It shook Patricio out of his trance, the notion of Única setting him up with a nice Cuban boy. He smiled and tried to imagine the inveterate cubanismo of her logic: if he's going to be a maricón he might as well be a maricón with another cubanito, porque mira, bien se sabe, que los maricones de Cuba son los mejores maricones del mundo! He hurried up

the side stairs. But by the time Patricio made it up to the apartment, around the side entrance, Lucas had thrown on a wrinkled T-shirt and a pair of khaki shorts over his boxers. The door
was ajar, so Patricio let himself in. Lucas was sitting on a spacious bed, struggling with the laces of his sneakers. Aside from
the waist-high bookshelves, crowded like a rush-hour bus, and
a black metal TV stand on which sat not a TV but more books
and an old computer, the bed was the only piece of furniture
in the room, the room itself not much more spacious than a
good-sized kitchen. In one corner, there were three long pairs
of Rollerblades leaning against the wall, as if resting, and a
mound of used rubber wheels whose various bright colors had
been dulled from their perimeters by use and were kept, it
seemed, as mementos of hills conquered and wicked curves
mastered and endless stretches overcome. The walls were
bare, except for various pictures, hastily taped on, of Roller-
blade racers in full gear, with their shiny skintight outfights
and aerodynamic helmets. There was a long row of louvered
windows that faced the decrepit yard, heavy curtains drawn
almost shut across it.

"Somebody else lives down there," Lucas said, not looking up.

"You're a Rollerblader?" Patricio raised one hand, signaling
he wasn't exactly sure at what—the pictures on the walls? the
mound of wheels that soon began to take on a ghoulish aspect,
like those mounds of objects, Patricio thought, that you see in
pictures of the concentration camps on the History Channel?
He didn't know how else to let himself into the room after the
goofy ogling he had done from below. He could have just as
easily pointed at all the books and said, so you're a reader, or at

the pond-sized bed and said, so you're a sleeper, or taken a deep whiff of the flowery racy scent rising from the bedsheets and from the little towelettes next to the bed and said, so you're a sex maniac.

"In-line skater," Lucas said, a little bit too seriously. "Roller-blade is a brand. Like Band-Aid or Clorox. Very important."

Patricio nodded unconvincingly, still standing by the door, even though he knew Lucas had meant for him to come in.

"Única didn't mention that, your . . . in-line skating thing. She *has* told me you love to read." And now he pointed to all the books, as if to prove he wasn't making things up.

Lucas stood and approached Patricio, his hand outstretched.

"Yeah, that too, my books." He took Patricio's hand and just as easily let it go. He stood about half a head shorter than Patricio and looked more compact and muscular up close, his hair messy and dark, like the pulp that surrounds a walnut, and it had been gelled and spiked up on top where it was thinner. And his eyes. Única had never mentioned his eyes to Patricio. Had she been so stooped over by her illness, by the brutal treatments that she had failed to look into them? They almost obliterated the rest of him, so dense and marbly in their greenness that they seemed unnatural.

Lucas got up. "You look shaky," he said. He came slowly towards Patricio, not taking his eyes from him. As if he were about to kiss him or something, Patricio thought, but he reached around Patricio, put his hand on the small of his back and gently pushed him into the darkened room. "Sit down."

Patricio went to sit where the bed was, missed the edge and landed on the floor. The gentle tingle from the Ecstasy spread from his lumbar region, as if spilling from something broken, to the ends of his limbs and the crown of his head. He giggled and then flashed his goofy smile.

Lucas stood above him. "Your grandmother is right; you are always smiling, no matter what." And then more serious, "What are you on?"

Patricio shrugged. Must be a good nurse. Usually people couldn't tell when he was buzzing. In high school, he would spend days strung out on cocaine and Miriam would ask him why he was so jittery.

Lucas sat on the floor beside him, their legs brushed and Patricio threw his head back on the bed. He reached beside him, took one of the small moist towelettes that were strewn by the bed and put it to his face. It smelled of mud and grease.

Lucas snatched it away. "I was cleaning the wheels," he said, pointing to the mound in one corner of the room.

"Oh, I thought that they were for something else."

"Why did you call me?" His voice grew concerned.

"I was curious. . . . Why did you ask me to come over?"

Lucas put his hand on Patricio's knee. This time he spoke as if to a child, pausing between phrases. "Curious about what? Why did you call me? It was about your grandmother."

Patricio lifted his head from the bed. "They've disappeared. They stole Miriam's car and they fucking disappeared." And then he sat up, a thought crossing his mind. "She could be dead by now. They could both be dead by now."

"They are not dead," Lucas said. Though even in his mildly euphoric state, Patricio knew that neither of them could be sure.

"Miriam has given me one day to find them."

"And so the first thing you do is get all fucked up?"

"Don't get holy on me. I can function on a lot more."

Lucas stood up and went to the crowded, midget bookcase and pulled out a CD and put it in the player. Pretty, Patricio thought. A jazzy emphatic piano. He stood up as if to walk away from the sound of the lonely music and paced around the perimeter of the small room, examining the pictures taped on the wall, reaching up one hand to each as if to get a better sense of them from their sleek glossy surfaces. Many were of Lucas, in pre-race poses, his arms tilted affectedly on each side, his chin cocked downward and his eyes flirting with the camera. As Patricio passed his index finger over the line of the curve that fell effortlessly from the small of the skater's back to the round of his buttocks to the slope of the back of his legs, he felt Lucas from behind him, wrapping his arms around him.

"Why don't you lie down for a while?" And though it sounded more like a command that an invitation, Patricio turned around quickly so that they were facing each other, and pressed his lips to Lucas's. He playfully passed his tongue over the edges of Lucas's pursed lips as if to tickle his mouth open, then up and down the ridge of his jaw to the underside of his chin.

"Stop," Lucas said. "You're slobbering." But he kept a tight hold of him and, as Patricio continued with his tongue, he readily picked him up and laid him on the bed, letting go just before he set him down. Patricio tried to sit up, but Lucas pressed a firm hand to his chest and held him down.

"Stay, boy."

"I know you want to kiss me," Patricio said, and folded his arms behind his head in a gesture of submission that was perhaps unnecessary, for the pressure of Lucas's hand on his chest made him feel yielding as the day's last light.

"What I want," Lucas said, "is not important right now. Come on, man! Coño, you came here 'cause your grandparents—"

"I didn't ask for your help."

"Then why did you call me?"

Patricio let out a belly breath. "I told you, I was curious."

Lucas frowned.

"And just how are you going to help, anyway?" Patricio said. "Put on your shiny superhero's outfit and get on your little roller skates and swish up and down U.S. 1 till you spot Miriam's Mercedes? How the fuck are we going to find them?" He took Lucas's hand by the wrist and lifted it off his chest and placed it on his crotch. "That, my friend, is what you are missing." Then he stood abruptly and made as if he were about to leave, but stopped just short of the open door. He patted his pockets, front and back, and looked for a moment at the spot on the floor where he had been sitting and then at the bed.

"Fuck," he said.

Lucas followed him down the side stairs out to Michigan Avenue, where Patricio's black '67 Mustang was parked under the shade of a bitter almond tree. The keys were hanging from the ignition, the windows rolled up, the doors locked.

Lucas peered into the passenger seat, and when Patricio asked him to go look for a wire hanger, he shook his head. "No, I don't think you want your friendly South Beach cop to ride by on his bicycle and look in there."

Patricio pretended to look in. "They're Modesto's."

Lucas cupped his hands on the window and peered in

closer. He seemed unconvinced. He pressed his three middle fingers just under the rubber lining of the vent window and with his other hand gave them one smooth slap. The little window swung open. He reached in and unlocked the door, took the keys and threw them at Patricio.

"Do you break into cars often?" Patricio said. He reached into the driver's seat and grabbed the pink cellophane bag among Modesto's medicine. He locked the door and shut it, examined the bag, counted the remaining pills and offered one to Lucas.

"No," Lucas said. "And if you take one more, you can go looking for your grandparents on your own."

Patricio slipped the bag into his pocket. He turned around and began to head back up to Lucas's apartment. "Let's hang out . . . and get to know each other." There was a cocksureness in his step as he headed up the stairs.

"Whoa," Lucas said, "we're not going back inside."

Patricio stopped, his back to Lucas. He unbuttoned his shirt and took it off. His body was in nowhere near as good a shape as Lucas's, but he could still do this sort of thing. He worked out two or three times a week, not because he enjoyed it but because it was good for business, just enough exercise so he wouldn't start getting flabby. No more, no less. But to date, it had never been a problem to attract others by simply doing what he had just done, slipping off his shirt and waiting for them to come to him. His clients always told him what they loved best about his torso. The tufts of fine hair around his dark nipples and in a wing-like pattern on his chest. The sheen of his suntanned belly. The constellation of tiny moles on the left side of his rib cage. The coarser hair swirling around his belly button.

"Is this the getting-to-know-each-other part?" he said, turning around. "Is that what you want? Do you want me to tell you about all the men that I've abandoned? Come here, I can show you a better way to get to know each other." His cock was half-hard under the fabric of his pants.

"Jesus," Lucas said. He was still standing by the Mustang. "I've gotta ask. Do you give a shit about your grandparents? At all?"

Patricio shrugged. "OK, I'm sorry. Let's talk about my grandparents." He looked up at the afternoon light as if searching for answers there. "That day she went into the water, how did you know where she'd gone?"

"I guessed," Lucas said. "She had spoken to me a lot about Elián and about Elián's mother, and how peaceful they say it is to drown. So I ran straight out to the beach, and there she was, still hanging on to the buoy rope when I hit the water and only when she heard me screaming for her did she let go."

Patricio cringed. "Good thing you're a swimmer." And then, almost to himself, "OK, then, if you know her so well: Where can she be now?"

"I don't know; hopefully somewhere like that day, holding on to that rope till she heard me." He reached out his hands for the car keys. "Why did you take those fucking pills!"

Patricio squinted and handed him the keys. "Así es. They amplify me. Can I kiss you?"

"No, you cannot kiss me." He opened the passenger door and motioned for Patricio to get in. "Give me your cell phone.

I'm calling the nursing home . . . though I doubt if your grandmother is checking in with them."

Patricio obediently sat in the passenger seat of his car and
leaned his head back and shut his eyes. He couldn't quite hear
what Lucas was saying into the phone. When Lucas hung up,
he threw the phone on Patricio's lap.

"Nada," he said.

Patricio opened one eye to look at him. "Now what?"

"Do you know the first thing your grandmother said to me
when I pulled her from the water that day, within seconds of
being dragged out by the undertow."

Patricio sighed, "No. What did she say?"

"You really don't care, do you?"

Lucas made to walk away, but Patricio reached out and put
a hand on him. "No, please, tell me what she said."

"'Don't tell, don't tell my husband,' that's what she said.
OK? And I only say it, because I don't think that she would do
anything to harm him."

"Oh, are you saying that we have time? That maybe I'll get a
message from her on my cell phone telling me where she is any
moment now?"

"Yeah, maybe, or maybe they just went looking for you in
Key West," he said. "She seemed excited about wanting to see
you for your birthday."

Modesto and Única had been to his house in Key West only
once, on the trip when he took them to visit the spot where
Dagoberto Masa's balsa had landed. Patricio roused up and
dialed Miriam on his cell phone. Lenny picked up. Miriam has
just taken a pill and gone to bed. She had not slept at all the
night before, Lenny said.

"But I thought you didn't find out till this morning?"

"No. She saw the Mercedes missing last night when she went to take her stroll in the garden. But she was afraid to call you. She thought you would blame her."

"Lenny, did Abuela say anything about coming to see me in Key West?"

Silence. Patricio could hear Lenny's unshaven chin brushing against the speaker.

"Lenny?"

"Yeah, I'm here. Look, your grandmother and I, we don't really speak much. I'm sorry. Maybe I should try to go get your mother up."

"No, don't. Let her rest, she needs it. Tell her we'll be in touch."

Not a minute after he had hung up, Lenny called back. "Look," he said, "if this helps. When I searched their room, I found a bunch of drawings, little maps of the keys drawn on scrap paper, your grandmother's illegible scribbles down the margin." But the maps weren't finished, Lenny said. They sort of stopped halfway down to Key West, as if the southern half of the archipelago had been swallowed by the sea. "I didn't think it meant anything this morning, but since you asked if they were going to Key West."

Patricio thanked Lenny, jumped out of the car and put on his shirt.

"Come on," he said to Lucas. "Unfortunately, it looks like we're not going to get a chance to get to know each other too well after all."

FLOATING LETTERS

ONE MORNING IN MID-AUGUST, BEFORE COMING TO BED, she removes the letters from the lining of the wicker suitcase. They are fastened with a navy blue ribbon. Later that day, when her husband asks her what she is doing with them, she says that she has nothing else to do, so in the afternoon, she sits on the wrought-iron bench out in the garden of the doctor's town house and pretends to read them. If her grandson asks her, she will not tell him that they are letters from his father; she will say that they are love letters from her husband and bundle them up in their navy blue ribbon and not read them to him.

That night, before she goes out, she puts them in the inner pocket of her midnight-colored coat; they are almost as heavy as the little stones that she has been collecting for weeks. She sits with her husband at the bar in the restaurant by the river. He has his brandy and she has her black tea. It's Eduardo's night off, so they don't stay long, for no one talks to them and they do not say anything to each other. On their way out, she goes by herself to the refurbished wharf. Her husband stays back, under a streetlamp by the old pier house that is now an ice cream parlor, his hands in the pockets of his oversized corduroy jacket, so she cannot tell for sure if he sees what she is doing. When she has reached the very edge of the wharf, leaning over the railing wound with verses of Whitman, she takes out the bundle of letters from her coat pocket, unties the ribbon and throws it into the water first, and then one by one removes each letter from its crinkled envelope, and unfolding it, casts it into the water as well, the letters first and then the envelopes.

She has every word of every letter memorized, no matter how offensive, how crude. Her son's words will live in her mind as long as her body holds out. After that, she thinks, it does not matter. No one else wants to remember him so precisely.

It takes a while for the current of the river, which is hesitant and swirly around the base of the pier, to realize what is going on, so the pieces of opened paper float nervously in the water like lost ducklings. But before long, before her husband has reached her to ask her softly what she is doing, all of her son's letters are swallowed up by the dark mass of the river.

A WAY BACK FROM THE SLAUGHTER

"I REMEMBER," Patricio said to Lucas as they rode south on U.S. 1, "the day I knew for sure that I would never see my father again." They had gotten caught in rush hour out of Miami, and by the time traffic eased up, it was late afternoon. He was still buzzing a little bit off the Ecstasy and wanted to get his mind off the reason why they were heading south on the narrow highway. Lucas had insisted on driving, and he was listening patiently, waiting, Patricio could tell, with a nurse's precision, for the hit of Ecstasy to wear off. Lenny had called twice, with the new details about the scribbles he was trying to decipher on the maps. One phrase certainly mentioned Dagoberto Masa, Lenny said assuredly. Miriam thankfully was still asleep, but they knew she might call soon to remind them that in the morning she was calling the cops. So Patricio was talking nonstop while Lucas drove. Every time they crossed a bridge into a key, Lucas slid over to the right lane and slowed down so Patricio could compare the road signs to the makeshift treasure map he had drawn from memory on a scrap of paper.

"I must have been—what?—eleven or twelve. It was the first time Miriam had the guts to go out on a date. Well, maybe not the guts, maybe it was the first time she'd ever really had time since we arrived in Miami. You gotta give her credit. . . . She worked like a beast, maybe to keep her mind off things. I think by then she must have known she would never see my father again. Abuela has told you, you know."

Lucas nodded without looking at him. He drummed his fingers on the steering wheel, his eyes intent on the road and on the areas surrounding it.

"So this guy comes to pick Miriam up. They met at school. She's taking night classes. Computer classes, so she can get a job at the travel agency. Night classes after she spends all day as an auditor for 7-Eleven. This is one of the nights that classes don't meet and this guy asked her out. So he comes to pick her up and he's taking her to Black Angus on Bird Road, the same steak house where Miriam always takes us—me and Única and Modesto—every other Sunday. Couldn't have been too romantic for her—but what do you want? She can't say anything. It's the first time she's been in this situation, you know, a romantic situation, with a guy since . . . bueno, since she didn't kiss Cándido good-bye while we boarded the bus for Mariel." They crossed a narrow rusty bridge and traffic slowed to a crawl. A car had run off the road directly up ahead, nose first into a rocky beach. Patricio climbed out of the window and stood on the ledge, then slid back in. "It's not the Mercedes," he said. "So, where was I? Yeah, this guy he comes to the little house we rent on Forty-third Street in Westchester and he sits with me in the living room while Miriam gets ready. He's so young, I think, much younger than Miriam, narrow-shouldered and flimsy-looking, like a sick plant. His hair is short and neatly combed, his face so pockmarked that there are certain sections he can't shave quite right, and his fingers long and thin like a woman's. He has a tiny gold crucifix hanging from his neck, and the black hairs sprouting on his chest. Miriam must have already told him our whole story because the first thing he does is start asking me if I remember Cuba. And then almost in the next sentence asking me if I remember my dad."

Patricio paused to gauge a reaction, but Lucas had his eyes intently on the redirected traffic ahead. So he went on. "Now, I don't want to be sitting there, but Miriam told me I had to, so I tell him the truth. I remember some things about Cuba, like the time I escaped from my playpen and walked out the front door and got hit by a bicycle on the street of our house." He leaned closer and showed Lucas the scar above his eyebrow. "And I remember Cándido. I remember how when he was painting he would dab his finger on the palette and then bring it to my nose. I remember how he rubbed his whiskers to my belly." He lifted his shirt and said that even today if he rubbed hard with a shoe brush, he could still feel his father's face there. "Cándido Duarte Aveyano is a very famous painter, I say to Miriam's date, and soon he is coming to Miami and we're going to be rich. He nods sympathetically and he smiles, unshaken by the mention of Cándido, or his supposed fame, or by the fact that I still think that I will one day see my father again. There are thin strips of dirt between his teeth, and he tries to make more conversation, he asks me how school is going, if I enjoy Sunday school, if I have a girlfriend, if I remember anything about the boat ride across the Florida Straits. But I'm an eleven- or twelve-year-old kid and I don't have much use for this kind of conversation, so in the end, we just sit there and wait while Miriam gets ready and all I can think about is what pieces of furniture I'm going to try to make my Evel Knievel motorcycle jump when I'm in the house by myself.

"And then they're gone to Black Angus. And I can't get my mind off of him. I don't even remember his name: Miriam's first date in the United States. But I remember the way he looked at me. How it was the first time any man ever looked at me like that, like nothing else interested him. I go in the back-yard and climb the narrow anón tree that twice a year is heavy with fruit. I go up as high as I can. I have been doing this ever since we moved to this house, to get away from Miriam, to be alone. And she goes crazy looking for me all over the house, thinking that I have left her like Cándido always left her. To make matters worse, every month I must climb lower and lower because the branches won't hold me. Soon she will find out about my hiding place. I pick a soft fruit and squeeze it open in my palm. Have you ever had an anón? It is the most deli-cious fruit in the world. The flesh has to be sucked out from around the little black seeds that are completely enveloped by it, but visible." He put a hand on Lucas's shoulder. "You know, like those very well-known but unspeakable secreticos every mariconcito has when he's a kid. So after Miriam's date left, I wait until it is dark and I stuff my mouth with the seeds. I eat one fruit and another and another, and let the sticky juices dribble down my chin, eat so many that I am eventually sick with their sweetness. And somehow, I understand that like Miriam, I will never see my father again and that I can stay up in the anón tree as long as I want and she won't come looking for me."

They passed the accident and both of them looked again to make sure it wasn't the backside of Miriam's gray Mercedes sticking up on the shoulder of the road. It was near dusk and they were almost to Isla Morada. The Ecstasy had completely worn off and it seemed a lifetime ago that he had taken it. Patricio rested his head on the windowpane and momentarily dozed off. He dreamt about the craggy face of Miriam's first date in the United States, about his concerned voice. When he was shaken awake, night had fallen and they were not moving. Lucas was saying something and for a moment Patricio could not remember Lucas's name or what he was doing driving his car. He's too young to be a john, he thought, but he tried to think back to where he picked him up. He reached out to caress his face (as if he were blind and needed to get reacquainted) and Lucas let him; he leaned his cheek into Patricio's hand and pressed his lips into his palm without kissing it.

He was pointing, whispering: "Mira, there." Lucas asked him a question and Patricio nodded, not quite understanding what had been asked, more in touch with the twitter of lips on the palm of his hand than with the meaning of the words. Lucas continued to point. They were on the shoulder of the road, under a salt-weathered sign that said UPPER MATECUMBE KEY. In the haze of the rudely wakened, the words meant nothing to Patricio, as if they were the volatile and scrambled syllables of other, more stable words. Lucas finally unfolded the piece of scrap paper that Patricio had crumpled up in his hand during his sleep and poked at the treasure map X at its center, repeating the first word on the road sign, *matecumbe, matecumbe,* as if it were a spell. Patricio sat up. "Shit," he said, "this is it. You found it." He had driven hundreds of times by that very road sign and had stopped only once, on the morning that he brought Única and Modesto to explore this spot. Patricio had stayed in the car listening to the radio. Dagoberto Masa had told Única and Modesto that when he had heard the name of the key, days later while lying in a hospital suffering from dehydration and third-degree burns, he had imagined it meant the way back from the slaughter. Única had always thought if that were the case then it would be the way back for her dead son.

Patricio got out of the car and looked ahead. There was a clearing somewhere, he remembered, and then a scattering of bumpy cracked streets, a clutter of collapsing bungalows and then the rocky beach. They drove slowly on, till they had reached Lower Matecumbe Key and then back up towards the northern end of Isla Morada. Night had fallen completely now, and a row of cars honked behind them. "Turn left, turn left anywhere," Patricio said, and at the first road, Lucas turned towards the ocean. When they reached the end of the street, a dirt road forked off to a weathered resort inn some five hundred yards north, but there was no sign of Miriam's Mercedes, so they got back on a small road that ran parallel to the highway and drove slowly south for a while. Lucas turned on the fog lights. And there it was—the gray Mercedes, parked with its backside protruding out into the road, leaning down into the small embankment that led towards the beach. It looked, Patricio thought, as if it had been left there by someone who had done one too many shots of tequila.

They pulled up behind it and Lucas ran once around the Mercedes, his hands passing over its elegant frame before he peered into the darkness inside. Both doors were unlocked. He ran around again and then climbed onto the trunk and onto the roof of the car. Lucas pivoted all the way around and looked towards the moonlit water on both sides of the key, but could see nothing in the darkness. Then he looked at Patricio. "They can't have gone far," Lucas said. He obviously didn't know Única too well. Sick and weak as she was, she could be miles from there.

Patricio felt the hood; it was cold. Then Lucas jumped off the roof of the Mercedes and without saying another word headed off down a narrow path that led towards the water. They walked south near the shoreline. It didn't take long to find them on the rocky beach. They were lying on a deflated yellow raft. Modesto was on his back with his hands clasped over his chest. His mouth was open. Única was nudged beside him with her arms under her head as pillow. The water had risen and ebbed again and left them there. Lucas put his fingers on her neck and then on Modesto's and then he nodded and whispered that they were fine, that they must be exhausted after their long night. He nudged Única on the shoulder, but she didn't stir, so he had to nudge her harder. She raised her head and looked up at him and then at the surroundings around the raft and then she laid her head back down on her arms. She did not see Patricio to the side of her and nudged closer to Modesto. Then she closed her eyes and was still again.

"Carajo," she said, before she raised her head again and looked wearily at Lucas, squinting, and then at the ebbing tide. "What the hell are you? My guardian angel?"

"Abuela," Patricio said. And at that word, Única became agitated and rose to her knees with the nimbleness of a young woman, as if she weren't ill at all. "¿Pero quién es ese? Who have you brought, my guardian angel?" She looked around but at first she couldn't see her grandson and she stuck her hands in the pockets of her housedress and nervously passed her hands on the bottom of the raft looking for her glasses.

Modesto stirred. He coughed. "It's cold in here," he said in Spanish before he opened his eyes. He raised his torso and rested the weight of his body on his elbows. He looked at Única and then at the two men and he pressed his lips tightly together.

Única found her glasses. The raft, she saw, had lost all of its air. Lucas was crouching by them, holding on to the deflated shell, as if he were afraid that they might still float away on it.

"Señora Única, how did you get this out here?" His voice was authoritative, or trying to be. Única didn't answer him. She was looking at Patricio. But at last she put a hand on Lucas's shoulder and got up on her bare feet, acting unflustered by their presence, trying to smile, her hands open, palms heavenward as in thanksgiving. Her shabby housedress was all wet and sticking to her belly. The scarf had come loose on her head and it hung on it like a shawl, part of her gray buzzed skull visible. She looked, Patricio thought, as if she had just stepped out of her own grave. When she tried to go towards him, she tripped on the shell of the raft and Lucas had to catch her. Her put-on joy fluttered away from her momentarily, like some bird she was holding on to by its feet. Then her body bent inward like a question mark as she pressed her forehead to Lucas's shoulder and sighed.

"A man helped us," Modesto said, and he repeated it to make sure Lucas understood. "He helped us fill it with air. She paid him. She told him that we were going after Elián."

Única ignored him. With great effort, she went to Patricio. She placed her hands on his cheeks and got on her tiptoes and planted a soft kiss on his lips.

"You are still getting taller," she said. "Happy birthday, mi niño."

He kissed her on the forehead and then hugged her and she grumbled about how bad she must smell. Like an open sore, she said. Patricio hugged her tighter.

Lucas helped Modesto get up. His knees were buckling under him, so Lucas had to walk him to the car, his arm around Modesto's waist. Única and Patricio followed in the same fashion behind them.

Única didn't know what she had done with the keys to the Mercedes, so they were going to have to leave it there.

Única and Patricio sat in the backseat of the Mustang and Modesto sat in the passenger seat while Lucas gathered up the ruined raft, carefully squeezing all the air out of it and folding it as if it were evidence. Modesto slumped to one side, his chin resting on his chest.

"I gave him a pill," Única said, "so he would sleep." She said that he would probably like some music, so Patricio stretched forward and turned on the stereo, which at first blared loudly with a sorrowful folk song. He pushed buttons till he found some classical music and Modesto touched his hand. He raised his head. "Ahí," he said.

Patricio sat back down and Única put a hand on his lap. "How old? How old are you today?" He told her. She said that when she was twenty-eight Castro had already been in power a whole year and Cándido was eight years old. She tapped Modesto on the shoulder and asked him if that was right, but Modesto didn't respond at all, so Única answered her own question. "Sí, sí, así es, your father was already eight years old and Fidel had been in Havana for a year."

"Chopin," Modesto said, "el concierto de piano, número dos." And then he rested his chin on his chest again.

After Lucas was finished with the raft, he grabbed Modesto's Walkman from the front seat of the Mercedes, and locked it up. He asked Patricio for his cell phone to call Miriam. When he returned to the driver's seat of the Mustang, he said the raft had a gash on one side, as if someone had slashed it with a blade.

"What did she say?" Patricio asked. "Miriam?"

"She was still asleep. I told Lenny."

"I don't want to go back to Miami," Única said.

Lucas was silent. Patricio told her that she didn't have to. He reminded her about his friend, the oncologist at Sloan-Kettering in New York. He asked her if she wanted to go see him, told her that maybe on the way they could stop and see Elián where he was being held in Washington. First, they would go to their house in Key West and rest for a few days. He told Única anything that would get her to agree to stay with him.

"She's not going to like this," Única said. "Your mother."

"It's not her life, abuela. She can come visit us in Key West if she wants."

No one disagreed with Patricio.

They sat there and listened to the elegant piano, till Lucas headed south on U.S. 1 again, towards Patricio's house near Key West. Patricio wondered how much money he would have to offer Lucas to quit his job and become Única's private nurse, to come with them to New York.

WATCHING

THEY WENT TO A RACE IN PROSPECT PARK, hundreds of skaters in their shiny skintight costumes, coursing through the hilly asphalt as if it were slick ice. They came as a family to watch Lucas—Única and her husband and her grandson and Dr. Abdel Alirkan. They cheered for him each time he passed by, every ten minutes or so, though he could hardly have noticed them, his every fiber absorbed in the precise movements of his body, the legs scissoring through the space ahead, the eyes reaching for some distant spot, the breath composed as if ignorant of the oppressive August heat.

After the race, while they wait for Lucas, the doctor walks them up a hill where a placard on a large boulder marks the spot of one of the most important battles of the yanqui revolutionary war. General Washington, he says, had almost lost his newly formed army and the revolution had almost been squelched a month after the signing of the Declaration of

Independence. From that very spot he was forced to retreat, through Brooklyn Heights and later the following night, under the cover of rain and fog, across the river into Manhattan. After losing all of New York to the British, he fought the rest of the war mostly by avoiding the more resourceful British army. He fought, Dr. Abdel Alirkan says, mostly by not fighting at all. Única translates for her husband, who for the first time that day takes off the headset of his Walkman, and she imagines the stoic general, huddled with his troops in the Heights where she recites the names of streets, waiting for the British army to finish them off, inventing drastic futures for all of them. Patricio is uninterested and he goes off to look for Lucas in the meadow where the racers are gathering. Única follows a few steps behind, leaving the doctor and his history lessons with her husband, who has put his headset back on even as the doctor continues to speak.

Patricio hugs Lucas and holds him long enough for other racers to stop what they are doing and glance once at them before they return to gathering their things or rubbing ointments on their bare calves and feet. But Única doesn't take her eyes off them, for she has begun to watch them like she watched her son in his makeshift home under the earth.

This afternoon she will sit out in the garden at just the right spot on the wrought-iron bench. After Lucas jumps in the shower, her grandson will bring out her forbidden cup of black tea. He will return later to collect the cup, which she hides among the potted begonias. He will leave open the curtains of the sliding glass door to their bedroom, leave ajar the bathroom door, and she will watch Lucas come out of the shower and towel off. Afterward, his side to her, so that she can make out the curves of his silhouette as if he were an ancient Egyptian drawing, he will remove the hand towel from over the mirror and examine his face for blemishes before combing his hair and rubbing his torso and face with skin lotion. When he reaches to rub lotion on his back and upper shoulders, the finger-like muscles that ridge the rib cage are exposed and it will feel for a moment as if she should look away. But she will not. He will replace the hand towel over the mirror, for it is the same bathroom she uses, and turn towards her and she will keep her eyes focused on no particular part of his body, though she will look at all of it, scrutinize it as if it were a precious work of art, as if it were something that she could possess had she the wherewithal. If he lifts his eyes and catches her watching him, she will not look away; she will let it be known with her eyes that this should be their secret, that she has begun watching him. But he will not lift his eyes, or even remember that she is out in the garden looking in on his simplest private acts as if they were extraordinary feats.

NEAR THE ZOO

BEFORE ARRIVING IN NEW YORK, in late May, they had stopped for four days in the nation's capital and Única had established a bond with the innkeeper of the Marcel House, the ill-kept bed and breakfast near the National Zoo. She sat in the still darkened dining room and kept him company while he busied himself with his uniquely unappetizing continental breakfast and poured her cup after cup of her black tea, sipping on the coffee that he periodically laced with brandy. And on the morning she disappeared, it was the innkeeper who noticed first and who, without consulting her grandson, called the police.

The night before, Única had sat up in bed and stared at the walls of the overly priced room which needed a thorough wash, she thought, if not a new paint job. Even with the dim light from the night table on her side of the bed she could see the grime and the fingerprints, around the light switches and doorknobs, like shadows of ill repute. Única wondered if the flamboyant innkeeper was looking for a maid and how much he paid whoever it was who wasn't doing her job very well. She hadn't seen a housekeeper in their four days there, so maybe he did it all himself. She was sure she could do it better for him. In the years that they had lived with Miriam, those years after her first death (that's what Miriam liked to call her suicide attempt—anything with Miriam as long as she didn't have to deal with the truth), Única had cared for the house so efficiently that for a while it was as if her daughter-in-law actually needed her. And although she had never given it much thought then, it had felt good having others besides her husband to toil for. She thought that perhaps the bed and breakfast needed a chef also; the pastries and overripe fruit the innkeeper served them in the morning were as dismal and unimaginative as the prudish couple from Ohio that they had been forced to share breakfast with, who had cowered at one corner of the table as if afraid of contracting the bubonic plague from them. They were the only other customers at the Marcel House during their four-day stay. She chuckled. This is what it had come to, to fantasies of becoming a maid and a morning cook at some shabby bed and breakfast in Washington, D.C.

Única was sitting up, with an extra pillow propped underneath her to ease the pain in her lower back. That morning, Elián and his visiting classmates, all in their starchy trajecitos de pioneros, had been at the National Zoo less than a mile away; but the pain in her back and hips had been so intense that it had been impossible for her to go get a glimpse at him, by midmorning impossible for her to lift herself from the bed without one of the boys on each side. Patricio and Lucas had gone to try to snap a picture, but had been kept back by a coterie of dark-suited Secret Service personnel, the little Cuban boy protected as if he were a president or a senator. Still, it was nice to know that they had been that close. Patricio had snapped three rolls of film from his distant spot and they would have their pictures the next day. That may have to be enough, he said, that may be as close as she would get.

As the day had passed, her pain had diminished, till she felt only its traces, like the hot breath that had persisted for days over the charred remains of her mother's house.

For the first night since they had fled Miriam's house, Modesto had fallen asleep easily beside her before she had turned off her own light. He was on his back, snoring softly, his arms splayed out, his long hands turned upward. Única had been leafing through a copy of an old magazine someone had left behind, had tried once or twice to read the articles, but the words bobbed on the shallow white lagoon of the page, and if she persisted they slowly sunk and left behind only a blur. And this seemed to her a crime, as if she were undoing the writer's considered loops and laces, so she contented herself with quietly leafing through the magazine from one cover to the other and then backwards. Since she was only looking at the drawings and the pictures, it didn't matter which way she went, and each time through she found one that she had missed. The magazine was dated almost a year and a half before, and because of this, when she had found it in the drawer of the nightstand, she decided immediately to keep it. To an outsider, she thought, it might seem as if she were trying to retain some relic from the world before she had been diagnosed. When this issue was published she had been (physically at least) as healthy as any other sixty-seven-year-old. But she had decided to keep it for entirely different reasons. At their little apartment on Meridian Street, she had always saved her copies of *¡Hola!* and *Vanidades,* stacked them in neat piles inside her pale wicker suitcase, aging them as if they were bottles of fine Bordeaux, till she could pull them out years later and gaze on faces that had been briefly famous, on fashions that the passing years had made absurd and on news features that seemed as inconsequential as fallen leaves. But yet, the further a world receded into the past, the more provocative it automatically became, the more incomprehensible, the more like a story anyone could have invented.

When they had moved into Miriam's house, her daughter-in-law had quickly banished this practice of hoarding old magazines, accusing her of building cockroach nests. And she made Única bundle up all the old magazines, tie them up with butcher's string and set them in the recycling bin. She had wanted to throw out the wicker suitcase as well. Where are you planning on traveling? she said. But that Única could not allow. There are things she still kept in there, she told Miriam. And that was that. She would take this old magazine, Única told herself, to start her collection again, wherever it was they were going. If she had told this to the boys or to Modesto, they would have considered it a very good sign: that she was planning for the future. So be it. Though she would never have put it in such simplistic terms.

She needed to use the bathroom. Careful not to wake Modesto, she slipped the bedsheets off and trudged to the bathroom, the magazine rolled up in one hand. Ever since they left the nursing home, she had been irregular. And often when she stood up from the toilet, she found it brightened with blood and nothing else. In Patricio's apartment in Key West, before they had set off on their trip, Lucas had turned her on her side, lifted her robe and checked her bum. He said it was just hemorrhoids, which the chemo had exacerbated.

The first time she had seen her own startling blood, straddling the bidet in her mother's bathroom, she had thought she was coming undone from the inside, and she sat there patiently for over an hour, drip-dropping her life away, till Dr. Esmeraldo Gloria, somehow intuiting what was happening, knocked lightly on the bathroom door and with one of her mother's napkins showed her how to care for her new womanhood. She had never been able to admit to herself how much she missed him. In the years after the fire in which the doctor perished, Modesto had arduously filled up the void left by her stepfather's absence. On returning from the law offices he filled their new house with stories, playing out for her entire court cases, not only relying on what had been said in court for his script, but on all the gossip that never could have been accepted as evidence (and that he related with the foreboding of a precious liquid drip dropping out of a vessel), till it seemed that she knew a little bit about everyone in their town and much too much about some. It was with these stories, acted out sacramentally by her husband in the baroque shadows of their courtyard, that Única learned to forget about the doctor, the way one casually forgets about any of the simple joys of childhood. It was only later, after they had learned of Cándido's death, that thoughts of Dr. Esmeraldo Gloria took up room in her mind again and that she began to summon his ghost in her dreams. And when he finally did come to her there, on the afternoon of her diagnosis, as she dozed off by Miriam's pool, he was still dressed in Agosto's ill-fitting linen suit. It was as if he had never been absent, as if it were his ritual to visit her daily in her dreams. He was eating one of his homemade pastries. She began to apologize to him, for keeping him absent from her thoughts for so long, but he raised his fork to silence her, and slowly made his way to her and offered her a bite of the *pastel*. She had thought that this was it, that he would never disappear again. But though she often thought of him, he had not appeared to her again. And now, every time she wiped her bottom and found the paper full of blood and stood to gaze inside the toilet, where it was as if a little animal had been gutted, she thought her stepfather might appear to her again, to console her as he had that first time.

When she came out of the bathroom, she could not go back to bed. The thoughts of another long night counting the whooshing lights from the noisy trucks on Eighteenth Street below inspired her to think of other ways of passing the dark hours. It was almost midnight. The innkeeper would not come down from his third-floor room to the kitchen for another six hours and breakfast would not be served for seven. Patricio and Lucas had already bid them good night. They were sharing a room on the floor above them, with the balcony facing the garden.

The innkeeper was a fey gangly man with a pencil-thin mustache, gummy skin and cloudy eyes like an old dog, and when they had checked in, he had twice asked them if they were sure they only needed one bed for the boys, and Patricio and Lucas had looked at each other and hunched their shoulders and said it didn't matter either way, and the innkeeper smiled while marking something down in the room journal.

"They are my grandchildren," Única had said, to quell his perverted joy. "Both of them."

"Cousins or brothers?" the innkeeper had answered, tilting his head and pursing his lips. "But you're right. Does it matter? I have a room, either way."

Única tried to guess the night when Patricio and Lucas had first made love. And though she so adored them, adored them both, the thought of them naked and kissing and . . . and carajo, that's it! She could not imagine other things.

She found her slippers and turned off the night lamp. She would spend the night elsewhere.

It was after breakfast that morning that her pains had begun in earnest. She was sitting with Modesto out on the porch as he read through the Spanish newspapers that Lucas got him every morning, when something seemed to crackle and catch on fire in the middle of her back and a blaze of pain spread downward through her hips and legs. They had been planning to leave for the zoo in less than an hour (through a friend of the innkeeper who worked for a well-known Republican senator, they had found out the exact time and place where Elián would be arriving), so at first Única ignored the pain, or at least didn't let on to Modesto, who hardly looked up from his paper. By the time Lucas noticed, the motley scarf around her head was saturated in sweat and she was holding back tears. He carried her

to their bed, rushing past the threshold of the front door as if
he were an overeager groom. Modesto followed behind, angry
at her, she knew, for not having said anything to him, for making him look like a careless husband who paid no mind. They
settled her in bed and Lucas gave her some pills. When the
fire in her lower parts slowly stopped raging, she pretended as
if nothing had happened, and asked for her shoes so that they
could go see Elián. Modesto came and sat by her and deli-
cately began to remove her scarf and, as Patricio and Lucas
and the innkeeper watched, he kissed her on the forehead and
told her that she wasn't going anywhere.

The innkeeper took the scarf and said he would wash it with
the morning laundry and then asked if there was anything else
he could wash for them. There was nothing else to do but tend
to them, he said; the couple from Ohio had left. And without
waiting for an answer he went to the closet and gathered their
dirty clothes and bundled them in his arms and left the room.

When Única tried to stand, to get her shoes herself, it was
as if a malicious wind stirred the brushfire of her pain and
forced her back down on the bed.

Patricio spoke. He had still been asleep when he heard the
commotion below and he wore nothing but a pair of sweat-
pants that hung too low on his waist, and his thick tangle of
black hair was standing on end, but even in her anguish, she
noticed what a beautiful man he had become. He was stern.
"You're not going anywhere," he said, "and we're leaving for
New York tomorrow morning."

Miriam had been calling tirelessly, threatening to send
Lenny after them if they hadn't made it to New York by week's

end. She said that Única was infecting them all, even Lucas, a registered nurse who should know better, with her lunacy. Each time she called she insisted on speaking with everyone, with Única and Modesto first, then her son, then Lucas. And her sermon did not vary much from day to day, emphasizing that a woman in Única's condition should not be orchestrating a crazy road trip as if she were a coed and that if they didn't make it to Sloan-Kettering by week's end she was coming with Lenny after them, and this time she was going to have them all committed.

As usual, Única thought that Miriam was right. She had even tried to be helpful and understanding when she had come to visit them in Key West, had washed all their clothes and packed their pale wicker suitcase, and in a pocket placed Modesto's classical music tapes. It was just the way she went about making her case that garnered no sympathy from any of them. And Única wanted to see the little boy just once before they shipped him back to Cuba and this was as close as she was going to get.

It would definitely be their last night in the capital. She grabbed her only sweater (part of the bundle of clothes that Miriam had neatly packed for them) and their set of keys. Then, shutting off her night lamp and holding on to the edges of the mattress and then the dresser, she made her way out of the room. In the dining room she opened a cupboard where she knew the innkeeper kept his brandy (which he nipped on during his breakfast preparations and niggardly served Modesto before they went out for dinner, or ordered in, as they had done that night) and poured herself three fingers' worth (almost half of what was left in the bottle) and gulped it down. It burned her throat as if it were her morning tea. She turned the glass back upside down and set it on the shelf and soon began to feel the effects of the brandy. Her movements became freer and her spine straightened. It wasn't anything like the effects of the egg-shaped pills, which made her feel airy, her body disconnected from the intricacies of gravity, her mind wide as the shell of an afternoon sky. In fact, it was the opposite: Each step she took made her feel more a thing of the earth, and though the remnants of that morning's intense pain were soon numbed and she was able to lift her chin and straighten her back, her steps grew heavier and her thoughts fleshier, as if they were tossing and rolling on the ground of her mind. She fumbled with the lock on the front door and was afraid one of the boys had discovered her when she heard a muffled voice from upstairs. But it was soon answered by another, and a small conversation ensued, filled with the kind of unchallenged lulls and grunted assents that are only natural to the darkness and to the bedtime hours. She waited a few minutes after the voices had gone silent and made her way out, leaving the front door unlocked.

LIKE GENERAL WASHINGTON

AT NIGHT, SHE CAN HEAR HIM when he leaves Lucas in his bed and goes up to see the doctor. After they are done with their thing, she listens closely and can make out, through the open window that faces the garden, fragments of their whispered conversation. He begs the doctor for a sunny prognosis. And the doctor says that he is sorry, but that that is just not the way things are, that when she starts the treatments again it will be long and debilitating and difficult. Then something she can't make out from her grandson and the doctor again. She will have to choose to fight, or else it won't work. He speaks this firmly, loud enough that she thinks it is meant for her to hear out in the garden. She wishes she could be like General Washington, to fight by choosing not to fight at all. But she will never admit this to him. Sometimes it seems that there is more at stake for the doctor in her survival than there is for her.

Dr. Abdel Alirkan sleeps almost as little as she does and he continues whispering, though soon she can hear the heavy breathing of her sleeping grandson. He will awake at almost the exact moment that she dozes off near dawn, at the time she hears the tap-tapping of the bronze horse, and return to his room down in the basement, to his bed with Lucas. She cannot fathom the arrangements that the three of them have made, though she is curious.

This morning she does not return to her bed with Modesto, and though immediately upon making this decision she feels a pang of guilt, can feel for herself the rushing sense of dread that will be her husband's when he awakes alone, she is resolute. She waits for Patricio to come down to his bed in the basement, waits to hear his heavy breathing again, waits for the first cindery shadows of day.

She is not furtive, does not take the trouble not to make any noise, and when she slides the glass to their bedroom open, does not take the time to slide it shut. They are sleeping with the covers wrapped below their waists. The doctor, accustomed to the balmy nights of his birth land, does not, he says, believe in air-conditioning.

As in, you don't believe it exists? her grandson asks.

Patricio is on his side, with one hand on Lucas's belly. Lucas is wearing boxer shorts. They are both snoring softly and she wonders how long her grandson can endure with his busy nocturnal schedule, how long Lucas will put up with it. She wishes she could be more moderna, as they say. To understand all this.

She stands by the foot of the bed, less than a yard away, and notices, as the morning gathers in the room, how much darker her grandson seems beside her light-skinned nurse. Patricio shifts, and for a moment she thinks that he is going to lift his

head and look up at her, but he does not. He snuggles closer to
Lucas and turns almost completely on his stomach, his forehead pressed against Lucas's shoulder. The covers have slid
now halfway down his legs and she can see that he is wearing
nothing. She turns her back to them and sits on the edge of the
bed, not because her grandson's nakedness has offended her,
but because she wants to get closer to them. She takes
her hand and places it on the back of her grandson's leg and
strokes it gently. His snoring stops short for one or two breaths
before it regains its rhythm. She turns her head to look at them
again and almost at the time she does, Lucas sits up abruptly
and stares at her, forcing his eyes to open wide. He glances
over at Patricio, at her hand resting on the back of his leg.
Lucas is befuddled. Questions are massing up like afternoon
thunderclouds in his head, but he cannot find the words to
frame any of them. So she speaks first.

I wanted to see, she says.

See what, señora Única? he whispers, still too flabbergasted
to move, to grab the sheets and cover her grandson's nakedness, to shoo her hand off his leg.

How you sleep.

His face is ashen. His eyes almost teary with uncertainty.

Patricio groans, half-awake, and Lucas is finally shaken
from his trance. He stands and takes Única by the hand away
from the bed and her grandson. In the kitchen, he makes her
the black tea himself. She apologizes for intruding on them
and he apologizes for overreacting.

It's almost, she says, as if I am not here already, isn't it? As if
I were a ghost sitting on that bed.

Lucas smiles. Mira, señora, he says, a ghost would have frightened me much less.

She asks him to sit by her, and she takes his hand. He will never love you outright, you know, she says. He will not be able to. The sooner you know that, the better off you will be.

Lucas nods. Gracias, he says, I think I know.

She wishes for a moment that she could protect him from all the torments that will invade even his most commonplace rituals, the emptiest pockets of his time. Yet she never thinks of her grandson in these terms.

But she will watch them both, watch them, if she can, from beyond her second death, watch them both, no matter how far apart they drift.

That is why she needed to see, she explains to Lucas as she takes her first sip of black tea.

GIRAFFE ON FIRE

THE WALK TO THE FRONT GATE of the National Zoo was brief, and with the aid of her cane and the boost from the brandy, she was able to make it there almost without incident, only once having trouble as she crossed the wide expanse of Eighteenth Street, the change in lights not quite giving her enough time to make it from one curb to another, so that a car had to come to a complete stop at the median while she finished crossing. The occupants of the car, a weary-looking young couple with a child asleep in the backseat, gazed at her apathetically, as if they often came upon such houseless creatures, wont to wander the lonely streets. After she veered left off Eighteenth Street, and through some leafy side roads, north, to where her guidebook marked the front gate of the zoo, it became darker and more deserted. Streetlamps disappeared and faint lights from porches and driveways gleamed from behind the gloomy vegetation that hid the homes. Without thinking too much on the lives that were carefully being constructed there, she quickened her pace, unsure of what she would do once she reached the front gate. Her housedress began to stick to the small of her back, an iciness there now that was the issue of that morning's pain. Rivulets of sweat trickled down her sides and evaporated with the breeze that glided under her floppy housedress. She was glad she had worn the sweater, though she must have been quite the sight. The weary-looking couple had been right in supposing what they did. She promised herself that she would return before the innkeeper started with his breakfast, she would just go as far as the front gate where Elián and his schoolmates had been photographed that morning. She would look around and see if any of them had dropped anything—a morsel of crayon, a candy wrapper, the clip from a pionero hanky, or the small cross his cousin had given Elián and that had not been seen hanging around his neck since the morning on which he had been taken—any memento to help her remember that she had been there at the front gate of the National Zoo not long after they had, then she would return and sit at the dining room table in the darkness and wait for the innkeeper to come down. And show him her find. She crossed a small wooden bridge that ran over a dry creek bed and soon came upon the massive shuttered gate of the zoo. She was now in almost complete darkness, the only illumination coming from the dreary caged bulbs outside the ticket booths. She searched the grounds, convinced that that was why she had come. She would find something. She picked through pieces of soft bark from the mulch of the exterior gardens. They crumbled in her hands and she smelled the unmis-

takable presence of her stepfather beside her, as if he wanted
to guide her now in the same manner that he had guided her
to find the remains of his own body many years before.

Four nights after the fire that had destroyed her mother's
home, she had gone searching for her stepfather's body. She
knew he had been there. She knew he had perished. But they
had yet to find his body in the gelatinous bog of soot and
muddy ashes from a day and a half of fire hoses. The fire had
burned with such intensity, with such endurance, the fire chief
had later said to her, waving one hand over the property, that it
was almost as if the flames had been feeding on some unfor-
given wrong. The only thing that had survived, it seemed, was
her mother's antique four-legged bathtub. It sat preposterously
in one corner of the property, where the bathroom had been,
its insides heavy with muddy ash and fragments of the fallen
house. Streaks of its old white porcelain coat were visible
around its rounded edges and on its sides, as if someone had
brushed some of the thick blackness away to see what, if
anything, lay hidden underneath. They had not found a body,
Única Aveyano thought, because they had not looked in the
right place. They had searched for his remains in every room of
the house, and in the three adjoining ones that had burned to
the ground, whose occupants had been saved only by the smell
that arose like a prayer from Marcia's old brick oven some
hours before anyone noticed the fire. It was nothing like the
acrid stench of something burning, or anything else that may
have caused great alarm. Instead, it was as if certain strange
fruits and nuts had been pierced to their very hearts and
released their inscrutable essences. The neighbors smelled

certain things for the first time, and knew them in the way they could not have known them before, in the way they lay hidden by the obstructive rind of the natural world—forgetfulness in the oily hard core of an almond, betrayal in the shredded flesh of coconuts and day-old love in the rainy sweetness of nísperos. They wandered out into the desolate afternoon streets and saved themselves from the unforgiving fire that was to destroy their homes. Some of these smells, Única noticed, still lingered out in the patio, near her stepfather's favorite spot, the brick oven, and she guessed it must have been from there that this fire of unforgiveness raged. When she led the coroner's men there and they began to remove the pile of bricks from the collapsed oven (its mortar dissolved like sugar from the fire's severity), they found the charred remains of her stepfather underneath, huddled into the same position that he had assumed after Marcia had whipped him mercilessly with her grandfather's wide leather belt six months before Única Aveyano was born. The gushing fire from the oven had encrusted his body in a finely detailed volcanic carapace, so that when they had removed the last brick from on top of him, they could clearly see the strands of hair that had come undone from his bald spot, veins in the back of his hands engorged from the boiling blood, the delicate weave in the fabric of his favorite linen suit, tattered and crudely mended at the elbows and kneecaps, and an upturned expression on his lips that almost expressed a final joy. Yet when they went to move it, the hollow mass crumbled in their hands as if it were made of a dry black sand. It was then that Única Aveyano heard her stepfather's ghost for the first time, as the coroner and his aides tried in vain to preserve the shape of what had once been his body.

"What are they looking to save?" His chattery voice mingled with the breeze that passed through the empty spaces of the pile of bricks, as the coroner's assistants continued with their futile efforts, each piece of her stepfather's volcanic cast disappearing into a pile of ashy gray rubble. And then, after so simply and mysteriously guiding her there, his presence vanished as definitively as had the carcass of his body.

In the intervening years, he never came to her again, and when he did at last, that indelible afternoon as she took a nap seated by the pool in Miriam's house, his baggy suit was still covered with a fine polleny dust, redolent of the hearts of almonds and the innards of coconuts and the syrupy flesh of nísperos. It is more difficult than she imagined, he explained, to rid a soul of the patina of its past lives. He had continued to age almost as if he were still among the living, the only hair remaining on his person a gray wispy goatee at the tip of his chin, his small black eyes buried in folds of bruised skin, his rosy skin now wan and grooved with wrinkles. But none of this diminished his optimism. Before Única could say anything, he went to her and took her in his arms and she buried her head in his chest, thinking in her dreams that for the first time since the diagnosis it would be all right to weep. When she awoke from her nap, the lush scent of Dr. Esmeraldo Gloria's death still perfumed the air as it had for weeks over the charred remains of her mother's house.

And then he disappeared again—until, that is, the madrugada when she visited the National Zoo. In the front gardens,

he wandered away from her and she gave up her search for a
trinket from Elián's group and followed him. Later, they were
to question her sternly on how she had made it onto the
grounds of the zoo, how she had evaded the night patrol, how
she had traversed the pits and thickets and wandered into the
giraffe enclosure, how she had seduced a young calf away from
its mother and coaxed it to fold its legs and lie down beside
her, so that when the keepers arrived at daybreak, she was
huddled almost entirely under the soft fur of its paunch, all to
which she would answer guilelessly, as if she were a child no
older than Elián, that she had simply taken the hand of her
stepfather and he had led her there. Which was not entirely
true. She had never quite been near enough to take his hand,
though she reached for it constantly as she aimlessly wandered
through the darkness of the zoo's paths, knowing he was near
by the inebriating fragrance that trailed him as decisively as it
had since the day of his death. She remembered waking under
the soft belly of the calf, and glancing up at its mother, grazing
from a tall acacia nearby. In the low scattered light of the
already feverish summer dawn, its dappled hide seemed to
flicker with hundreds of little flames that threatened to engulf
it, but unlike in Cándido's mad dreams, it did not race across
a barren plain, but peacefully stretched heavenwards for its
breakfast, its body taut, its only movement the grinding of its
jaw and the gentle rocking of its giant conical skull. The calf
shifted and turned its head to look at her; it batted its lashes,
which were wide and long as blackbird feathers. She could
feel it adjusting so that all its weight would not crush her. By
all accounts, they told her later as they frantically escorted

her out of the enclosure, poking the calf on its soft belly with a prod, she should have been dead.

"Yes," she answered, though under the belly of the calf she'd felt as safe as she had in years. "I know."

Four times during the moonlit night, the calf had struggled up to suckle, and four times it had returned to her, clumsily kneeling on its front legs as if it were about to pray, before lowering its haunches and readjusting itself beside Única. The mother glanced indulgently at them. Única knew that in the wild she would have never allowed the young calf to do this, to settle on its haunches to sleep. And even here, in the safety of their enclosure, where no predators roamed, she did so only grudgingly, emitting a tuba-like moan each time her daughter wandered away from her after suckling. She knew that the intruder posed no threat to her calf, but she kept a close watch anyway, sleeping on her feet in such impossibly brief spurts, that her dream world, Única thought, must have been a place where stories barely had the nerve to get started.

Única had not slept much, so she attributed the visions of that night partly to this, and partly to the stiff glass of brandy she had poured herself before leaving the Marcel House. A woman, barefoot and in a moth-eaten nightgown, her long dark hair loose, wandered to and fro in the fields of the enclosure. In her hands she held a white porcelain teacup that she intermittently sipped from and set back on its saucer. She seemed vexed with having to carry it around with her; but from the frequency and thirsty manner with which she sipped from it, casting it aside was clearly not an option.

Única followed the woman's rambling as she drifted from a spot by the trunk of the acacia to a vanishing point on the

precipice of the pit that surrounded the peninsular enclosure
on three sides. Once or twice, it seemed as if the figure had
cast herself into the pit, but as Única waited to hear the thud
of the landing, the shattering of the teacup, the figure floated
again into her vision, muttering to herself and addressing the
gnarly trunk of the acacia as if it were an animate thing and
sipping incessantly from the venomous cup.

By her ragged nightgown, by the manic way she sipped her
tea, Única recognized the woman, but her mother made as
little note of Única's presence as she had during her whole
life. Marcia was as young and beautiful and wretched as on
the morning on which, after patiently sipping half a gallon of
tea brewed from the crushed leaves of the rhubarb that her
lover grew in the gardens of the yanqui naval base, her heart
had stopped. When Dr. Esmeraldo Gloria found Marcia that
afternoon on returning from his day at the clinic, his beloved
slumped in his reading chair in the parlor, barefoot and dressed
in the same nightgown in which she now wandered through
other worlds; the empty teacup and its saucer were neatly balanced in her lap. The house was infested with the rancid smell
of old urine; it had trickled down her legs and spread beneath
her. Not knowing what else on which to take out his rage, Dr.
Esmeraldo Gloria smashed the cup and its saucer to bits and
tossed the shards into the fires of the brick oven. He sat by his
beloved, took her stiffened hand and slipped off the thin platinum band with which Christophe Evesque had promised his
eternal love, and he ate by himself all their afternoon pastries,
imploring Marcia how it was that he should tell of this to Única,
who had been out all afternoon, alone, searching for a bargain
wedding dress.

When he was done with the pastries, he flushed the remaining tea and crushed rhubarb leaves down the toilet. He washed Marcia's body twice, brushed her long hair till it was dry, and changed her into a simple white cotton dress, embroidered elegantly at the collar. After he laid her on the bed, he dabbed her neck and the back of each wrist with perfume and placed one hand over the other on her belly. It was as if she had died peacefully while taking a siesta. No one doubted his word when he said that when he had come home, her heart had already stopped. But from the moment that they buried her, he could not escape the smell that had confronted him as he came home on the afternoon of her death. It followed him from Camposanto, through the long walk down Perdido Street, and into the house on Narciso López Street, so that for a moment he thought her soiled body was there again. And it would go on like that for days, no matter what he was doing or what room of the house he retreated to, from one breath to the other he would abruptly be surrounded by the stink of her urine, by the pestilence of something left uncared for. That's how he knew Marcia had been at Única's wedding, for after they had made their vows and the congregation had dispersed, Dr. Esmeraldo Gloria had returned to the church to light a candle for Marcia's soul. As he was doing it, a putrid air settled in around him, but just as quickly it dissipated. It was then he decided to tell Única the truth of how he had found her mother, for he had made up his mind to be with Marcia again. "She must not be all gone," he whispered to Única during the wedding feast, slipping her mother's thin platinum engagement ring onto Única's pinky as he began the story. "Some part of her is call-

ing for me." On the day of the fire, it was suspected that Dr.
Esmeraldo Gloria was well into his mission to reunite with
Marcia. He had been experimenting with aromatic combus-
tibles that hid the stench of her presence and was rehearsing
the day when he would disinter his beloved and take her with
him into the raging blaze of the brick oven, but he had lost
control of the experiment and perished before he ever had a
chance to reunite with her.

But the figure in the giraffe enclosure seemed as little concerned with reuniting with her lover as she did with making
contact with her daughter, huddled under the belly of the calf.
Her struggle was with the teacup and saucer. If she could
make them levitate in the air beside her and have them follow
her around, reaching for the cup when she needed it, she
would be content, it seemed. Once, she held cup and saucer
at arm's length in the palm of her hand, and Única thought that
she was about to remove her hand from under the saucer—
abruptly, the way a magician pulls a tablecloth from a set dinner table—to see if it would do just that, float in the air beside
her. But the figure was not so bold; she retrieved her hand
slowly, cup and saucer safely on it, and sipped some more, as
if it were her duty. Única wondered what coldhearted deity
would so condemn a creature to perform its most cherished
act again and again, till, through sheer monotony, it had lost all
semblance of originality, through dulling repetition, all power
to please.

By the time her mother ended her own life, Única Aveyano
knew, she had long forgotten the reasons why it was proper
for her to do so. She had banished the memory of Christophe

Evesque from her heart. The only remnant of his presence in their lives, aside from his daughter, was the hand-colored photograph that Única Aveyano learned to hide from her mother lest she destroy it. She took it from the house on the eve of her wedding—along with her three favorite Christmas ornaments—and thereby saved it from the fire. Marcia had settled into a fretful domesticity with Dr. Esmeraldo Gloria and had, more to please her lover than from any motherly affection, agreed to let Única marry a man whom they hardly knew. Her life was not then and never had been her own, though she must have thought, as she peacefully crushed rhubarb leaves and brewed her last pot of tea, that perhaps the way that she left it could be. As if anything, anything at all, could be all our own, Única Aveyano thought. Her mother had no more invented her death than she had invented any of her life, and with this thought Única was able to stop watching the pitiful roaming phantom, and by the time they found her under the belly of the calf, the figure of her mother had long disappeared, the nervous rattling of cup on saucer long silenced.

As they prodded the calf away from Única, other keepers distracting the mother, she noticed for the first time how young it was, the blotches on its buff hide much lighter than its mother's and its frightened gait ungainly as a child just learning to walk. Her own state was no less precarious: there were bruises on her thighs and scratches on her arms and lower legs, and from this they presumed that she must have made her way into the enclosure through the thickets on the far side.

"If I can get in, then there's a problem," she said, evading all of their questions except what her name was and where she was staying.

"A problem?" the keeper said.

"Yes, a problem," she said, raising her voice as if the transgression had been theirs and not hers, "for then the animals can get out."

"No, no, you see, they don't want to get out. They are perfectly happy here. All we have to do is put up some barriers, you know, dissuade them from thinking about it."

Única wondered if it worked the same for all animals, or if some, like the giraffe, were more indolent and accepted their fate more easily. Can you dissuade the lioness from attempting to flee? The black leopard? But she realized she hadn't, quite, asked the questions out loud.

The head of zoo security and two police officers questioned her in a tiny room of a doll-like brick house. Their voices sizzled in the hot air of the windowless room like the spill of toasted coffee beans. She had no answers aside from the ones she had already given them. When she refused medical help, even as they were bandaging the scratches on her arms and legs, they took her in a patrol car to the Marcel House, though she was sure that the officers weren't expecting anyone to claim her there and were more than prepared to take her to the nearest mental ward.

There were three other patrol cars there when they arrived, and aside from Modesto, the innkeeper seemed the most discomfited. It was he who had awakened everyone to announce that Única was missing, he who had called the police without consulting anyone.

As he came to her with a shawl and wrapped her in it even though the temperature was already in the eighties, Lucas spoke briefly to one of the officers, who soon demanded to see

a relative. Until then, Patricio had been sullenly loading suitcases in the trunk of the black Mustang, which was backed
into the driveway, ignoring the police and Única's arrival
entirely. He walked over to the officer grimacing and scratch-
ing the back of his head, and answered a round of questions
simply by nodding after each one. Then listened, biting on his
nails, to the story of the night before. When he was finished,
the officer took one brief look into the Mustang and then, sat-
isfied, walked over to Única and put a hand on her shoulder.

"Hang in there," he said.

Patricio stayed motionless by the passenger side of the Mustang as he watched the patrol cars drive off. For a moment,
Única thought he was going to wave good-bye.

They left for New York in the early afternoon, leaving the
Marcel House officially empty. The innkeeper wept as he said
good-bye to her, and promised to say only good things about
her to the reporter from *The Washington Post* who was on his
way over. In the passenger seat of Patricio's car, Única waited
for their barrage of questions, but they never came. Modesto
asked her once if the scratches on her arms and legs were still
bleeding, and she touched the bandages and said they felt fine.
He then put his hand on her shoulder and left it there for the
rest of the trip. Lucas told her that perhaps she should take a
nap and adjusted her headrest. Patricio was silent, and though
she could not look at him, she felt him taking his eyes off the
road and glancing at her momentarily, as if afraid that she
might vanish from her comfortable spot in the speeding car.
When she dozed off, they were talking about the inconve-
niences of the Marcel House, the dribbly showers, the concave

mattresses, the slanted floors, about how much nicer it would be in Dr. Abdel Alirkan's town house, as if nothing extraordinary at all had happened the night before. There was no one in her dreams, and she sat in a colorless room waiting for them, her mother and her teacup, her stepfather in his ashy linen suit, until she remembered that they were not coming, that this was not the hour, not the hour at all. When she awoke, they were crossing a long bridge. Patricio said that he was sorry, that he had wandered too far up north, that he should have taken the tunnel directly into the city, though Única thought that an unseemly way to enter a place that she had never been to before, through a tunnel like a mole. As it was, they seemed to be coasting in across the gray river on a low-flying plane. To the south, the towers of the city crouched in the distance, and it would not be till they were almost upon them that she would recognize their immensity, the audacity with which they stretched upward towards the ochre vastness of the twilight, each with its own peculiar daring. It was as if this gray island between two rivers (so different from their lush Island in the sea) depended on their exact positioning for its balance, as if one were shifted a foot or two, the whole thing could go belly up. And as they began to drive through its streets, countless pedestrians spilling into the crossways, she thought of all those that did not come to her in her dream of the colorless room, and she wondered if they could ever come to her in such a man-haunted place as this.

SECOND DEATHS

SHE IS ALONE AGAIN. She did not go into the bar of the restaurant by the river on purpose. But when Eduardo comes out through a side door of the bar to smoke his cigarettes, Única gets up from her spot on the refurbished pier and joins him. He offers a cigarette and she accepts. There are stains on his vest and on his pants and she takes the hand towel that is hanging from his waist, still moist, and wipes them off. They silently watch at least three different wedding parties amassing by the edge of the river for photographs. She notices how the brides size each other up, their dresses, their future husbands. The boys, the grooms, chat casually while each bride takes her turn with her back to the river. They are all uncomfortable in their garish costumes, with posing for all their future generations.

I wonder, she says, what they'll remember most when they look at these pictures years from now.

Eduardo finishes the last drag of his cigarette and flicks it into the river. You're assuming that all of them will stay married, he says. Why don't you come in, sit at the bar, keep me company?

No, not tonight, I think.

I'm keeping an eye on you. He winks and smooths out his cleaned vest. Thanks, she says. Before he goes back inside, he offers her another cigarette and, with the same flair that he always uses with customers at the bar, lights it for her.

She stays by the side door of the restaurant barge and, as it darkens, waits for the wedding parties to disperse. She takes out one of the larger stones from the pocket of her coat and puts out her cigarette. She will save the other half for later. She returns to the pier and sits and waits for Eduardo's next break. It will be his last one. The bar will get too busy after that.

I am starting the treatments again, she says when he offers her a cigarette this time; and as if she was implying that this meant she could no longer smoke, he pulls the cigarette pack away from her. She adjusts the scarf around her head. The doctor says it is time, she says, that I am strong enough to withstand them.

He blows out smoke and nods. You look . . . He is stuck for a word. He points at her with his cigarette hand. You look, vaya, rapturous. He nods again, to convince himself that he has used the proper word. It will come out well, I can feel it.

She is silent. She looks at the river, at the band of orange hanging off the edges of the sky like a flounce.

You will let me know how it goes?

She nods, and before he goes back inside, she kisses him softly on the cheek. She will never, she thinks, see him again.

She waits for hours, watching the bustling bar from her spot on the pier. Eduardo sometimes stands at the end of the bar to look out on her, but he is too busy. She has not felt the presence of her stepfather in days. She is glad that Modesto did not want to come with her. She is alone again.

She walks to the edge of the pier and slowly takes off her midnight-colored coat. It is so heavy with stones she can barely hold it aloft in front of her. She leans over the railing and holds the coat with both hands over the edge of the pier. Some of the stones slip out of the pockets as she does this, and their noise catches the attention of a few passersby who have come to admire the spangled city across the way. But no one comes to her. She reaches the coat as far out as she can and lets it drop. It falls headlong into the river, but when it hits the waters it opens up, its flaps spreading wide in the surface, more of the small stones scattering from its pockets. And then the current grabs it and drags it down. It bobs up once, as if struggling for air, and then sinks again, never to reappear.

In her housedress, feeling as if she has just peeled off a layer of skin, she returns to the streets that she roamed when she first arrived.

There is Cranberry and Orange and Pineapple, she begins.

And does not return to her garden till it is near dawn. She knows the boys will be out there, has heard them from her room, many times before, as she slipped into bed with her husband. They are there now, mounted on the bronze horse as if they were children. She watches from a far corner of the garden, hidden by a wall of morning glory. The summer is almost over and the vines are in full bloom. Her grandson is in front, his arms wrapped around the horse's rearing head. He is crouching like a catcher on the horse's bare back, near its withers. Lucas is behind him, his legs dangling to each side, one arm wrapped around her grandson's belly, the other around his chest, his cheek pressed to her grandson's back. They are as naked as the bare horse is naked, their eyes closed, their minds shuttered, their voices kidnapped by some breath from low within.

She watches them and she prays that they will not forget this part of themselves. She watches them as she will watch them from beyond her second death. She waits till they are spent on the back of the bronze horse, splayed one on top of the other like bodies being brought back from a battle, before she returns to her husband's side.

She slowly removes her scarf, her housedress, her slippers, and lies on top of the covers. She passes her hand over the thick buzz of her hair, over her breasts, over her thighs that have become sturdier from so much walking, and she tries to invent words with which to tell the kind doctor that there will be no treatments. He is the only one who will understand her decision, for even her nurse, even he has been blinded by his affection for her.

She will bathe. She will remove the hand towel and look at herself in the mirror for the first time in ages.

Then. Then she will look, she thinks, rapturous.

ACKNOWLEDGMENTS

Stories are never told by one person alone. So I am deeply grateful to all those who helped me with this one. . . . For time and space and a few tips on how to build houses, the Blue Mountain Center and Jack; for their support, encouragement, close readings and a few jobs here and there, Eduardo Lago, Gerry Geddes, Dennis Abrams, Marcia Morgado, Cuqui Tornes, Juan Abreu, Robert Fowler, Michael Denneny, Margaux Wexberg, Linsey Abrams and Mary LaChapelle; for the wedding present, Islam Towhidul; for their magisterial works on Cuban history, Hugh Thomas and Tad Szulc; for being the kind of editor I couldn't have dreamed up on my best day, and for keeping me honest, Robin Desser; for too many things, but mostly for being my Brooklyn family, Tom, Elaine, Julia and Laura Colchie; for teaching me and inspiring me, Mat Johnston; and for filling my life with all those little joys that matter, and letting me borrow, for a little while, all their stories, Tati, Marita, Lou, Phil, Lisette, Rafa, Marquito, Lily, Angela, Antonio, handsome Ricky, Nicolas, Mike, Candy, Heidi, Heather, Rob, Auden and mi Andrew.